REBEL FALLS

Also by Tim Wendel

Fiction

Castro's Curveball
Escape from Castro's Cuba
Habana Libre
Red Rain

Nonfiction

Cancer Crossings: A Brother, His Doctors, and the Quest for a Cure to Childhood Leukemia
Summer of '68: The Season That Changed Baseball—and America—Forever
High Heat: The Secret History of the Fastball and the Improbable Search for the Fastest Pitcher of All Time
Down to the Last Pitch: How the 1991 Minnesota Twins and the Atlanta Braves Gave Us the Best World Series of All Time
Buffalo, Home of the Braves
Far From Home: Latino Baseball Players in America
The New Face of Baseball: The One-Hundred-Year Rise and Triumph of Latinos in America's Favorite Sport
Going for the Gold: How the U.S. Olympic Hockey Team Won at Lake Placid

Books for young readers

Night on Manitou Island
My Man Stan

For my parents,
who taught me to look to the morning sky.
For Sarah and Chris,
who keep me laughing and proud.
And for Jacqueline,
who always believes.

CONTENTS

Part 1: A Haunted Look   1

Part 2: Along the Border   39

Part 3: Among the Rebels   95

Part 4: At the Precipice   171

Epilogue   245

Acknowledgments   251

Author's Note   255

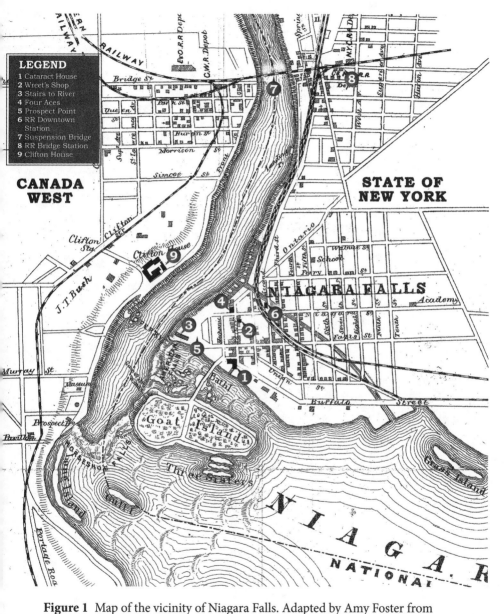

Figure 1 Map of the vicinity of Niagara Falls. Adapted by Amy Foster from an 1870 map printed by Burland, Lafricain & Co., Montreal.

PART 1

A Haunted Look

Here was the last point on which North and South agreed: anyone who still believed in compromise—exemplified by the doomed bargain of 1850, of which the fugitive slave law was the crumbling keystone—was at best a foolish child, at worst the devil's spawn.

—ANDREW DELBANCO, *THE WAR BEFORE THE WAR*

1

In the summer of 1864, those close to my family, and many more who claimed to be, attended my uncle's burial at Fort Hill Cemetery. The Sewards had ensured that Uncle Frank was awarded a plot in the most cherished resting spot in Auburn, New York. Secretary of State William Seward himself was there, along with his son Augustus and his daughter Fanny, who has been my best friend since I can remember. They stood alongside me as Pastor Harris drew out his closing prayer in solemn, measured tones. When I gazed up at the blue sky, barely a cloud to be seen, Fanny drew closer and rested a hand on my forearm.

"O Lord, accept our prayers on behalf of your humble servant, Franklin Hawes," said the pastor. He added, "And let us beseech our heavenly Father that this war may soon end. For too long, our nation has wandered in the wilderness."

Thankfully, the ceremony soon drew to a close, and the expensive coffin—which the Sewards had paid for, too—was lowered into the ground. Pastor Harris looked to me, silently asking if I wanted to throw the first shovelful of dirt upon the cherrystone casket. When I didn't move, Augustus Seward, attired in his Union Army uniform, stepped forward and scattered a shovelful upon the coffin. With that, I abruptly turned, and the Sewards fell into step alongside me. The townspeople, easily one hundred of them, followed us down the hill and into town.

A few blocks ahead of us, at the Sewards' home on South Street, I knew that tables of food and drink awaited our arrival. Fanny was determined to see that such occasions were done to the letter, even with a flourish whenever possible. Once inside their house, I tried my best to be hospitable, moving among the well-wishers, attempting to focus on their nervous words of condolence. Yet my attention soon drifted, and I felt the anger and disbelief rising up within me once again. I couldn't believe that a comedy of errors and miscalculations had taken my uncle, the last of my immediate family, from me and our town.

Almost three years before, after a series of skirmishes near Harper's Ferry, tensions along the Potomac River near Washington rose markedly. The battle lines, which had been stable since the debacle at the first Bull Run, began to move and blur once again. The Confederates occupied the Virginia side of the Potomac, while the Union held the Maryland side. After dusk in late October, a half-dozen members of the 15th Massachusetts crossed the river with orders to scout the area. In the moonlight, they came upon what they believed to be a row of rebel tents. With no sentries or campfires to be seen, the encampment appeared to be ripe for the taking. Based on such faulty reconnaissance, the Union command decided to attack before dawn, with the leading force and subsequent reinforcements ferried across the Potomac in a handful of small boats.

Climbing uphill from the river, Uncle Frank's unit soon reached the supposed camp, only to discover that what had been mistaken for rebel tents in the moonlight was actually a line of evergreen trees. Just beyond those trees were pickets with the 17th Mississippi, an experienced band of Confederates. Without hesitation, the 17th Mississippi sounded the alarm and in the steep terrain the outnumbered Union troops were unable to make a stand. Too soon, they found themselves with their backs to the fast-moving river they had just crossed.

While my uncle had been born and raised in Auburn, he was technically a member of the 1st California Regiment at the Battle of Ball's Bluff. The outfit had been formed to encourage California men throughout the United States to enlist. In actuality, the regiment had its origins in Philadelphia, where Uncle Frank himself had signed on.

With only four small boats at hand, many in the 1st California, including my uncle, plunged into the fast-moving waters and attempted to swim back across the Potomac. Very few made it safely across, with the rest carried away in the current. More drowned than were shot that day, and some bodies were found far downstream, close to Washington, almost thirty miles away. My uncle somehow survived the retreat and drifted ashore several miles downstream, on the Maryland side. The terrible wounds he suffered to his legs and back invalided him out of the army and he was never the same. Indeed, I felt that for my uncle, death had been a relief.

I had learned much of this—more than most families would gain about the circumstances that took their fathers, sons, brothers, or uncles from them—because I'd had the gall to ask. Then Fanny Seward used her father's influence and sought out the particulars from the War Department in Washington. One could say that the Sewards will miss my uncle as much as anyone, for he regularly worked the grounds at their estate here in Auburn. Sometimes gardener, other times handyman, my Uncle Frank knew this place well.

"Rory, you should go home," Fanny whispered. She had once again slipped beside me. "You've done enough today."

"No. I'm fine."

"About as fine as a potted plant in need of water. Your mind's elsewhere, which is perfectly understandable."

Fanny led me by the elbow up the staircase, above the crowd in the parlor that overflowed into the kitchen. Many of them were simply curious to catch a glimpse of the Sewards' home, the grandest in all of Auburn. Fanny and I gazed down upon these people, many of whom I had known since I was a child. Among them were the Conleys and the Ledbetters. Their patience with the war had run out long ago. They had lost loved ones, too, and believed that peace should be made with the South. The sooner the better. They were whispered to be Copperheads and would undoubtedly vote against Abraham Lincoln in the upcoming presidential election.

"I cannot believe they're here," I whispered to Fanny.

Below us, in the crowd, chatting away was Daisy Conley. She was a year or so younger than Fanny and myself, and her brother had fallen at Antietam.

"Best to forgive and forget," replied Fanny, making it sound so easy.

"And if Robert E. Lee appeared outside your door," I said, surprised by my anger, "Daisy and her kind would usher him inside with a smile and holding out a full plate."

"Hush now," Fanny said. "Let's take one last pass through the babble, and that will be enough on such a day. I'll have the carriage take you home."

It was dark by the time the Sewards' rig dropped me off at the two-story home Mother had rented the autumn we returned from Niagara Falls. The modest dwelling was on Owasco Street, on the poor side of the tracks, as some would say. Mother had passed away soon after the war began, and I knew that's why Uncle Frank was so determined to fight in it. To honor his only sister. Some would say that Mother and Frank were both in heaven now. But I didn't put much credence in such notions. All I knew was that my funds had dwindled to a pittance, and I didn't want to ask the Sewards for any additional assistance.

Four long years. That's how long the war had been going on. Ball's Bluff, Shiloh, second Bull Run, Antietam, Fredericksburg, Chancellorsville, Vicksburg, Gettysburg, Chattanooga, Wilderness, Cold Harbor. Each a nightmare unto itself. Each tragedy chipping away at the best intentions any of us once held.

For a moment, I lingered by the quilt hanging on the wall inside the front door. A colorful swirl of blue and green and a dash of red, it was fashioned from scraps of cloth Mother had gathered during our time in Niagara Falls. It reminded me of something you might glimpse through a child's kaleidoscope, and for that reason alone I'd hung it here, the only adornment that these walls still held.

Burrowing deep under the covers of my unmade bed, I wanted to be done with this wretched day, let it lift away from me. While I somehow fell asleep, in the end the respite did little good. Too soon, a dream came upon me in which I found myself in the countryside. At first, I thought it was a scene from *Wuthering Heights*, *Jane Eyre*, or *Ivanhoe*—novels Fanny and I have enjoyed since were young. Yet on this evening events soon turned strange and curious as Uncle Frank appeared at my side. We were dressed for cold weather in Mackinaw coats, gloves, and hats, and both of us held our hunting rifles. Uncle Frank was the one who taught me to shoot. He and I used to patrol the fields outside of Auburn in the autumn for pheasant and grouse. That's what we appeared to be doing again with the skies overhead turning foul with cloud and wind.

As the breeze grew stronger, swirling the leaves on the ground, we continued to walk away from the village when deep down I wanted nothing more than to turn back, return home. With Uncle Frank leading the way, we were intent upon reaching a stand of cedar and oak on the far side of the rolling field, and too soon we were somehow there, on the edge of that thick growth.

There I did stop. Even in this dream, which was fading into a strange vision, even a nightmare, I feared going any further, straying too far into that realm. But when I looked beside me, perhaps for confirmation from my beloved uncle, Franklin Hawes was no longer by my side. Somehow the forces had taken hold of him, and now when I gazed back to the thick wood, I saw that he was already there—spirited ahead of me. As I watched, he turned at the edge of the wood and nodded to me, beckoning for me to follow. For a long moment, I held my ground, refusing to be drawn any closer, until I saw another figure appear from out of the trees. It was Mother, and she came alongside her only brother. Both of them looked at me with what appeared to be impatience and restlessness.

That's when I awoke, with my skin flushed and slightly feverish. This long war wouldn't let me go. I decided it was time that I tried to do something, anything, to find my proper role amid such chaos.

Down in the kitchen, I found Mother's long shears. Clutching them in one hand, I went back upstairs and by candle light in the bedroom, I began to pull the pins from my hair and shake the locks free. The black tendrils reached my shoulders, framing my face's reflection in the mirror. For a moment, I simply regarded myself. How distraught and unhappy I had become.

I knew I would never be what some would call pretty. Yet my hazel-green eyes weren't reluctant to hold anyone's gaze. My face, with its upturned nose, longish chin, and small mouth, could offer the world a pleasant enough countenance when I remembered to smile. Still, I knew that my height, the way I towered over many people, wasn't helpful, as Mother would say. Once the tomboy, always the tomboy, Fanny Seward liked to add. If that was so, I decided that I might as well use such assets to my advantage.

With another deep breath, I cut away the first long section of my hair. Methodically, with growing purpose and resolve, I continued until my labors with the scissors made sure that most of my locks were gone. When I finished, I set down the shears and gazed again in the mirror. The only feature that appeared familiar was my eyes. They were as troubled and as haunted as before.

2

The rifle they issued, the Springfield Model 1861, felt comfortable enough in my hands. Some complained about its action, how the kick could bruise the shoulder, or how quickly the barrel grew red-hot with repeated firings. Still, when I cradled it in my hands or rested it on my shoulder for parade march and even shifted from one hand to the other for double time, I decided it would suit me well enough.

Unlike many Union troops, we received a measure of drills and target practice. Sergeant Russell Walters had gotten permission from Major Fergus Bards for such activity. Walters had a brother who had seen action at Malvern Hill and Gettysburg, and he wrote home that the lack of such training proved disastrous on the battlefield, how too many Federal units were like lambs to the slaughter. That's what had us target practicing again in the afternoon.

The drill was simple enough. Our unit was divided into two rows, all of us facing an array of paper targets that had been nailed to boards, about a man's height, which were surrounded by hay bales. As one row of men fired, the row behind them reloaded, ramming the minié ball down the barrel and then fitting the weapon with another cap for detonation. Our goals were accuracy and pace, with the person who had reloaded exchanging places with the soldier who had just fired. When he was fully reloaded, ready to squeeze the trigger again, he tapped his partner's shoulder, and they switched places again. I was usually paired with Barry Peters, a sweet enough boy from Seneca Falls, a small town west of Auburn.

On this afternoon, only days before we were said to be heading south, to the war, Colonel Garrett Oliver had joined Sergeant Walters to take in the proceedings. By the disgusted look on his face, we could tell Colonel Oliver wasn't pleased by what he was witnessing. While the Springfield rifle was said to be accurate from several hundred yards away, few of our regiment's attempts hit the targets. Such accuracy suffered even more when Sergeant Walters urged us to reload faster, picking up the pace.

As Peters and I switched places again, I saw Colonel Oliver give our sergeant a mouthful and then spin on his heel, leaving Walters saluting his back. Within minutes, the remainder of the afternoon's drill was called off.

Sergeant Walters walked through our midst as the men dispersed. "He calls it a waste of bullets." Walters mumbled, almost to himself. "But we need to be better."

As we moved past him, Sergeant Walters gazed upon the white-paper bull's-eye targets, which were flapping in the breeze. His eyes ran along the row of them, more than thirty in total, before he settled on the one Barry Peters and I had been intent at firing at. It had a good many strikes, if I do say so myself.

"That your work?" Walters asked, and Peters stood in place, unsure what to say.

"Hold it here," the sergeant ordered as he strode into field. We had no choice but to wait for him, and as we did so I saw that Sylvester

Cobb and Archie Blake, the regiment's rabble-rousers, were watching him, too.

As Sergeant Walters returned with our target in hand, a hint of a smile spread across his face. "This is splendid," he said. "I'll show this to Major Bards. Maybe this can get us more of the training we need."

He glanced at us and then back at the target. "I count more than a dozen quality hits. Now, if we can see one shooter with this kind of success, instead of the efforts of two, we're actually making progress."

"Sir, it is one shooter," Peters blurted out.

"What do you mean, son?"

"I'm like most of them here," Peters continued as he shifted uneasily from one foot to another. "Lord knows I need the practice and sincerely hope you're able to deliver us more of it, sir. The idea of marching south with barely the wherewithal to load and aim a gun, especially under those conditions. Well . . ."

"If it wasn't the pair of you, then," Walters began.

"It was Hawes, sir," Peters said, nodding in my direction. "He's a much better marksman than me."

Sergeant Walters smiled, becoming more excited. "All right then. Both of you come with me."

As we approached camp, Sergeant Walters led us past the officers' tents. They had been set upon a small hill, and down the other side was another shooting gallery—a smaller setup, with more elaborate stacks of hay bales and a few select targets.

"Hawes, if you're a fledging Hawkeye," Sergeant Walters said, "a marksman in the making, let's see what you can do with this piece."

He handed me a rifle that was lighter than the Springfield, with a better scope attached to its barrel.

"It's a Whitworth," Walters told us. "British-made. The rebels have a few, but we've been promised more. Plenty more. The idea is to take the best marksmen from our units and designate them as snipers. Have them pick off top-ranking braids and bars."

"Hawes could do that," Peters said. "He's got a keen eye."

"Let's see it at work then," Sergeant Walters said, nodding for me to take the elegant weapon.

Gingerly I balanced it with both hands. Trying to take my time, I brought it up to my shoulder and spied through the telescopic sight. Magically so much more came into focus. So clean and precise that I felt as if I could reach out and touch what lay many yards away.

"See the bull's-eye on that oak tree, Hawes?"

"Yes, sir."

"Have a go at it."

Taking a deep breath, I let the air slowly flow out of my mouth. As the last of the sigh ebbed away, I concentrated fully on the target and gently squeezed the trigger. Just as Uncle Frank had taught me.

Compared to the Springfield, the Whitworth had barely any kick at all, and the bullet made a shrill whistling sound. Behind me, I heard a stirring as Walters had a pair of spyglasses out.

"Dead center," he said. "All right. How about the piece of paper flapping in the pine tree to the right?"

With the scope, it was easy enough to spot.

"Careful now, Hawes," he said, moving closer, almost like an angel settling on my shoulder. "The breeze is rustling, so this one won't be as easy."

But I knew enough to fully gauge things, wait for the right moment. I nailed that target with little trouble as well.

As our session continued, I hit every target that Sergeant Walters asked of me. While I had been comfortable enough with the Springfield rifle, the Whitworth was already feeling like an extension of my arm and eyes, a part of my very heart and soul.

"I will tell Major Bards," Sergeant Walters said as our session ended. "Hawes, you may have a new role in Abe Lincoln's army."

Afterward, Peters and I hurried back to the main camp, eager not to miss dinner.

"So, you're Walters's new darling," a voice cried out as we approached the cook fire.

It was Sylvester Cobb. He was hanging with Archie Blake and several of the others, downing their grub as fast as they could.

While I didn't answer, Peters couldn't resist telling them about the Whitworth rifle. How well I'd fired it. For some reason, he was more excited about my success than I was.

"Is that so?" Cobb said, stepping toward us. He held out his metal plate, and one of his laughing boys took it from him. "You're going to be a sniper. Hiding in the trees, while the rest of us do the hard work. Gunning down men like so many deer?"

"It's not like that," I replied.

"What's it like then?" Cobb lashed out, his forearm driving hard into my chest. As I fell backward, the sting of it rang through me, but I scrambled to my feet, eager to fight him, knowing that I couldn't show any cowardice or reluctance to grapple. Thankfully, Peters held me back, and others did the same for Cobb.

"He's nothing," said Cobb. "Simply a tall boy that topples over hard."

Yet I saw a look of confusion, followed by disbelief, steal across his face. Cobb's eyes momentarily grew wide, then narrowed with a newfound realization that he had brushed against my bosom. After several weeks of hiding my true identity, had I been discovered on the eve of our regiment's entry into the war?

Later, walking to the tents, Peters tried to advise me about fisticuffs and the art of boxing. Growing up, I'd wrestled when I was too young to know better. But the gentleman arts? I was at a loss.

"Cobb's right," Peters said. "You're a tall one, but that won't stop them from going for your chin and your nose. So, why not surprise them? When they do, duck down low. They'll grumble about how you're not fighting proper. How you need to stand upright. But don't pay them any mind. With any set-to, the biting and head butts begin soon enough."

I nodded dumbly.

"So, fight 'em dirty," he continued. "No place for a pretty face in this witless world."

"Private, would you kindly remove your jacket," the colonel ordered.

I looked to one side and then the other, realizing other men were moving in on either side of me, with several more blocking the tent entrance.

Reluctantly, I undid one button as Colonel Garrett Oliver and two of his subordinates drew closer for a better look.

I had been brought to the large canvas tent, the regiment's command center, at gunpoint. Rumors continued that we would soon be pulling out. That the order to move south was imminent and with it our official entry into the war.

They nodded for me to undo another uniform button, but I refused. That's when somebody pinned my arms behind me, forcing me back onto a camp table. Oliver stepped forward with a cruel smile, reaching for the next brass button himself. One of his subordinates pulled the jacket away from my shoulders, while another ran a dirty fingertip downward from my chin.

"Soft skin," he whispered as everyone drew closer. "Softer than mine, that's for sure."

Even though my bosom was wrapped as tight as the Christ child's swaddling clothes, even here the prying fingers found their mark, beginning to pull away the cloth in the half-shadows of the command tent.

I shoved them away as best I could, but around me the men began to snicker and pressed in closer as if they had stumbled across some rare diamond amidst so much rubble.

"It's been a long time since I've seen me a woman," one soldier said.

More hands reached forward, peeling back the uniform jersey, revealing my bare shoulders and naked back. All of which may have been as muscular as any man's but now left little doubt that such characteristics belonged to the female of the species.

That's how things would have continued if the tent flap hadn't parted as another man strode into the shadows. He wore a long riding coat and slapped his gloves against his open palm.

"Attention," someone shouted, and the men stumbled away, leaving me to roll off the table and pull my clothes back over me.

"He's a woman, sir," someone else said, as if that declaration made everything acceptable. "A woman right here in our midst."

Major Fergus Bards continued to tap the riding gloves against his open hand.

"Indeed, gentlemen, Franklin Hawkes was badly wounded at the Battle of Ball's Bluff," Major Bards said. "An unfortunate calamity in which bodies floated down the Potomac River. Some were carried all the way into Washington itself, I'm told. Franklin Hawkes eventually died of his wounds, and I came upon that official notice in town."

"So, if this isn't Private Hawes, who is it then?"

"His niece," I told them as defiantly as I could.

"One Rebecca Chase," Bards said. "It seems she wants to take a measure of vengeance against some unsuspecting Rebs."

"And I can do it, too."

"No doubt, good lady," Bards replied. "While I admire your courage, I'm afraid that the Union Army remains man's work, and Lord knows what could have happened if your true self had been discovered on the back roads of Virginia, closer to Richmond."

"Enough," I said, taking a step toward him, watching how the good major and his officers retreated ever so slightly at my advance.

"You're to stay here, under guard," Bards said. "After midnight, you'll be released and allowed to walk back home to Auburn."

"But that has to be fifteen miles away," I protested.

"Where I expect you to be back in a dress and petticoat by evening."

With that, Major Bards stepped closer. "Do I make myself clear, Miss Chase?"

All I could do was nod and then, as a small token of protest, raise my right hand to salute. The major stared intently at me and didn't return the gesture.

Small campfires dotted the wide fields and rolling hills where we had been stationed for the past week. The regular men did their best to make a proper meal for themselves from the meager rations that were divvied out. Here, closer to the officers' mess, the smells were much more mouth-watering. Later that night, Sergeant Russell Walters talked his way past the ones guarding me.

"Here, I brought you something to eat," he said, holding out a metal plate of blackened chicken and stewed carrots.

I eyed his offering with suspicion.

"Please take it," Sergeant Walters said. "You're going to need your strength."

"That's it, then?" I asked as my stomach rumbled. Despite my pride, I accepted the plate of cold food.

"Yes, sometime before dawn two sentries will march you out to South State Road and you'll be set free. What you do after that is up to you."

"I'd like to say good-bye to a few of them."

Sergeant Walters shook his head. "That's impossible. If you come near the 138th again, orders are to shoot on sight. Major Bards has construed such a situation as spying. I don't understand it myself, but those are his words."

I tore apart the chicken, stripping the meat from the bone with my dirty fingers.

"I'm sorry," Walters said. "I should have brought you proper utensils."

Stifling a laugh, I couldn't believe how he was now acting in my presence.

"Why? Did I become some delicate flower after being discovered for what I truly am?"

The sergeant sighed, refusing to take up the argument, and I returned to eating the morsel of chicken and then the carrots until the plate was empty.

"You were a good soldier," Sergeant Walters said. "A crack shot. What you could have done with the Whitworth . . ."

Then he paused before daring to ask, "Why did you do this?"

I looked down at him and realized I had no idea what he was thinking. Was I now an embarrassment to him? Had he sensed something was amiss all along and now berated himself about not doing enough to investigate? But then I saw that all he really wanted was some kind of explanation. Who was this woman, and how had she come to serve under his command?

"I did it to honor my family," I told him. This seemed to reassure Sergeant Waters, for he nodded. To him, it had to sound more proper, something a woman might say. But what he didn't realize was that deep down I was angry, and I vowed one day I'd gain a measure of revenge.

"They deserve better," I continued. "Of course, you could say that about anyone killed in this ungodly war."

Sergeant Walters blinked at the word *ungodly*.

"May we pray that it all ends soon." He extended his hand, taking the metal plate of bare chicken bones from me.

"It won't," I said. "We both know that."

Sergeant Walters stood in front of me, holding the metal plate in one hand. "The sentries will come for you shortly," he said. "You're not to make any argument or protest. If you do, you will be gagged and treated harshly. Just go with them and let it be, understand?"

I nodded, almost feeling sorry for him. A pleading tone had crept into his voice.

"Thank you, sir," I replied, but he was already striding away from me.

Most may mind, even fear, the dark. But since my mother's passing, I've come to enjoy the particular solitude that can only be found late at night. Back home, I'd heard the whispers. How I'd become a crazy woman, too often seen in the shadows around Auburn well after nightfall, walking by myself, sometimes talking to the stars and the moon. Not that long ago, such talk would have embarrassed me. But now I didn't care. Not one iota.

That was my state of mind as I walked the South State Road in the early morning hours. The half-moon shone above, and the first hint of hot summer was carried on the breeze. I tried talking to Mother and then Uncle Frank on the long walk, as if they were right there with me, step for step. But for some reason neither one of them was speaking to me tonight.

Alone with my thoughts, I imagined that the lights of Auburn would appear when I crested the next hill. When they didn't, I knew it would be midday, maybe even later, by the time I reached home. And what would I do then? I had to be a sight. Something to get the tongues wagging again. Still in my Union blues, at a distance I might pass for a soldier, except for the missing rifle, which had been taken from me when I was banished from the 138th Regiment. My hair, which I had shorn close to the skull, would soon grow back, thick and soft. Reluctantly, I would return to skirts again, almost eager to be back in the shadows and contemplating my next move.

3

One barely needs both hands to count the Celtic nations of the world: Ireland, Cornwall, Wales, the Isle of Man, Brittany, and Scotland. Centuries ago, many of these lands were beyond the fringe of the Roman Empire and their inhabitants relished being renegades, pushing against the forces of history.

And that is how Bennet Burley pictured himself when he arrived in America from Glasgow in 1862. Another renegade, a would-be soldier of fortune. The northern states were thick with factories and mills, with businesses capable of bringing more bullets and cannon to the Union side. As Burley traveled south by horseback that first time, the smokestacks eventually faded away, replaced by fields of crops and cattle. The green fields and wide rivers of the hinterlands reminded him of home. Yet as he listened to the conversations around him in the taverns along his route, he could not miss their worries about where this war was leading.

"More of them march down my road every day, heading to the fight," a farmer somewhere below the Mason-Dixon Line told him. It was dusk, his third day out of New York City. "I know they're green, and everyone agrees that they can't hold a candle to those fighting under Lee's or Jackson's command. For some that's enough to disregard the likes of them. But I try to tell folks, like I'm telling you now, the bluecoats never stop coming. They may not be the best of soldiers, but there's so many more of them. That will mean something someday. It has to."

The elderly farmer asked if Burley was headed to the fight, and the Scotsman said that he was.

When the man heard that, he eyed the stranger and said solemnly, "They're a haughty people. Thick with pride, they are."

At first, Burley wasn't sure if the farmer was talking about the rebels or the Yankees, but it soon became apparent he meant the Confederate leaders in Richmond.

"They're the ones whose forefathers got away from the old country and fought the British for their independence," he told Burley. "So, it's easy for them to say this war is like that one, that they're just fighting for their kind to be able to do whatever they want, whenever they like. But I'm watching those bluebellies march down my road, day after day, more and more of them heading to the fray. All the Confederates' pretty words, all their notions about what's just and proper, won't stop the likes of so many boys in blue."

The old sod was kind enough to offer Bennet Burley dinner and a place for the night in his barn. For the days and weeks that followed, what the farmer had said continued to rattle around in Burley's head. What if the Romans hadn't been content with sitting pretty in London Town or hiding behind Hadrian's Wall? What if they had kept building their roads deeper into Scotland? That Celtic heritage that Burley took such pride in wouldn't have stood for long against such marching legions and cruel intent. It isn't preordained that any place on earth will stand and others fall. As he headed toward the epic struggle, the war being talked about even an ocean away, Burley reminded himself to remember the old farmer's words.

4

As dawn approached, a few wagons appeared on the road. The farmers were heading into Auburn for market, and I moved to one side, keeping my head down, giving their "Morning" greetings a half-hearted wave. That's how things continued as the sun edged above the horizon, until I saw the carriage with a pair of regal horses coming toward me from town. As the rig drew closer, I knew who it was. Somehow word had already gotten back to her.

"Is that you, Rory Chase?" she called down.

"You know it is, Fanny Seward."

When I was a girl, Mother was the only one who called me Rory. She told me it was Old Celtic for the "Red King" who fought the Norman invaders in Ireland centuries ago. Somehow Fanny, and then the rest of the Seward family, began calling me that soon after Mother passed.

"C'mon," Fanny said as she came around and pulled the carriage alongside. "I don't see how you can put one foot in front of another after everything you've been through."

I scrambled into the seat beside my childhood friend, and we were off at a canter toward home.

"How did you know?" I asked.

The morning breeze in our faces, so much now passing in a blur, never felt so good.

"Reports are always coming into Father," Fanny Seward replied, letting loose the reins. The horses broke into a trot. "When they mentioned a woman being found in the ranks, I knew it had to be you."

"Have I become that notorious?"

"No, simply as stubborn as ever."

At the village limits, the horses slowed. Around us, Auburn was stirring to life, preparing for a new day.

Fanny added, "Thank goodness we hadn't left for Washington yet."

"You're accompanying your father again?"

She pulled back slightly on the reins. "Has it become that predictable?" she asked. "My mother's bouts of melancholy timed to our next trip south to the capital?"

I tried not to smile. The daughter was fulfilling more of her mother's duties as the war raged on. Anyone who knew the Seward family could see it.

"Mother doesn't get along well in Washington, I'm afraid," Fanny continued. "Lord knows that she's never happy there. Always complaining about being away from her beloved Auburn."

"And what do you think of Washington?"

Fanny smiled, dark hair framing that angelic face of hers. At first glance, it was easy to underestimate Frances Adeline ("Fanny") Seward. Easy to believe she was just another young woman from money who was doing well despite such tumultuous times. Yet when one heard her talk about the places she had been, the people she had met, it was apparent that she knew better than anyone how to make her way in the world.

"I'll happily go in her place," Fanny said, making it sound matter-of-fact. "Play the woman of the household in Washington again. My father needs me there, and I can witness the goings-on. I must admit, I've come to enjoy it all."

Fanny guided the horses off South Street and up the gravel drive to the family mansion and the carriage house around back. When I was growing up, it was a fine enough house but not as impressive as it was now, with the gabled roof and two-story tower erected along one side. As the power and influence of Fanny's father had grown, so had the family home in our community.

"Let's find you some proper clothes," she said.

"I don't mind," I told her. "I've become rather accustomed to wearing trousers."

She pretended not to be shocked. "You're certainly determined to be a part of this war, aren't you?"

"And what if I am?"

"There are better ways than the 138th."

"They are becoming a good enough unit," I maintained, surprised by the measure of pride that crept into my voice. "They have been drilling hard. Ready to do their part with honor."

Fanny shook her head at this. "That's not what I meant. And anyway, most of them will fall in some forgotten field in Maryland or Virginia," she said, suddenly overcome by emotion. "Men are dying in such vast numbers in this war. The battlefields are killing grounds. I've seen the reports that come across my father's desk. My brother Augustus . . . Will he end up in command of an ill-fated group like the 138th?"

Ahead of us, a few lights still glowed from the Sewards' home, as if the estate was a beacon calling my friend back from the wilderness.

"All I know is that I cannot stay here," I said, in a softer voice. "I need to do something."

Fanny regained her composure. That calm way she liked to carry herself through the world. "The misguided angel needs a quest?" she asked.

Slightly stung by the accuracy of her comment, I tried to smile. "You make it sound so childish."

"No, if anything it's admirable. It truly is, Rory. If our generals were half as determined as you, this war would have been over long ago."

We pulled into the yard, and a stable hand stepped from the shadows to take the horses.

"What are we to do with you?" Fanny said.

As she spoke, Washington came to mind. Perhaps there would be something there, I decided. Yet Fanny was already ahead of me, like she knew what I was thinking.

"We will have you to the capital soon enough," she said. "But you didn't seem to enjoy it all that much last time."

I almost argued with her, but why bother? My childhood friend often knew my leanings better than I did myself.

"C'mon, Father's been up for hours. I'm sure he has an idea."

5

"Miss Rory, I admire your determination to serve your nation," Secretary of State Seward said. "But the infantry? I don't believe that's your true calling in life."

"So it would appear, sir."

"There are plenty of opportunities here, on the home front, as they say."

"I can do more than make bandages, Mr. Seward," I told him, daring to raise my voice. "I'm sure of it."

"I see." He briefly gazed out the window as Auburn readied for another day. Then the secretary turned his attention back to me. "You lived for a time in Niagara Falls, right?"

"Father," Fanny interrupted. "We've been over this."

Secretary Seward glanced at his only daughter, then paused again, seemingly uncertain how to continue. The three of us were in his home, where almost every sliver of space was taken up by something impressive and important. As I sat there, I recalled that the small-sized Congressional desk had been used at George Washington's inauguration. The parlor's fireplace was constructed by a young carpenter named Brigham Young, who later became a prophet of the Mormon Church. Everywhere hung family portraits and engravings of world leaders, including Napoleon and Queen Victoria, while any remaining wall space was lined with bookshelves. Even the ivy plants along the walkways to the Seward mansion were distinctive.

They came from Sir Walter Scott's home in Scotland and had been presented to Secretary Seward by Washington Irving. Growing up, Fanny and I had read Scott's *Ivanhoe*, among other classics that others might deem too romantic for such sophisticated young women. Yet sitting there, in the secretary's study that morning, I suddenly had a longing to reread Scott's most famous work. Pretend that Fanny and I were young enough, still naïve enough, to escape into that tale about the Saxons and the Normans from long ago.

As the room fell into an uncomfortable silence, I tried to hold the secretary's gaze. I sat in the dark leather chair across the polished mahogany desk from him. Stacks of paper covered the desk's surface, and anyone who didn't know better would think that it was a hodge-podge of letters and official correspondence. Still, at that moment in the country's history, Secretary Seward was as organized as anyone in government, as busy as any general in the field. He was a man who had a finger in every pie, as the locals liked to say.

Only a few years earlier, many had thought he would be the next president. After all, he had made a name for himself in Washington and throughout the nation as a US senator, as outspoken as a politician could be against slavery. (Though word had it that his wife, Frances, was more adamant about such things than he was.) Secretary Seward appeared to have the inside track for the presidential nomination when the Republican Party opened its convention in Chicago in 1860. But a young politician from Illinois, unknown to most in the New York delegation, outmaneuvered Seward's backers and won the nomination on the third ballot. From there, Abraham Lincoln went on to capture the White House, and soon after his election the southern states seceded from the Union.

While another man might have sulked and even plotted his political revenge after losing the nomination, Fanny's father accepted Lincoln's invitation to be secretary of state. (He did let the new president stew for a few days before doing so, but what politician wouldn't have done the same?) Since the war had erupted at Fort Sumter, and the months had drawn into years, Seward and Lincoln had formed a close friendship. Many now regarded my best friend's father to be the second most powerful man in what was left of the United States of America.

For some reason, something told me not to let this moment go. To continue through whatever door, the secretary, a longtime friend of my departed mother, held open to me.

"Yes, we lived in the Falls," I said as Fanny stirred behind me. Once again, she was worried about my well-being. I could tell.

"I remember now," said the secretary. As the two of us watched, he stood up and walked over to one of the bookshelves.

William Seward wasn't very tall. I'd grown to tower over him, and his youngest child now came up to his shoulder. Still, with his head of white hair, his booming voice, the man would always be the cock of the walk, as they say.

"I cannot help thinking you'd be well suited for the border," he said, pulling down a full-sized volume with a dark-red hard cover. "You have some history there. With your heroic mother."

"The border?" I asked.

"Yes, with British Canada."

He placed the atlas down on the desk and began flipping through the pages.

Canada? I had no idea what he was speaking of. All the battles we had been following were well to the south, in such places as Antietam, Gettysburg, and Ball's Bluff.

"Of course, you don't know the seriousness of the situation there," said Secretary Seward. "And how could you? We're not sending armies to the northern border, even though President Lincoln fears we'll need to someday."

"Has it become so desperate?" Fanny demanded. "That we need to bring this up with Rory?"

I looked from my childhood friend to her father, sensing the beginnings of a possible argument between the two of them. Yet the bond between this particular daughter and father ran deeper than most, and even though they briefly glared at each other, they quickly turned their attention toward me. As if the direction the conversation had taken was somehow my fault.

"Perhaps our Rory could be of service," he said as he sat down. Then he glanced at his daughter. "Close the door, my dear," he said.

The atlas remained open as the secretary gathered up a stack of papers, maps, and small photographs, the newer ones called *cartes de visites*. The popular calling cards.

"All of this needs to go with us to Washington," he reminded his daughter.

"I know," Fanny said as she moved around to her father's side of the mahogany desk and nodded for me to join them. "But if you're going to involve Rory, she needs to know more. Much more."

The atlas was opened to a map of the eastern half of the United States, from the Mississippi River to the eastern seaboard.

"To win this war, we must retake the South," Secretary Seward said. "The Confederacy needs no such victory. They simply require us to give up our attempts to drag them back into the Union. There have been some serious feints by the Confederates into the North—Antietam and, more recently, Gettysburg. Attempts to create war weariness among our ranks and people. But the president and I believe that such threats have been stymied, hopefully forever. That Lee and his army have been worn down and in Ulysses Grant we finally have a general determined to finish the job."

"Unconditional Surrender Grant," Fanny said.

"Yes, the man is a fierce warrior," her father murmured. "As a result, after years of bloodshed, the end may be in sight. That's why we cannot allow anything to upset the balance."

Here the secretary flipped the pages to a map of the Great Lakes—Superior, Michigan, Huron, Erie, and Ontario.

"In recent weeks, we've focused our attention on Erie and Ontario," he said. "Their southern shores are well populated, and if there was any kind of threat to these regions, it could be catastrophic for a final resolution to the war, as well as the president's re-election chances."

"And that's exactly what's happening," Fanny said.

Secretary Seward nodded. "Our sources tell us that the number of Confederate spies along the border increases by the day. In turn, they have joined up with mercenaries from other nations. These so-called soldiers of fortune." He spit the words out in disdain. "Some have gathered in Halifax and Montreal, others in Toronto. Now I don't want to overstate this. All of these groups together couldn't mount an offensive. Far from it."

"But they remain dangerous," Fanny said, completing her father's thought.

The secretary glanced at his daughter. "Especially since we don't know what they're up to. Perhaps that's where Rory could help."

"That may be," Fanny said. "But being a courier—some would say a spy—is perilous work."

"Agreed," the secretary replied. "But we're badly outnumbered in these areas. We're desperate for more eyes and ears."

"Lakes Erie and Ontario," I said, leaning closer to the map, "means cities like Detroit, Buffalo, the Falls?"

The secretary nodded gravely. "Yes, and any remaining units in that region are strictly Home Guard. Nearly every warship or larger vessel that could be of service is now part of the blockade in the Atlantic and the Gulf of Mexico. As I said, we are desperate for more information from our northernmost border. Perhaps that is where you could play a part. You proved to be an able member of the 138th—"

"Until she was discovered," Fanny reminded her father. "And she nearly paid dearly for that, didn't you?"

I kept my eyes on the atlas in front of us, my lips tightly closed.

"Still, you lived in Niagara Falls, on the American side, for a summer not that long ago," the secretary began again. "So, you already know the area."

"A bit, sir."

"A bit? From what I understand, your dear mother, God rest her soul, was a major help to the Underground Railroad there. She worked with Harriet Tubman, and if I remember correctly, you were of some service, even though you were how old at that point?"

"Sixteen. Just sixteen."

The secretary gave me a curious look. "Why are you being so modest, Rory? According to records kept by Mrs. Tubman herself, more than seventy-five runaway slaves passed through Niagara Falls to freedom on the Canadian side that particular summer, often with the catchers right on their heels. Your mother was part of the elaborate operation, was she not? Operating out of the Cataract House hotel as the Negroes were spirited across the Suspension Bridge or ferried across the Niagara River. And you assisted her during that pivotal time."

"Yes, I helped," I told the secretary and his daughter. "But . . ."

"Yes?"

"There was more I could have done. Should have done."

Secretary Seward waited for me to go on. When I didn't, he glanced at his daughter, unsure how to continue.

"You have a haunted look about you, Miss Rory," he said. "That troubles me."

Fanny remained quiet at this, and I knew she was concerned as well.

"Still, there's no denying that you know the town, the river, both sides of the Falls itself," he added, setting aside his concern. "And that is how you can be of service to your country. So, please consider relocating there for a time on our behalf."

His hands rearranged the stack of papers on his desk. He reminded me of a wizard conjuring up one illusion after another. The secretary placed two photographs of men dressed in fine suits atop the maps in the middle of the table. The images were about the size of someone's palm, mounted on cards.

Speaking as if I had already agreed to his plan, Secretary Seward tapped one of the photographs. "We believe these were taken in a shop on the American side of the Falls. From there, they eventually found their way to me."

"Father has his methods," Fanny said, with a hint of pride, and her father tried not to smile at this.

The three of us studied the images. The first was of a man in a well-tailored suit, sporting a neatly trimmed beard, as he gazed with intensity at the camera lens. The man in the second one seemed larger physically, with what could only be called a smirk on his face. He too wore a three-piece suit, but it did not fit him as well.

The secretary continued. "The first gent is John Yates Beall, spelled B-E-A-L-L, although he pronounces it 'Bell.' A graduate of the University of Virginia, he had been conducting raids in the Chesapeake Bay. That's where we apprehended him, but then he was returned to the South in a prisoner exchange. A most unfortunate series of events when you consider what has transpired in recent months. His partner is one Bennet Burley, a Scotsman, who fancies himself as a soldier of fortune. He was with Beall during the raids in the Chesapeake, and this Burley character is an expert in explosives and nautical torpedoes."

I asked, "And what are they doing now?"

"We only know what they've done in the past," Secretary Seward answered.

"Stealing boats, blowing things up," Fanny added, with a note of disgust.

"And now they have been sighted along the Niagara River, on both sides of the border between the Falls and Buffalo," the secretary said. "We can only assume that they are determined to do something similar there."

Fanny glanced at one photograph and then the other. "What an odd couple," she declared. "One serious, the other a bit of joker."

"Whatever the case, we need to know what they're up to," her father said. "President Lincoln and I have talked privately about the fearsome possibilities along our northern border with Canada. How an international incident could bring the British into the mix. Something that bleeds men and equipment from our ongoing campaigns in the South."

"I could do this," I told them.

"You're sure?" Fanny asked.

Yet her father had seen an opening, and like any good politician he was eager to capitalize on it. He held out the *cartes de visites* for me to have a better look.

"As I said, I need to take these with me to Washington," the secretary said. "In cabinet meetings, I pretend not to care, but I'm deeply concerned about this threat on our northern border."

"It's Stanton's responsibility then?" Fanny asked, always eager to learn the true reason behind what appeared to be random circumstances. Stanton was Edwin Stanton, the secretary of war.

"Yes, technically this is Stanton's domain," replied her father. "But you know how I feel about his methods. How he can blow hot and cold. Ignore the larger picture."

In listening to it all, I wouldn't have been surprised if Secretary Seward had gotten ahold of the pictures without Edwin Stanton being the wiser.

"They are the only copies that I have," Fanny's father said, turning toward me. "But I can leave them with you for the morning. To study and memorize as best you can."

"Rory can do better than that, Father," Fanny said. "If she's certain about this."

Only after I nodded did Fanny briefly disappear from the study, soon returning with a sketch pad and several pencils.

"You've forgotten, Father," she said, placing the materials alongside the images. "Our Rory is an accomplished artist."

"I don't know about accomplished," I told him. "But I do like to draw."

I took up the pencil. As the Sewards watched, I focused on the first one's face, the man called Beall. He had such dark eyes—the kind that could bore right through a person. He seemed to be filled with purpose and duty, a combination that could be especially dangerous during the times we found ourselves in. He was the kind of person one would recognize across a crowded room or along a busy street. He simply had that air about him. In comparison, the other rebel spy, the one called Burley, had to be the renegade of the two, the one who could come up with outlandish plans and was more eager to take chances.

As I sketched, the pencil moving faster now, the secretary and my longtime friend receded from my thoughts. Instead, I found myself pulled further and further into what I was drawing.

"Her sketches do have a flair," I heard Secretary Seward say.

"Let her be," Fanny replied, almost in a whisper. "I'll speak with her before we leave."

6

Too often I don't see the worth, even the purpose, in my own work. Mother used to tell me that. Still, as I looked upon one sketch and then the other, even I couldn't deny that the likenesses were of high quality.

"Are you hungry?" Fanny asked.

She was watching me from the doorway to her father's study. I felt as if I was again coming out of some kind of trance. Since I was a child, I've had such moments, where I allowed myself to fall deeply into the waters of whatever may be at hand. Often that happened when I began to draw.

"What time is it?" I asked, returning to the land of the living.

"Going on eleven," Fanny told me. "You've been working away. Father was impressed."

I gazed about me, realizing I had taken up the secretary's study. "I hope I didn't disturb things. Being here, where all his papers are."

"Nonsense," Fanny said. "Father is more adaptable than many give him credit for. Besides, with the way you were working away, your 138th could have paraded through and I don't think it would have mattered to you. That's how intent you had become."

I smiled at her mention of my old regiment. I missed being in their ranks. How much easier things would have been if I had been born a man, instead of so often having to act like one!

"Your father is certain?" I asked. "That I could be of help in the Falls, along the border?"

Fanny tried to appear noncommittal. "Of course, it's up to you. Still, you know the towns, the river there. I have to agree that you'd be well suited for the assignment."

"Hardly," I said, trying to smile.

Fanny stepped closer and looked at the sketches I'd done of John Yates Beall and Bennet Burley.

"It is fine work," she said. "I'll fetch a cylinder, something to put them in."

"You know I so want to help," I said. "But of all the places? Niagara Falls?"

Fanny pulled up a chair and huddled close with me.

"You've never told me everything that happened to you there," she said. "All I remember is that you were gone with your mother for that summer and into the fall. Then you were back home with us in Auburn."

I nodded. "It was nothing."

"I don't know about that, Rory Chase. For when the topic comes up, the look on your face? Well, I believe Father is right. Haunted may be the best word for what comes over you."

"It's difficult to explain," I said.

"You can tell me," Fanny said. "There are no secrets between us."

I considered this and realized there was no disagreeing with her.

"Mother was working at the Cataract House. We lived there that summer when she was helping with the Underground Railroad. Between such doings, the carnies and barkers, the very Falls itself, the place was as checkered as anywhere I've ever been."

"It had to be," Fanny said. "After the Fugitive Slave Act became law, the slavers were emboldened to chase the escapees right up to the border itself."

"But the staff at the Cataract was there to help them get across the border."

"The hotel workers?" Fanny asked. "Father says many of them are escaped slaves themselves."

"Yes, the owner of the Cataract House, Mr. Chapman, a white man, had abolitionist sympathies. Mother said as much."

I looked out upon State Street, and in my mind the years peeled back to that long summer when we were in the Falls. How Mother helped escapees reach Canada, on the opposite side of the Niagara River. But not everyone was so lucky.

"It was a few days after the Fourth of July," I began. "Hot as blazes, and this rich family from Charleston arrived at the hotel for the week. They had two young women in their service. They looked like sisters. They were called Mary and Bessie."

"And the wait staff spoke to them?" Fanny said. "Seeing if they wanted to escape across the river to Canada?"

I nodded. "The head waiter at the Cataract House was John Douglas. Mr. Douglas. Perhaps he's still there. All I know is he was polite as could be on the outside, but always with a plan and at the ready. He had a rowboat at Ferry Landing. That's about a quarter-mile from the back door of the hotel. It was docked down a ragged set of wooden stairs that were always slick from the mist coming off the Falls. That's how close it was."

"So, he approached this Mary and Bessie?"

"Yes, and an opportunity presented itself. Mr. Douglas informed them that the time was right—a chance to escape across the river, to Canada and freedom. Mary immediately said yes, she would go. No questions asked, and soon she and Mr. Douglas were making a beeline to the stairs down to the river and his boat. I happened to be helping Mother at the hotel that morning, and Bessie couldn't decide what to do. She dithered and dithered until Mr. Douglas and Mary were away, and then she decided she would go, too."

"Oh, no."

"I took her by the hand and led her across the hotel lawn, running for the stairs and the river. But her owner by then had caught wind of what was going on, and he and several others were soon on our heels. I can still remember him howling for someone, anyone, to help him save his property. Those were the words he used—'help me save my property.' That soon drew a crowd, and in short order a mob was right behind us.

"We had almost reached the stairs down to the river when they caught up to us. Bessie was pulled away from me. Then they took pot-shots with their pistols at Mr. Douglas out there in the middle of the rapids, pulling on his oars like a madman, with Mary huddled down in the rear of the craft. I knew Mr. Douglas was working those oars faster than he would have liked against that fierce current. He must have been a waterman in another time, in another life, because no one knew the Niagara River like he did. And on that day, in the shadow of the Falls itself, the waters nearly capsized him several times. How the slave owner and his kind would have cheered at that sight. As I said, it is about a quarter-mile from the Cataract Hotel to the Ferry Landing, another quarter-mile across those raging waters, and then up the embankment to the Canadian side and freedom."

"And did they make it?" Fanny asked.

"Yes. Somehow Mr. Douglas kept his boat afloat and got safely to the other side. Soon afterward, the mob on the American side dispersed, with Bessie in tow. Several in the mob threatened me, and by the next day, Mother was making plans for us to return home to Auburn."

After my story ended, the two of us sat quietly in the Sewards' parlor.

"The Cataract House, Mr. Douglas, crossing below the Falls," Fanny eventually said. "I didn't know the place was so much a part of your past, Rory."

"I wish it wasn't."

Fanny stood and briefly rested a hand on my shoulder.

"All I know is that if you could go there, simply look around, it would help our effort so much," she said.

I nodded.

"But nothing more," my friend said. "After that you come home, back to Auburn. You promise?"

"I promise, Fanny."

A dozen or more people stood alongside the train scheduled for Washington, waiting for Secretary Seward to address them. I carried my mother's small suitcase, its sides scraped and scarred like a beaten mule, to the other side of the station platform for the train heading in the opposite direction—west to Buffalo and beyond.

The good secretary would never disappoint an audience, and he soon came to the rear of his train, looking upon his supporters. Many applauded his appearance. Over his shoulder, I saw Fanny survey the crowd, always watching out for her beloved father. Our eyes briefly met, and she waved, just a flutter of the fingers. Then she disappeared into the last car of the train, which was reserved for the secretary when he traveled south to the nation's capital.

Secretary Seward told his gathering about how it had been a long fight, certainly longer than either the Union or the rebels had expected. But he believed that with the victories at Vicksburg and Gettysburg that "history's unpredictable pageant has now turned in our favor."

Those words brought a round of applause and some hearty cheers. As one who had heard Secretary Seward speak on more occasions than I could remember, I half-expected him to stop there. He so enjoyed ending things with a slight crescendo, as Fanny would say.

Yet this time he said a bit more, telling his impromptu assembly to "be ever vigilant. To not be lulled into the misconception that all our battles lie hundreds of miles away. Sometimes the most vexed, the most difficult ordeals lie closer to home, festering at our back door."

As he spoke those words, he was looking past his well-wishers— his eyes only on me.

7

Almost every day I find time to gaze upon the river,
And when I see those roiling waters, it gives me hope.
Cesar tells me that the ravine from the edge of the Falls
Has moved back almost six feet during my lifetime.
Eroded away by those fast-flowing, green-blue waters,
And while that may be too rosy for me,
There is no denying the power of water upon hard rock.
How what we may consider solid and impenetrable
Can be worn away over the years and centuries.
It is water over stone, relentless and every day,
And I believe in the power of such notions,
More than anything else I've ever encountered in my days.
Water over stone. I bear witness to the process daily
And I've been an active participant in this holy war.
Water over stone. Believe. Just believe.

JOHN DOUGLAS

Wreet Thayer opened the small white envelope that had been slipped in with the morning mail. Outside the skies promised light rain and perhaps sun in the afternoon. If the heavens did brighten, she would walk to the Falls and then visit the Cataract House and thank Mr. Douglas for his latest page of verse. Such offerings always gladdened her heart.

Rereading the poem, lingering over it like a fine wine, she would later file it away in the scrapbook where she kept such gifts from her old friend. As the war stretched on, Mr. Douglas had been writing more, which she took as a good sign. Even though the way stations for the Underground Railroad stretched far from western New York, such activity had slowed to a halt. Nothing like it was in the decade before the firing on Fort Sumter and the start of the war. Back when the Fugitive Slave Act made it the law of the land that local authorities were required to assist slavers in retrieving their so-called property— even if the poor wretch was within the shadow of the Falls itself. Back when the Niagara River, which was only a few blocks from Wreet's door, just over by the Cataract House itself, had been literally the last river to cross.

Wreet knew that Mr. Douglas still kept a longboat tethered to the small dock down the flights of stairs in the mist and shadow of the American side of the Falls. How many had crossed there or via the Suspension Bridge north of downtown, high above the gorge? She had lost track long ago. Still, Mr. Douglas would know. He kept ledgers of such attempts. Those that ended well and those that didn't. Those who escaped and the others who were led back into slavery.

If Wreet's days became too long, she would flip the sign on the front door from OPEN to CLOSED and retire upstairs to sit on the small balcony that looked toward the Falls, where she couldn't quite make out the raging waters but could regularly spy the clouds from the cataract billowing to the heavens. She was tempted to do so this morning when a knock came on her shop's front door.

It was Ronnie, the errand boy from the telegram office. Although Ronnie wasn't much of a boy anymore. The younger ones had been drawn south, like moths to the flame, to fight the Confederates.

Opening her door, hearing the familiar bell atop the frame jingle, Wreet took the message and tipped him a coin. Back inside, she saw that it wasn't a conventional gram. Instead, it was a letter on official letterhead from Secretary William Seward. She hadn't received one of those in months.

She read the letter and then reviewed it, noting the important passages. More rebel spies were now in the borderlands. Well, that was nothing new. If anything, the secretary was repeating information that Mr. Douglas and others had relayed to the secretary in the first place. What was novel here was that the good secretary had sent a new courier to help them. This one would be arriving soon.

Certainly, they could use all the help they could get. She, Mr. Douglas, even the others at the Cataract House weren't getting any younger. Still, whoever was sent their way had best be on their toes. While the Falls billed itself as an escape from the everyday world, the war had encroached here as well. Their struggle wasn't with armies and firepower, at least not yet. Instead, it was about disguise and stealth and whom to ultimately trust.

PART 2

Along the Border

To have Niagara before me, lighted by the sun and by the moon, red in the day's decline, and grey as evening slowly fell upon it; to look upon it every day, and wake up in the night and hear its ceaseless voice; this was enough.

—CHARLES DICKENS

8

The Suspension Bridge that spanned the Niagara River had two levels, one sitting over the other. "A grand wedding cake of construction," Mother used to say, but I remembered it as something more beguiling and dangerous than anything of true beauty.

The top level supported a railroad branch line, connecting the northern outskirts of Niagara Falls on the American side to the less populated Canadian side. At the Bridge Station on the American side, a second rail line traveled south a short distance to the larger terminal in downtown Niagara Falls. From there, it continued south to the prosperous city of Buffalo and the way back east to Auburn and Albany and eventually to New York City. Or, from Buffalo, one could go in the opposite direction, sweeping along the southern edge of Lake Erie toward Cleveland and Chicago.

From the bridge's upper tier, the enormity of the Niagara Gorge revealed itself beneath the structure, and when crossing over the abyss the mist from the Falls often hung like a veil. When those clouds did part, the distant smoke from the factories closer to Buffalo could be seen. Off to the other side, the Niagara River flowed north past sheer cliffs until it soon emptied into Lake Ontario. In the early morning, mist could hug those shale-green walls like ghosts from some forgotten cemetery.

After checking into the Cataract House, I walked over to Prospect Point to view the American Falls. Even here, next to one of the famed wonders of the world, the region was parceled out and broken into contrary pieces. The American Falls are smaller in size than their Canadian counterpart, due to Goat Island and the necklace of Three Sisters Islands that stand like a small fortress reaching toward the middle of the Niagara River.

Walking along those glittering green-white waters, I recalled the summer a few years before when Mother came here, ostensibly to work at the hotel as the assistant supervisor of the cleaning staff. Actually, she came at the request of Harriet Tubman, her friend from back in Auburn. In the time before the war began, Mother did all she could for Miss Harriet and the Underground Railroad.

These memories crowded my mind as I turned and took in the Suspension Bridge, which towered above the river, just downstream from the Falls. In the distance, the bridge rose like something from a madman's fantasy. Soon enough, I'd have to cross over to the other side, to British Canada. It was expected for the work I would be doing. Spy work. But on this afternoon, the day of my return, I watched the train chug across on the top level and remembered that day almost five years ago when Mother decided we wouldn't wait for the next train. Instead, we crossed on the bridge's lower level in a hack from the hotel.

As we approached the Suspension Bridge that afternoon, I got my first glimpse of the bridge's bottom rung, which rolled out as a long dark tunnel, an opening of shadow and malice. Framed by the wooden beams overhead and along both sides, the lower level traveled directly beneath the railroad tracks, with only a few feet overtop for clearance. At the entrance, Mother paid the few pennies toll as men in long coats and wide-brimmed hats eyed our rig.

"Bystanders," the cabbie muttered. "Looking for no good."

"Looking for what?" Mother asked.

"Anyone they decide shouldn't be crossing, ma'am. That they can blow the whistle on."

Before we could ask anything more, the cabbie gave the reins a flick, and we were off.

Gaps in the wooden frame allowed us to see some of the river below us and the mist that billowed up from the Falls. It was an extreme, even disjointed landscape, so unlike the rolling hills and tranquil long lakes near Auburn.

We were almost across when a commotion broke out behind us. A moment later, a man, a Negro, ran past the carriage. I edged forward for a better look.

"Make room," shouted a white man atop a horse standing at least seventeen hands high. He galloped up behind and then past us. As he rushed by, I stood, leaning alongside the driver for a better look.

"Missy, you best sit back where you belong," he warned.

"What's this about?" I demanded, sounding older than my sixteen years. Once he saw that I had no intention of returning to my seat next to Mother, he nodded at the Black man running as fast as he could for the far side of the bridge.

"Another runaway," the driver said. "The Bystanders back at the toll entrance must have sounded the alarm."

I turned to see more figures moving about at the entrance to the bridge's tunnel-like passageway.

"He'll be safe if he makes it to the other side," I said.

"But that ain't going to happen, young one. Not today."

Our driver was correct. The man on horseback was soon pulling alongside the fleeing figure. With a practiced motion, he tossed his lasso high into the air, and it settled over the escaped slave's torso. With a tug, the man tied the rope to the saddle horn, and when the horse braked, the Black man toppled to the ground like a small tree going down in a windstorm.

"He was nearly to the other side," I protested.

"And what of it?"

"The boundary line must be the middle of the bridge, right over the heart of the river. By that measure, he had already made it to British Canada."

The cabbie chuckled. "Nobody has ever fully sorted out such things, let alone drawn a proper line down the middle of the Suspension Bridge. You know how the slavers work. They always hedge things in their favor when it comes to the fugitive laws."

Soon afterward, the poor creature, his hands now tied behind him and pulled along by a second rope around his neck, was led back to the American side. Back to captivity.

That was years ago, I told myself, *and so much has changed since then. War now rages across the country, and President Lincoln has declared all the slaves to be free.* Still, as I gazed past the rising mist, toward the Suspension Bridge, the buggies and carriages crowding the adjoining streets, I saw the so-called Bystanders still milling around the entrance to the tunnel-like passageway, and I knew I had once again fallen into a world where past and present could swirl like the raging waters of the Niagara below. While history may march on, as learned men like Secretary Seward like to say, this part of the world can conjure up more ghosts than any philosopher or scholar or statesman will ever explain away.

Returning to the Cataract House, I gazed upward at the sky, which one was prone to do in these parts. Due to the proximity of the two Great Lakes, Erie and Ontario, the weather could change in barely a glimmer. *Barely a glimmer?* How did that expression of my mother's somehow fall into my head?

For a moment, I stood there and realized that this world, this one from my past, was framed by two architectural wonders. The Suspension Bridge rode the northern view, always to be found by following the Niagara Gorge downstream from town, while directly upriver, hard by the waters racing toward the precipice, stood the elegant, some would say opulent or even gaudy, Cataract House. Five stories tall, with a wide veranda sweeping up two sides, the cupola tower rising out of the rear bank of rooms, it was both elegant and imposing. But I had already decided I would rent a room somewhere else in town—some place smaller, more common—as soon as I got my bearings here. Even years later, the Cataract House held too many memories for me.

Approaching the hotel's front entranceway, I sensed that someone was watching me. Another glance upward, and I saw a dark face gazing down at me from one of the upstairs bedrooms. Yet she disappeared before I could determine who it really was. Inside the front foyer, I appeared to be alone until a soft whisper called out to me.

"Miss Rory? Is that you?"

It was the face from the upstairs window. Her eyes studied me from the half-open doorway to the stairs off the entranceway.

"Sissy?"

"Yes, ma'am," she said, edging briefly into the foyer. But then she stole a look around before backing toward the stairwell. "You've returned. But why?"

Why, indeed, I thought.

"We heard about your mother's passing," Sissy continued, and I had little choice but to take a step closer, to better hear her. "Such a hard loss."

"I'm just visiting," I said. The older woman only smiled at this.

Sissy had been working at the Cataract House for many years, ostensibly as a maid under my mother's direction during our time here. She was as adept at helping souls escape across the border to Canada as anyone, except for Mr. Douglas.

"And we heard about your uncle, too," Sissy said. This was already becoming too much for me, and I was eager to leave.

"Is it all right if I tell the others, Miss Rory?" Sissy asked, briefly resting a calloused hand on my forearm. "Cesar, Aran, and, of course, Mr. Douglas?"

"Yes," I said with some reluctance. "Tell them we'll talk soon."

With that, she excitedly clapped her hands together, one-two. Although an elderly woman, Sissy Morris still carried a youthful enthusiasm about herself, especially when the world delighted her, even in a small way.

"Oh, they will be so happy to hear that, my child," she said. "So happy."

9

Before entering the shop, I stopped to study my reflection in the window, smoothing the loose strands of my short hair back in place. It was growing faster than I expected.

A small bell above the door rang as I entered the two-story store, which was located a few blocks from the Cataract House on the American side of the Falls.

"Be with you in a minute," a woman's voice called from the back.

Venturing further inside, I studied the framed photographs of various sizes that lined the walls on either side of a glass showcase. From the street, the shop might be easily passed by, as small and dark as it was. Yet the more I looked about the interior, the more convinced I became that the work was top-notch. Perhaps as good as anything one would find in New York or Washington. The larger photographs, the so-called Imperials, were done with the "wet plate process" from England, expansive and more detailed than most painted portraits. A few of the daguerreotypes, which were quite the rage a few years ago, were to be found, too, while on a nearby table was a box of stereoscope offerings. I peeked through the viewfinder, where the two images came together to form a lifelike vision of Niagara Falls.

A counter ran along the back wall, and behind it stairs led to the second floor, which I surmised was for the pose studio, with the usual skylight or two. That said, much of that space was shielded by a theater-style curtain. As I waited, a bolt of light flashed from far back in the darkness, through a sliver in that dark veil. For a moment, it reminded me of the spring thunderstorms in Auburn, before I left home the first time for the Falls. Back then, Fanny and I would rock together on the Sewards' front-porch swing, giggling at the passing world and the gathering clouds overhead.

In time, an elderly woman, with a dark-blue shawl draped over her narrow shoulders, emerged from behind the curtain, wiping her hands on a small rag.

"Sorry to keep you," she said. "How can I be of service?"

While her voice had almost a playful lilt, a touch of Irish to it, her eyes were tired, as if she had already put in a hard day. Even though I had rehearsed this moment in my mind, I couldn't decide where to begin. Was this truly a person Secretary Seward trusted? A member of his fledgling spy network?

"You have some impressive works here," I stalled.

"That we do, darling," the old woman replied. "I hate to say it, but the war has been good for business. Even here, hundreds of miles away from the front lines. Now, what can I do you for?"

"I'm looking for Mr. Thayer."

"You a friend of his?"

"Not exactly, but I need to talk with him on a matter of the utmost importance."

"I see," the woman said and turned back to the counter, which was topped with butcher block paper and corner pieces and fasteners to assemble more frames. She tore off a bit of paper and held it out, with the stub of a pencil. "Be a good dear then, and jot down your name and where you can be found. I'll be sure he gets it."

I took the paper from her but hesitated. "When is he due back?"

"I can't say."

"I need to talk with him, face to face. It *is* important."

"So you said, darling."

"Will he be back later today?"

Slightly exasperated, the woman flipped the rag toward the counter, and both of us watched it flutter through the air before landing softly on the floor.

"What do you want, my dear?"

I wasn't sure how to answer.

"C'mon now," the woman said. "I don't have all day."

"The Sewards. I'm a friend of the family. Fanny Seward, specifically."

"The secretary's daughter?"

I nodded, fearing I had already said too much.

"They sent you?"

I nodded again, and the old woman brushed past me, turning the small sign in the front window from OPEN to CLOSED. For good measure, she bolted the door, too.

"I'm Mrs. Thayer," she said. "My friends call me Wreet, short for Marguerite. I reckon you can, too."

"And Mr. Thayer?"

"There is no Mr. Thayer. At least not above ground anymore."

I nodded dumbly at this news.

"Things have already been muddied up but good," Mrs. Thayer said. "Come, it's best if we talk in the back, out of view."

"But I was told to ask for your husband, Mr. Thayer."

"My husband, God bless his soul, died three months ago. Obviously, that hasn't drifted back to the powers that be. I run the operation now. And, like I said, you can call me Wreet."

The old woman pushed aside the black curtain, and I followed her into a small room with trays of pungent chemicals arranged on a series of tables. Glass plates were stacked against the far wall. Wreet took a jug of a chemical solution and poured a splash into one of the trays. I hung back, barely able to make out the hand in front of her face.

"That will do," she said. "Follow me."

Down the narrow hallway was a small table with two chairs. We settled in on either side as Wreet lit a small candle that flickered to life between us.

"You're a tall one, ain't you?" the old woman said as if she was taking me in for the first time. "How did you get caught up in all of this?"

"I wanted to help my country, saving the Union, bringing those rebels to heel," I said.

"High-sounding enough words. But why you?"

For some reason, I began to tell her about my Uncle Frank. How he had been seriously wounded at Ball's Bluff, less than two months after leaving home. How his body had floated down the Potomac River and how he was never right in the head after that tragedy. No matter how much those of us back in Auburn tried to nurse him back to health.

As I finished, Wreet began to run her right index finger along the edge of the table. She did so in a slow, delicate manner, as if she was running the digit down the keen edge of a knife. Then she nodded, as if she had reached a decision. She stood up, and I watched as she went along the tables, gently rocking the trays, one after the other.

"The chemicals can separate if you're not careful."

I didn't answer, just watched her.

"You've got eyes and ears, child," Wreet said. "I'll wager you won't disappoint your friend or her famous father."

"But I don't know what I'm looking for."

"It doesn't take much to pick Johnny Rebs out of a crowd. At least not in these parts. They like to think they are safe and above it all, which they can be, especially on the other side of the border. They're well dressed; they have money and ain't afraid to flash it."

"Are there places they like to congregate?"

"Congregate," Wreet chuckled. "Now there's a highfalutin word. Well, one of their favorite places is a stone's throw from here—the Four Aces. You may have passed by it on your way here."

"I don't remember that name."

Wreet shrugged. "It's well hidden but with a little bit of everything. Music, drinking, den of ill repute. We will stop by there tomorrow."

"Why not tonight?"

"Closed on Monday, lass. The only thing still open for business this evening is the water going over the Falls."

She sat down across from me. "Who are you looking for in particular?"

"A pair of them. One's called John Yates Beall. He was with the rebel army."

"A dangerous one."

"The other is named Bennet Burley. A Scot."

Wreet shook her head. "Never heard of them."

"We think they had their portraits done in this shop."

"Well, that takes in about half the surrounding area by now. Any poor lad going off to the war wants to be remembered in his uniform. It usually doesn't matter if it's a tintype, a *carte de visite*, or if they have the money, an Imperial. They want their loved ones to have a portrait of them. That's why those tent studios are following the troops. And that's what my dear husband was doing until he died."

"Maybe this will help," I said as I reached into my bag and took out the cylinder with the sketches done in the secretary's study in Auburn.

I unrolled them on the tabletop, and Wreet leaned in closer, a flash of recognition in her eyes.

"You've seen them?"

"Maybe so," the older woman said.

"Any idea where they're staying?"

"I cannot say for certain." Wreet picked up one of the sheets of paper and held it closer to the flickering light. "But Mr. Douglas, at the Cataract House, needs to see these."

10

"Mr. Burley, what part of this has upset you so?" Captain Beall asked.

It was early in the evening of August 21, 1864, and the two had gathered in the lobby at the Clifton House, secure on the Canadian side. But they were about to take another trip across the border.

"It's Booth, sir."

"Burl, he's nothing more than a means to an end."

"An ongoing distraction that puts us in danger," Bennet Burley answered, and he saw the captain's face momentarily cloud over.

"He's a bagman. Nothing more," Captain Beall said, lowering his voice, as the hackney carriage pulled up to the Clifton entrance and they climbed aboard.

John Wilkes Booth was scheduled to perform soon in Buffalo and supposedly had funds for their operation from Richmond. He was only in the area for a few days before heading back east. But to meet him meant the rebel spies needed to travel from British Canada, the safe side of the Falls, to the American side, where they were in danger of being apprehended. Arguably, they had already made too many such crossings in the weeks that they had been here. So many eyes always on them.

Besides, Booth was a slippery one. Too much so for Burley's liking. Perhaps that was part and parcel of being an actor, plying one's trade in front of full houses night after night. It could make a man too full of himself, even downright delusional. For his own reasons, Booth wouldn't come to them, so Captain Beall and Bennet Burley needed to make another visit to the Four Aces this evening, making sure all was in order for Booth's arrival tomorrow.

"Interesting how events can turn," said the captain as they pulled away from the Clifton House. As was his wont, when he became philosophical, even melancholy, his voice, which was such a commanding instrument, dropped a tad in register. Even though Beall would never admit it, he would have been a fine actor himself.

"Sir?" replied Burley as he kept an eye on the passing scene. Their ride was gathering speed, heading toward the Suspension Bridge's lower level, which rolled out in front of them like a tunnel straight down to Hades itself.

"What I mean is that for so many years, the darkies were coming from the other direction, out of the South, and this was the last obstacle in their path," Beall said, nodding at the bridge's silhouette looming before them. "This was the final hurdle to their so-called promised land. And now it is an obstacle for us."

"One that's easily managed," Burley replied, trying to put a brave face on things.

Captain Beall nodded. "How I wish I shared your confidence, Burl. Perhaps that comes from the narrow escapes you've had."

"You've had your share, too."

"That may be, but yours seem somehow more colorful, dare I say even more romantic. Perhaps it's the way in which you tell them."

Yes, Burley could tell a good yarn and admire a better lie. Perhaps that's why he was at home in these parts, at least on the Canadian side. While the American side of the Falls sported more industry, a growing hulk of commerce that sent ample supplies and cannon to the bluecoats, the Canadian side was "high carnival," as the locals liked to say. A swirl of hucksters, carneys, and mountebanks with Malacca walking canes. On this side of the border, small stones painted white by clever peddlers were hawked as slivers of congealed mist from the Falls itself. And, my goodness, people bought them. To venture outside, at almost any hour, was to be propositioned by Irish prostitutes, their cheeks aglow in rouge, and hack drivers, like this one, eager to take you to the next big show in town for which they undoubtedly received a cut. That all existed within sight of one of the natural wonders of the world, somehow doing a brisk business despite the free and often glorious views.

From Burley's room at the Clifton House, one could see Niagara Falls and glimpses of the Union land beyond the border. His room was so close to the roaring cataract that if the wind freshened from the east, the encroaching mist enveloped the very establishment. But even closer to the ravine's edge stood Thomas Barnett's Table Rock House, as well as Saul Davis's Table Rock Hotel. Burley had talked with both of them at length, and he found Barnett to be far more honorable. Barnett brought a measure of class to his hucksterism. The barkers outside his establishment were as loud as anywhere, but his museum did offer genuine curiosities and his walkway down to the base of Horseshoe Falls took a backseat to no other scenic view in town.

Barnett's rival, Saul Davis, had a reputation as a swindler and a cheat—and deservedly so. Davis also offered guided tours down to the river, promising a rare peek behind the raging sheets of water, and his employees were at hand to take one's likeness in the adjacent studio—all of which fetched good coin. If one was reluctant to pay, Davis's enforcers received a good sum to help overcome such disinclination. Of course, they knew better than to threaten Burley.

Captain Beall and Mr. Burley were on the Suspension Bridge now, moving at a good clip. To either side, the view fell into darkness. Only glimpses of the mighty river, raging at all hours, were visible.

"I have nightmares about this place," the captain said. "Specifically, this location, crossing the Niagara border. In my bones, I fear that I'll be caught on the wrong side when the reckoning comes."

"This place can put the best of men on edge," Burley agreed, and for a moment he entertained such concerns himself. There was something about this place—the narrow gorge beneath them, the ever-changing vistas of the Falls itself—that could enchant a person. In this landscape, a faint, incessant voice was sometimes carried on the night breeze. Burley heard it as an almost mournful tune, reminding him that little ever went as planned, that even carefully choreographed events could run away from him.

"We'll get the job done," said Burley, as much to himself as to Captain Beall.

Up ahead of them, the lights of the American side were coming into view, and the two rebel spies shifted their attention to their latest task.

"Yes, Burl," his commander agreed. "The way the war is going, we don't have much choice."

11

When I say that I talk with my mother, it's not that I hear or even expect any spoken words in response. I have not lost that much of my mind.

It is as if I send my concerns and worries out to the world through her. Usually mumbled under my breath, so no one thinks I've become completely possessed. But after doing so, I'll carefully observe the world around me. Did the wind suddenly strengthen or shift? Did the clouds begin to build, for no apparent reason, upon the far horizon? Perhaps in such deviations or transitions, another answer to what bedevils me can be found.

This is what I was doing late that afternoon, after meeting with Wreet. I was talking to Mother with a keen eye on what the world might next bring my way.

Daylilies and summer snapdragons decorated the sides of the trail leading to Prospect Point, the closest vista on the American side, and I heard the low rumble of the Falls before I saw it. Overhead, banks of gray clouds were bearing down from the northwest, and a smattering of seagulls pinwheeled and cried above the fast-moving river. Here the Niagara River itself accelerated, seemingly devouring everything in its path as it raced, faster and faster, for the precipice.

At the vista point, I gripped the rail with both hands. I've never been afraid of heights, but the sight from the overlook was almost too much to behold. Well below me, the green-blue waters roiled and waked, and I felt as if I was stranded on a trestle and a train was bearing down on me. For an instant, I realized how easy it would be to simply step off and be done with it all.

Talk to me, Mother, I thought. *Show me some sign.*

It was then I heard the woman's voice, "Are you all right there?"

I turned to see a regal lady dressed in a full-length coat and a small hat, with a neat strand of pearls around her milky-white neck.

"You were so riveted by the view," the woman added, "that we grew concerned for you."

Over the woman's shoulder, I caught sight of a gray-haired man nodding in our direction. His polished black shoes were protected by spats, and his coat glistened from the moisture in the air.

"I'm fine," I insisted, although I knew I was very much out of sorts.

"Here, come sit on this bench," the woman said, taking me by the elbow. "The view can be overwhelming sometimes."

"Yes, ma'am."

"Please, I'm Leila Beth—Leila Beth Kidder. Ma'am sounds so formal and makes me feel older than I want to be."

Mrs. Kidder brought me to the bench, and we sat down together. The man shuffled closer, standing behind us, as if he was trying to protect us from the mist rising from the river below.

"Many a visitor to Niagara Falls is caught up in the splendor, the sight of it all," he said. "Charles Dickens comes to mind. The same with the woman who wrote *Uncle Tom's Cabin*."

"Calvin, please don't mention her." Mrs. Kidder frowned. "That damn book helped bring on the war."

"That may be. But she was as enthralled with Niagara Falls as anyone."

Ignoring him, Mrs. Kidder asked me where I was from. When I blurted out Auburn, still too agitated to conjure up a proper lie, Mrs. Kidder replied that they were from Covington, Kentucky. "Right across the river from Cincinnati. The war is thick in those parts, and we simply had to get away."

"And then we discovered there's no real escape," Calvin said. "Isn't that right, my dear?"

Mrs. Kidder nodded. "I fear the world has gone quite mad. Even in London and Paris all anyone can talk about is our grand war. Tongues wagging about Lee and Lincoln and Grant. The whole lot of them rolled into some kind of comet bursting across the heavens. I fear we have become a world on fire."

With that pronouncement she smiled and asked, "What brings you to this part of the comet in the sky, child?"

"I wanted to see Niagara Falls," I replied. "For myself, you know, instead of hearing others' stories."

"A fine idea," Calvin said. "In such times of upheaval, gazing upon nature, especially one of the wonders of the world, can be so reassuring."

"Please," Mrs. Kidder said. "If I hear another word about this war, I'll start to cry. I mean it. I surely will."

With that, she patted my arm. "Take in the sights, sweet one. They are something to behold," she said. "But be careful that you don't draw too close to the edge. These times can beguile and perplex the best of us."

12

The sign displaying the four aces of the playing-card deck swung lazily in the evening breeze. As we stepped inside, Wreet held out an elbow, a scrawny chicken wing, and I gratefully latched on. The bartender, dressed in a starched white shirt and red bow tie, nodded in Wreet's direction, while the men at the bar nursed their drinks and eyed our reflections in the large mirror above the rows of bottles and glittering glasses. As we drew closer to them, Wreet whispered, "No chatter or rash moves now, Miss Rory. Just follow my lead."

Dutifully, I stayed in step with her as we neared a second door, a smaller one located at the end of the bar. Wreet pushed it open, and we headed down a narrow hallway, where the din of conversation and the notes of music became louder with every step. Soon we found ourselves at the edge of a ballroom, with a wide bank of tall windows overlooking the Niagara River and the Canadian side of the border. On stage, a clarinet, bass, and piano played, and under the spotlight was Mrs. Kidder. She was decked out in a long evening gown that hugged her elegant form, and the very image sparkled as she swayed back and forth with the slow beat.

"Mrs. Kidder?" I asked.

"You know her?" Wreet asked as she nodded toward a small table well away from the dance floor.

"We met at the overlook. Down at the Falls."

I didn't mention that we had met because the rushing waters and rising mist had momentarily gotten the better of me.

"She's a real peach," Wreet grumbled. "Likes to play the field against the middle."

As we sat down, Mrs. Kidder began to sing "Home, Sweet Home," the tender ballad that both sides of the war claimed as their own.

"An exile from home," she sang in a beautiful alto voice. "Splendor dazzles in the rain."

Around us, I saw some of the patrons mouthing the words, finding solace in the tune, which harkened back to the days before the war had driven the country apart.

"She came to town for a weekend engagement," Wreet said, "and she's become popular enough that the Four Aces has kept her on. Or so she claims."

Mrs. Kidder finished her set with a down-tempo version of "Dixie." It began with her and the piano, with the rest of the instruments eventually joining in. To my surprise, it was greeted by a smattering of applause, and no one appeared miffed at all. The song moved ahead, slow and deliberate, almost like a prayer that a child would recite before going to bed.

When the piece was over, Mrs. Kidder smiled and stepped down from the stage as the band fell into an instrumental number. Mrs. Kidder slowly wove her way among the tables until she drew near to ours.

"I thought I saw some familiar faces," she said. "Even if they are hiding too far back in the shadows."

"You're in fine voice this evening," Wreet said.

"Ah, listen to you, Mrs. Thayer. You just want me to spend more money down at that little shop of yours. Lord knows I've given you enough business, from *cartes de visites* to your larger prints."

"Stop by any time, Leila Beth. You do make a striking likeness."

"As would your friend here," said Mrs. Kidder, turning to me. "Who knew that you two were acquainted?"

"Family, actually," Wreet lied. "Some kind of niece, twice removed, isn't it?"

I nodded, not knowing what to say.

"And what did you think of our little production?" Mrs. Kidder asked me.

"I especially enjoyed your version of 'Dixie,'" I replied.

Mrs. Kidder beamed. "I'm told that Mr. Lincoln himself appreciates the tune as well. Perhaps that can give us a sliver of hope, even with the current state of the world."

Wreet grimaced as if Leila Beth's comment was the most ridiculous thing she had ever heard.

Up on stage, the music swelled, and Mrs. Kidder turned to go. "No rest for the wicked," she said. "Especially in these parts."

We watched Mrs. Kidder make her way back to the stage. As she passed a large table, near the lip of the stage, several men in suits rose to greet her.

"See that one," I whispered.

"Aye, Rory, he did sit for a likeness at the store," Wreet replied. "He's from one of your drawings, isn't he?"

"Yes, I'm sure of it."

The man in question briefly took Mrs. Kidder's hand and kissed it.

"And the tall one. Right next to him."

"The Scotsman joker," Wreet added. "All full of mirth and merriment. I remember them now. They came to the shop almost a month ago. They must have been fresh to town then, with money to burn."

Everyone at that table, including a pair of women and several other gentlemen, rose along with the pair of Confederates. They remained standing as Mrs. Kidder strode back on stage.

As everyone grew quiet, ready for the next song, Wreet gazed about the ballroom with its glittering chandeliers, and I followed her eyes. "What are you thinking?"

"That it's a marvelous illusion, young one."

"Illusion?"

"When you've lived in a place as long as I have here, you know where the skeletons are buried, the ghosts that can inhabit a place. I couldn't help thinking that a few blocks from here is where Charlie Benson grew up. You know him?"

I shook my head.

"Of course, you wouldn't. Few here even do. But he was a chap obsessed with the river and seemed to have a sixth sense for it. Wasn't much for school as a boy. Instead, he spent his days down by the river, throwing in anything that would float—twigs, cans, scraps of paper."

"To what end?"

"To see how the currents ebb and flow. When someone drowned in these waters, he was the one most apt to find the body."

"The body?"

"We don't go long without a mishap in this part of the world, Rory. Our Mr. Douglas knows that as well as anybody, and he was well acquainted with Charlie. Sometimes Mr. Douglas helped with the next search party."

After her last set, Mrs. Kidder took a seat at the table with the rebel pair and what was left of their group. It was getting late, and the ballroom had begun to empty out. A few waiters stood back in the shadows, waiting to clean the remaining tables.

"We could go over," I said. "See if she invites us to join them."

"No, best to bide our time," Wreet said. "We've found them and now look—"

The party was saying its good-byes, calling it a night. Already the waiters were moving in like crows to tidy up the mess.

"We'll trail them," Wreet said. "I betcha they're at the Clifton. On the other side of the border. But it's best to be sure."

I paid our check with money that Secretary Seward had given me before leaving Auburn, and the two of us headed for the door. Outside, the only constant at this late hour was the roar of the Falls a few blocks away. We moved across the street, hanging back in the darkness. Soon the shorter rebel, the more dapper of the two, exited the Four Aces. But the taller one was nowhere to be found.

"Where he's gotten off to?" Wreet wondered.

Together we watched the one called Beall say good night to the remaining folks in his party. A carriage rolled up to take them away, but Beall begged off, saying a walk would do him good and he would find a ride closer to the bridge. Alone he began to walk up Ontario

Street, and we stayed on the opposite side, following him. We were coming around the corner when a figure stepped out of the alleyway. It was the taller of the two. The one called Burley.

"Late to be out, isn't it, ladies?" he asked. "It could get tongues to wagging."

"What business is it of yours?" Wreet snapped and attempted to push past him. But Burley held out an arm, stopping her.

"I'm not done talking with you yet, luv," he replied, his accent growing thicker.

"Get away from us, you fool," Wreet said.

Up ahead, I saw Beall turn and approach us, curious about the commotion. Before he could arrive, I knelt down and swept my hand along the sidewalk until I found a fair-sized stone. I stuffed it inside my small handbag. Standing up, I headed straight for the taller one, swinging the bag angrily in front of me.

"What's this?" Burley exclaimed.

Wreet broke free, and Burley lunged again for her. That's when I struck him a smart blow upside the head and followed with another good smack to his shoulder. Burley stumbled backward, stunned by the attack.

"You harpy," he growled.

As he lunged for me, I dropped low, almost on my knees, and his arm sailed over the top of my head.

"Stay put," Burley ordered.

Of course, I had no intention of doing so. Rising up, with both hands on the strap of my bag, I swing wildly and yet somehow struck him again. This time across the bridge of the nose. Gasping in disbelief, Burley flailed at me, allowing Wreet to drive every ounce of her petite frame into his lower back, which sent him hard to the ground.

"That's enough," Beall ordered, and his voice was so commanding that all of us froze in place.

"Why don't we declare this skirmish a draw?" Beall added. "Live to fight another day, shall we?"

"I can handle these two," Burley said as he struggled to his feet.

"Not tonight," Beall said. "Please stand down, good sir."

Burley did as he was told, backing up a few steps.

"Who are you?" Beall asked, focusing on me. "That you can hold your own against one of my top men?"

"One who believes that good folk should fight for what they believe in," I replied.

"Good folk?" Beall repeated. "You come to hear our Leila Beth Kidder sing sweet songs of America, especially the South, and yet you moralize like a Yankee statesman?"

"Are we always bound by allegiances and borders?" I asked.

Beall smiled at this notion. "It all depends upon where one's true allegiances lie, now doesn't it?"

I felt as if I was back in the fight, parrying more blows. But unlike his partner, Beall used the dubious code words and questionable logic shared by the secessionists.

"Perhaps parts of the nation should be left alone," I continued, knowing my friend Fanny Seward would find such lines pathetic, even comical. "Allowed to take the desired path based solely upon individual choice."

"Individual choice?" Beall smiled.

For a moment, the four of us stood there, uncertain of what would happen next. Beall looked over at his taller friend, who dabbed at his bloody nose with a handkerchief, and then he returned his attention to me.

"Who are you?" he wondered aloud. "Some Amazon come to life? Another Joan of Arc?"

"My name's Rebecca Chase. But my friends call me Rory."

"And where are you staying, Miss Chase?"

"With me," Wreet interrupted.

"With you?" the taller one said dismissively. He dabbed at his nose once again and folded his linen handkerchief away.

"I have a fine guest room," Wreet said.

"I can only imagine," Burley replied. "Something akin to the Tower of London, I'd suspect."

Beall stepped alongside his friend and rested a hand on his forearm. With that, Burley grew quiet.

"We're staying at the Clifton, across the river," Beall told us. "Would you like to join us there for tea tomorrow?"

"Why would we do that?" Wreet asked. "After your hooligan accosted us on the street?"

"It was a simple misunderstanding," Beall said.

"Misunderstanding?" Wreet replied, refusing to be placated by the hypnotic tone of the rebel's words.

"I'm sure it was," Beall continued. "For our Mr. Burley can sometimes blunder into things. Isn't it so?"

"Yes, sir," Burley answered with downcast eyes.

"Tea would be fine," I said. "But let's meet at the Cataract House, on this side of the river. It's closer to Mrs. Thayer's."

Although Beall grimaced, in the next breath he reluctantly nodded in agreement. "You must be busy at your little store?" he said to Wreet. "There's no need for you to come, too."

"I can find help," she said. "I'll reserve us a table."

"No, allow me the honor, dear lady."

"For all of us," I said, gesturing at Burley. "Him, too."

A bemused look spread across Beall's face. He waited to hear more from me, but I remained quiet, letting him decide what to do next. After a long moment, he said, "Very well. It will be a full cast of characters. At the Cataract, then. Say, two o'clock tomorrow afternoon?"

He tapped the brim of his derby hat with his cane and turned away. Burley fell into step beside him.

We watched them go, heading for the Suspension Bridge and the next train or hack carriage that would carry them across.

"What a devious little man," Wreet said.

She began to walk toward her shop, and I fell into step alongside her.

"I wasn't leading you on, child," Wreet said. "You can stay with me. I have room. I don't mean to be rude, but the Cataract may be a touch too fancy for you."

"Thank you. I'll think about it."

"Child, don't be polite," Wreet said. "Anyone who can fight like you I'm keeping by my side. I don't know where you learned such tricks, but they can be put to good use around here."

I shrugged, refusing to answer.

"You think I'm making small talk, even flattering you," Wreet said at her front door as she fished for the key. "But we don't have time for such things. Perhaps you thought you could spend a week or so here, return with a few rumors and stories for the Sewards, and then be on your way. But my intuition tells me that those two, Beall and Burley, are real trouble. Like it or not, I hope you'll stay here for a spell. At least until we can figure out what they're up to and how best to stop them."

13

The next afternoon, as we entered the dining room at the Cataract House, I saw Mr. Douglas standing, erect and alert, just inside the dining room entrance. He immediately recognized me and nodded in my direction. The years had treated Mr. Douglas kindly. He remained a presence here, the knowing force in this part of the world. The one who had worked closely with Mother in bringing so many escaped souls across the border.

The expanse of long tables with fresh linen, sparkling pitchers, and polished silver was managed by the precise movement of a dozen waiters, all dressed in black jackets and creased pants, white shirts with starched collars and cravats. The wait staff was entirely men, and their skin was as dark as their waiter suits. Rumor had it that many were escaped slaves themselves.

As we stepped farther into the vast room, with its glittering chandeliers, Mr. Douglas nodded toward the table in the corner. John Yates

Beall was stationed there and stood as we entered; walking toward us was Bennet Burley.

"I'd like to formally apologize for my actions of last night," said the taller of the two rebels. "It was unacceptable."

Wreet smiled as if she didn't believe a word he was saying.

"I mean it," Burley said. "It was conduct unbecoming a proper gentleman."

"Proper gentleman," Wreet scoffed. "The other one must have put you up to this."

"Captain Beall doesn't force me to do anything. While I admire his leadership, I don't take orders from anyone."

"How reassuring," Wreet replied.

"It's fine," I told him. "All is forgotten and forgiven."

With that, Burley nodded in appreciation and led us into the dining room.

John Yates Beall was seated on the far side of the table, where he could see anyone entering or leaving the dining room.

"Ladies," he said, rising from his chair. "How good of you to join us."

In comparison to Burley's sober tone, Beall's manner carried a lightness, even a sense of play. After we settled in, one of the waiters placed a small kettle of tea in the middle of the table, followed by another waiter who delivered scones, a third with clotted cream, and a fourth carrying a decanter of juice. It was another well-orchestrated presentation at the Cataract House, and Mr. Douglas oversaw it all.

"Thanks for meeting us here," I said.

"Undoubtedly," Wreet added, "it would have been more convenient for you on the Canadian side."

"How kind of you to be concerned about our schedule," Captain Beall replied. "There's no need, though. With the proximity to the Suspension Bridge, we manage well enough. And to view this glorious establishment . . . well, it does take one's breath away, doesn't it?"

For a while, we sipped our tea and eyed each other. We did so until Wreet couldn't stand it any longer. "What brings you here?" she asked. "A Southerner and a Scotsman."

"A Virginian, actually." John Yates Beall smiled. "Mrs. Thayer, you were much more accommodating when we visited your shop, ready to part with our hard-earned coin."

"You're one of many," Wreet replied dismissively.

"And maybe that's the problem with the world today," Beall continued. "Too easily everyone becomes one of many."

"And any inherent rights," I offered, "are lost."

Beall raised an eyebrow. "Do you believe that's what's going on in the world, Miss Chase?"

"I don't know," I began, trying to conjure up the rhetoric that Daisy Conley and others like her back in Auburn used. The talk of the Copperheads or Peace Democrats, those who were so tired of the war that they were ready to make any kind of agreement with the South. "All I know is that whatever is taking place can't continue. If it does, we'll all go mad. The conflict has gone on too long. It's torn the country apart."

Beall raised his teacup, blowing on the hot surface, before setting it back down without taking a sip.

"I agree with you, Miss Chase," he said. "Anyone can see that the United States is a broken construct. An idea or a theory that doesn't function any longer. Four years of war have done irreparable damage."

Beside me, I heard Wreet take a deep breath, eager to debate such points. Yet somehow she held herself in check.

"What do you think of there being two nations, Miss Chase?" Beall asked. "Each allowed to go its own way."

I turned this over in my mind, unsure of how to play out the string. "I'll be honest, kind sirs," I told them. "As I said, I don't rightly know. I'm not as well versed in such arguments as you appear to be. All I'm certain of is that we can no longer continue like this."

Here I racked my brain for something more, something more convincing, and I fell back on the phrase Mrs. Kidder had used when we were at the overlook, high above the Falls.

"We can no longer be a world on fire," I told him.

"A world on fire," Beall repeated. "Such an appropriate phrase, Miss Chase."

As we watched, he reached alongside his chair and raised his cane. It was an impressive instrument, made of black lacquered wood, topped with a knob of shining crystal and a gold band.

"I need this to make my way in the world now," Beall said. "For I've learned that a bullet fired under any circumstances can cause as much damage as one fired at Manassas or Fredericksburg."

He briefly held the cane in one hand before letting it slide back to the floor. "There's no way I could be with a regular unit in the field anymore," he said.

"So, what brings you here?" I asked. "To the Falls?"

"I appreciate your directness, Miss Chase." Beall smiled. "Let's just say that perhaps I find myself at the Falls, truly one of the wonders of the world, for many of the same reasons that likely brought you here." Then he turned to Burley and said, "As for me, I've decided to follow Mr. Burley's lead. He has family near Toronto. We'll soon head that way and ride things out until the world returns to its senses. Isn't that right, Burl?"

The Scotsman nodded. "As you say, Cap'n. We'll take in the sights here, then move on."

14

"Forget about the old lady. I know she gets your goat," Beall told Burley. "It's the young one who fights like a banshee. She intrigues me."

The two of them dared to linger at their table in the Cataract House dining room, with its high ceiling and elongated, sentinel windows, after the women had left. Burley was ready to take the next train back across the Suspension Bridge to the Canadian side. A sixth sense told him that spending too much time on the Union side wasn't the wisest course of action. Not now.

"Her heart may be with the cause," Burley agreed. "But why even consider her? It's another wheel to the cart."

"Because our cart needs more wheels," Beall replied. "I have to move on to Detroit soon enough and make sure Maxwell has held up his end: assembled more men, checked the ferry schedules. As we've discussed, you'll be in Sandusky, making sure Cole is in position."

"But how could she help us?"

"I'm thinking we could place her in Sandusky, with you and Cole," Beall said. "Even if it's only for a few days."

"I don't know."

"Oh, my dear Burl, you're as transparent as the curtains in a brothel sometimes. Admit it. You don't like that she more than held her own in that tussle with you."

When Burley refused to answer, Captain Beall glanced at the Black waiters, picking up the last of the plates and cutlery, shifting the expansive room over to a dinner schedule. "We need more eyes and ears, like they have in this establishment," the rebel leader added. "See how they serve the meals in regimental order? All of these heathens have a job to do. And along the way, they're listening, always listening, to what transpires. It is an amazing operation they have in place here."

"Many a slave made his final escape from this location," Burley said, following his gaze. "That's what the carney operators tell me. More often than not, they say it was the waiters here that helped the darkies get across the river, either via the bridge or even by small craft from one side to the other."

"I can well imagine," Beall agreed. "They do appear to be a crafty lot. Much more enterprising than the ones back home."

Both of them took a moment to consider the wait staff at the Cataract House, reluctantly impressed by how they went about their business. For the soup course, they entered six to eight at time, all in step with the head waiter's soft bell, and placed the bowls, multiple ladles, and steaming cauldron of the day's offering in the center of each table. The dining room at the Cataract House stretched out in long tables, almost everything served family style, running the length of the place. As the hotel visitors finished the first course, the soup dishes were cleared away, with the waiters bringing out the main course—usually roast beef, boiled potato, succotash, and an array of greens in ornate china dishes with matching lids. Every matching plate, serving basin, or accessory for the evening's meal had a white gleaming surface with classic blue highlights along the upper edge.

The waiters moved back and forth from the sides, as precise as any honor guard, always there if something was needed by a patron. Most of the time, though, they hung to the side or moved back into the kitchen to prepare the next round. Through it all, they regularly advanced and retreated in single file as they went about their duties. It was only for the dessert course, the final round of the evening, that they called the slightest attention to themselves as they wheeled carts from the kitchen to the soft trill of their boss man's order bell. Even on a full belly, those carts were enough to make anyone cast a longing eye, as they were weighed down with cakes and pastries, puddings, and cream confections. Of course, a second set of carts arrived with the coffee and tea, with those small silver spoons rattling ever so slightly as they approached.

"Then why do we come here?" Burley asked. "If there are eyes and ears everywhere?"

"It remains a captivating setting, don't you think, Burl? Besides, with a break here or here, we can bring the war to this part of the world. So much so that the locals maybe don't call it Niagara Falls anymore. Perhaps something more fitting of the times."

"Rebel Falls?" Burley offered.

"Or something even better, my friend," Beall said. "Between us we could conjure up a more fitting moniker, couldn't we? Say, Lee's Falls or the Stonewall Cataract. And we'd built a statue to Robert E. Lee himself right out front, facing those raging waters."

Once more, Burley found himself astonished by his leader's audacity. How his grasp of reality sometimes was tenuous at best.

Captain Beall stood up and briefly surveyed the room. For a moment, every waiter stopped what they were doing and glanced at him. Then, like the workings of a fine watch, they went back to their respective duties, seemingly paying him little mind.

"Don't worry," Beall told his partner. "We'll be done with this place soon."

"And what of Miss Chase?"

Beall pondered this a moment. "Perhaps you're right," he replied. "Time is running out. We need to find a way ahead without her."

15

A floor below the Cataract House's vast dining room, Wreet and I huddled with Mr. Douglas in the small sitting room of his apartment.

"I'm told they are leaving as soon as the day after tomorrow," Mr. Douglas said. "My friends at the Clifton say reservations have been made for the train out of Buffalo, heading west."

"It's just as Secretary Seward feared," Wreet said. "They're expanding their operations."

"Maybe we could trail them," I said to Wreet.

"And what happens when they catch sight of any of us, dear one?" Wreet asked. "Whatever lie we come up with won't play then. They don't trust you enough, at least not yet, to smooth over any kind of coincidence."

"Trust?" Mr. Douglas said softly, almost to himself.

The two of us looked on as the head waiter became momentarily lost in thought.

"Trust?" he repeated as he rocked slowly back and forth in his chair. For a while, everything around us grew quiet, and I heard footsteps far down the hall and more on the floor above. The hotel, with

its ebb and flow, was changing over from daytime bustle to the eloquence and cadence of the dinner hours.

Soon enough, Mr. Douglas returned to us, blinking his eyes.

"Trust," he said one last time. "There may still be a way to win
Beall over."

"But how?" I asked, feeling my memories and worries about this
world well up inside me again. How could I do any good in a place
that held so many ghosts for me?

There was a knock at the door, and Mr. Douglas opened it. In the
hall, I saw two familiar faces. Mr. Douglas nodded for me to follow
him outside.

"Sissy must have told them," Wreet whispered.

Realizing I had little choice, I made my way toward the two men.
They were both dressed spit and polish in their waiter uniforms,
ready for the dinner shift at the Cataract House. The solidly built one
smiled and nodded in my direction.

"Aran," I said as Mr. Douglas headed further down the hall.

Behind Aran, the taller, gangly one studied me with a solemn
gaze.

"Cesar," I said in his direction.

The two of them had escaped bondage years before, during what
some called the war before the war.

"Sissy said you were back," Aran said. "I didn't believe her, but
I see I owe her an apology."

"Not that you'll say you're sorry." Cesar glanced at his longtime
friend.

Aran shrugged in reply.

"You're helping our Mr. Douglas?" Cesar said.

"Trying to," I told them. Down the hall, Mr. Douglas was returning, likely from checking the shift change at the dining room, and
Aran and Cesar became slightly nervous in their boss's presence.

"It's good to have you back, Miss Rory," Cesar said, in a lower
voice.

"Yes," Aran added. "It brightens the day."

With that, they turned away, and I went back inside with Wreet. Once we were settled again, Mr. Douglas closed the door. He then took down a thick leather-bound book from high on his shelf. With both hands, he held it out for me.

"This may be a jumble to you," he told me. "You were young your first summer here. But your mother, our Miss Meredith, was a part of so many of these moments here, Rory. It's time you realized that."

I opened the heavy work, not sure where to begin. Yet Mr. Douglas and Wreet stayed silent, watching me flip through a few pages. Every one contained two columns, one narrow and the other much wider, all done in neat cursive script. The left column of each page gave a brief notation of the date for an escape attempt, while the wider one on the right detailed what had happened.

"Miss Rory, your mother was between here and Auburn more times than you can imagine," Mr. Douglas said. "Often she was with Moses."

"Moses?"

"Mrs. Tubman," Wreet answered.

"As you know, the Niagara was often the last river they had to cross, sometimes with the slavers on their heels. Look there," Mr. Douglas said, his long fingers turning to a few of the entries from the summer and into the fall when I was here with Mother. "See for yourself."

As I read, the dispatches rolled out, one after another:

August 1, 1857: Nancy Clemens arrived from Memphis in the company of her Masters, Mr. and Mrs. Cox. When they left the hotel the next morning for a carriage ride along the Gorge, Nancy locked her mistress's trunk and placed the key under the woman's pillow. Nancy's plan was to get across the Niagara, but when she came downstairs to the hotel lobby her fears got the best of her. She began to tremble and cry. That's the state I found her in, and I steered young Nancy into the garden, away from prying eyes. By then JD had been alerted, and he caught up with us as we walked toward Ferry Landing. If Nancy Clemens wanted to cross over to freedom, now was the time. In all likelihood, this would be her only chance. I walked with her down the stairs to the landing, where JD rowed her across. Glorious day, glorious day.

September 3, 1857: Slavers everywhere in the town. It must have been in the air that so many were trying to cross the Niagara to Canada at this time. I talked with several of the worst ones, their pistols showing outside their trousers, knowing they had bribed the Bystanders at the Suspension Bridge to help them with their efforts. I spoke with them like you would to a fierce beast—soft and slow, eyes holding theirs—while several waiters helped take a family of four down to the landing late that afternoon. JD rowed them across as a light rain began to fall.

September 13, 1857: Joe Bailey arrived here with the slavers on his heels. Moses told us that wanted posters for his likeness were posted well above the Mason-Dixon Line. When Bailey arrived at the hotel, the river was too furious to ferry him across by boat. So, I decided we could go by the bridge, in a delivery buggy. With no time to waste, Bailey was put inside a barrel and arranged with other barrels under a large tarp. At first, the Bystanders at the entrance wouldn't let us pass, but I talked our way past. On the other side, Moses was waiting for them. "Joe, you're in Queen Victoria's domain now," she told Bailey, who had tears running down his face. "You're a free man."

I stopped and ran my thumb through more of the pages. The entire volume, perhaps two hundred pages, was filled with such accounts.

"That's why I cannot help thinking it's God's doing," Mr. Douglas said. "That you're here to follow in your mother's footsteps. To help us finish her work, once and for all."

"I remember the stairs down to the Ferry Landing," I said, as much as to myself as to Mr. Douglas and Wreet. "Mother took me down them once."

"Your mother had your build," Mr. Douglas said. "As nimble as a dancer upon those steps. Of course, the steps down to the river, 290 in total, don't see much traffic these days. Not with the war on."

Mr. Douglas paused and looked to Wreet and then back to me. "But my favorite story concerning your mother isn't in that book. You know of what I speak, don't you, Miss Wreet?"

Wreet nodded.

"There was this young woman, who had escaped from the South years before," Mr. Douglas began.

"Cindy Sue," Wreet added.

"Yes, that's right," he said. "She was working here. Had been for several years. Late one afternoon, after her shift, she was heading home to her husband in the Falls. You see, she had begun a new life, about to start a family of her own. She was walking away from the Cataract House, into town, when this white man, all dressed to the nines, stepped down from a carriage and asked her, 'Don't you remember me?'"

"It was her old owner," said Wreet. "He had hunted her all the way to the Falls. That would have rocked many a soul, but Miss Cindy was a smart one."

"That she was," Mr. Douglas continued. "She turned on a dime and began running across the lawn, heading for the river and the landing, ready to cross over the Niagara just like that. No looking back."

"And from what I remember," Wreet said, "her old master was having none of it?"

"Indeed," Mr. Douglas said. "He started to yelling and carrying on, telling anyone who would listen that he'd give one hundred dollars to anyone who would help him fetch back his property. Your mother heard the commotion, Rory, and soon enough, she was right down in the middle of it. That's what I always appreciated about her. She was ready to act.

"Soon enough, your mother was alongside Cindy," Mr. Douglas continued. "Both heading down to the river. Fast enough to get ahead of the growing crowd. The two of them hurried down those stairs, three steps at a time in some places, and jumped into an empty rowboat."

"As if God himself put it there," Wreet said.

Mr. Douglas tried not to smile. "Except in the winter, we always had a boat at the ready," he explained to me.

"But you cannot guarantee an oarsman, now, can you?" Wreet teased.

"Few are perfect in the eyes of the Lord," Mr. Douglas replied.

"So what happened?" I asked.

Both of them turned toward me. "What do you think your mother did?" Wreet asked.

"She manned the oars herself?" I said in disbelief. "She got Cindy Sue across? Through the rapids and the current to the other side?"

Mr. Douglas gazed past me, as if he could still picture Mother pulling the oars through the mist. "That she did," he replied. "Never an easy task, rowing across such a tempest sea."

The three of us sat alone, not saying a word for a time. I never doubted that my mother was courageous. But as we sat there, considering that momentous crossing, I couldn't help but wonder how much bravery, determination, and purpose she had truly passed along to me.

"What can we do now?" I asked them. "With the rebels slipping away?"

"I have an idea," Mr. Douglas replied. "But you'll have to trust me."

Wreet and I watched Beall come down the front steps of the Cataract House and walk into the town itself. The other one, Burley, had left minutes before, undoubtedly sent on another errand by his captain. For a moment, we feared that the rebel leader would grab a hackney across the Suspension Bridge to the Canadian side. But after taking a glance at the clearing sky, he decided to walk, cane and all, to the nearby railroad station. I assumed his intent was to ride to the Bridge Station and catch the spur-line shuttle to the Canadian side. The next train north was due in ten minutes, but it sometimes fell behind schedule, waiting for the connector from Lockport. That's what we were counting on to make Mr. Douglas's plan come together.

We followed Beall to the platform, keeping well back in the growing crowd, watching until he sat down and checked his pocket watch. As he did so, we saw Aran and Cesar, dressed in Union uniforms, coming down the platform. The two in Yankee blue didn't say a word, but they slowly surveyed each passenger, giving them the once-over, before moving on. Many of the passengers didn't think anything of it. Yet for a Reb spy, like our Beall, it would be enough to strike terror to his very core. Here was the nightmare of any diehard secessionist come to life: Negroes wearing a uniform.

"He's seen them," Wreet said. "It's your time now, child."

I quickly moved toward Captain Beall, weaving my way through the crowd, my skirt skimming past this person and that, until I was right in front of him. Beall had been so concerned with Aran and Cesar moving down the platform that he hadn't seen me draw near.

I said, "They're on to you, kind sir."

Beall looked up, and I knew he believed me.

"Follow me," I told him. "I can get you away from here."

I held out my elbow, and he took it; then the two of us were off, fading into the crowd, away from the train platform, with the Black men in blue uniforms edging closer. We went down the backstairs that Wreet had shown me, reaching the street and moving at a brisk pace away from the railway platform. Only then did Beall come around.

"Where are we going?" he asked.

"To the river," I told him. "It's your only escape."

Down the steps along the embankment we went, with me leading the way and Beall laboring to keep up. He had been right. While he may have been a fine foot soldier once upon a time, in step with the famed Stonewall Brigade, Captain John Yates Beall would never serve in the infantry again. Still, by bracing himself with his ornate cane, he kept up with me, down the 290 steps to Ferry Landing, where

Mr. Douglas had arranged that a rowboat would be waiting, with a white, not a Black, man at the oars. Only here, in the shadow of the mighty Niagara Falls did the rebel hesitate. Yet I was ready for any protestations.

"Up there," I said, nodding at the top of the slick stairway we had taken down. "See them?"

Beall turned to follow my gaze. He so wanted to believe what I'd told him. He peered up through the mist and the roar and the madness held in the shadow of the Falls, and he somehow convinced himself that the Black men in uniform were still after him. Of course, there was no one up there, no one on his tail. Still, the mind often believes the lie. We all so want to believe the lie.

We clambered into the rowboat, with John Yates Beall and me hunched over in the stern. We pushed off into the surging waters, and I had to admit this was the only part of the plan that truly concerned me: that someone other than Mr. Douglas was at the oars. In a perfect world, it would have been the head waiter from the Cataract House. But a Black man at the helm? Captain Beall never would have fallen for such a ruse, so instead we had to make do with someone else, a workman with white-enough skin. As our small craft began to pitch and roll in the angry waters, I briefly closed my eyes, praying that we would be all right.

Too soon, though, I knew everything was amiss. Our oarsman couldn't handle the Niagara's fast-moving waters. Already he was breathing hard, struggling to control the oars, as the current seized ahold of us, pulling us too quickly down the river, bearing toward the larger whirlpools that would capsize us for sure. Beall was gazing crazily about, and he soon saw that we were in deep trouble, too.

Sliding forward on both knees, I came face to face with the craft's operator and took ahold of the long oars as well. Together, the two of us started to work in tandem—pushing harder on this oar and now the other. Panic rose in the man's eyes, but as we began to edge through the flashing white water, the Canadian side finally beginning to draw closer, he regained control of himself and then our battered craft.

"Thank you," he whispered as we reached the shadow of the far side.

16

"It appears the bait has surfaced a big fish," Wreet said the next morning. She held out the small envelope addressed in his neat cursive to me.

"When did this arrive?"

"I don't rightly know," Wreet said. "It's ahead of the regular mail. On Clifton House stationary to boot."

I peeled open the envelope and glanced at Wreet in surprise. "How did you know he'd be asking us to dinner?"

"John Yates Beall may be a scoundrel from the backwoods of Virginia," my friend replied, "but he tries so hard at being a proper gentleman, doesn't he?"

"Dear Miss Chase," I read aloud. "I would be honored if you and Mrs. Thayer would join us tonight at the Four Aces for another performance by our talented Leila Beth Kidder. I have reserved two seats for you at our table."

It was signed *Captain John Yates Beall.*

That evening, the rebels' table was more uproarious, and the champagne flowed freely as Wreet and I entered the Four Aces' ballroom.

"Despite all the heartbreak in the world, the party never stops with this lot," Wreet muttered as she pulled her shawl tighter around her shoulders.

I surveyed the table, my eyes settling upon a dark-haired gentleman with a thick mustache and piercing eyes. He sat next to Captain Beall, and I realized that I had seen him somewhere before.

Burley approached us, his face flush with excitement and alcohol. "Good news," he beamed.

"Has the war ended, dear chap?" Wreet asked sarcastically.

"Almost as good," Burley said, trying his best to be in on the joke. "John Wilkes Booth is here."

"The actor?" I said, now recognizing the man next to Beall. The two of them were caught up in their own conversation.

"One and the same," Burley replied. "He and the captain go way back."

Several years ago, before the war, I had accompanied Fanny Seward to Syracuse to see Booth in the role of Romeo in Shakespeare's play. While Booth was better known for playing more clever parts, Mark Anthony in *Julius Caesar* and the lead in *Richard III*, both of us came away impressed by how well he had carried the role. Despite the longing looks, the ridiculous way a first love can make a person appear to the rest of the world, Booth's manner carried a hint of mischief and even melancholy. As Fanny later remarked, it helped that he was so handsome, with his jet-black hair and devilish eyes.

Tonight, as we drew closer, I recognized that same air about him in real life. How Booth could slide close toward a person he was with, in this case John Yates Beall, and appear to be hanging on his every word. Yet his mind was elsewhere, scheming and preparing for what was next.

"Ah, here they are," Beall said when he saw us, accompanied by Burley. "Added fuel for our cause, Wilkes."

Booth rose, took Wreet's gloved hand, and brought it to his lips.

"We've met before?"

"I doubt it," Wreet said.

"No, no, I'm sure of it," the actor continued. "The captain says you're from this part of the world?"

"Born and raised in Buffalo."

"And you've been to the theater there?"

"Once in a blue moon."

"The last time I was through this part of the country was as Romeo, speaking so many heartfelt, dare I say boyish, utterances to his beloved Juliet."

I almost mentioned that I had seen the same production in Syracuse, but I bit my tongue.

Wreet nodded. "Yes, I was at that show."

"You were sitting down front, stage right, I believe."

"How can you remember that?"

Booth beamed. "Every actor has his tricks, the sleight of hand to get him through another performance in fine stead. From the lip of the most stages, I can make out faces in the first few rows. That allows me to lock onto the eyes in front of me. I can pretend that we are the best of friends, and we share such confidences. Some lines I'll speak directly to the person right there, in front of me. Dear woman, I undoubtedly opened my heart and my very soul to you that evening in Buffalo, and you didn't even realize it."

That brought laughter from all around. Booth nodded, dismissing Wreet, as he turned his attention to me.

"This is Miss Chase," Beall said. "The one I've been telling you about."

"Suffice to say that if Miss Chase had been in the front row for *Romeo and Juliet*," Booth began. "Well, I would have never forgotten her lovely face."

Even though I knew it was all an act, I couldn't help but blush at such attention.

Throughout the evening, Booth became the hub of the wheel, the one everyone turned to. Only his example was followed. So much so that Leila Beth Kidder eventually came down from the stage and took a seat at the table, realizing that she couldn't hold a candle to the famous actor. The band played on as background music to Booth's tales, jokes, and monologues. As the night drew to a close, the actor couldn't resist one last performance. Climbing onto the stage, he urged anyone left in the ballroom to join him.

"Now let's imagine it's the dawn before another great battle," he said, "perhaps Manassas or Chancellorsville."

I prayed that he didn't mention Ball's Bluff. That would have been too much for me.

"Now gather round, in groups of two or three," Booth said. "We're in our encampment, fearful but resolute. It's one of those times when words can mean a lot."

As everyone drew close, the actor gazed out on the nearly empty ballroom. Once again, our party had gone late into the night, and soon Booth's voice began to fill every corner of the place.

"'I'm not covetous for gold,'" he said. "'Nor care I who doth feed upon my cost . . .'"

His voice became a shade louder and richer, soon a soaring entity unto itself. "'But if it be a sin to covet honor, I am the most offending soul alive.'"

Heads turned toward him, enthralled by his web of words.

"'This day is called the feast of Crispian. He that outlives this day, and comes safe home, will stand a tip-toe when the day is named, and rouse him at the name of Crispian . . .'"

I recognized this was more Shakespeare—the speech before the final battle in *Henry V*. What the embattled British king told his vastly outnumbered army before the Battle of Agincourt.

"'This story shall the good man teach his son,'" Booth continued, "'and Crispin Crispian shall ne'er go by, from this day to the ending of the world.'"

Here Booth shifted his gaze from the ballroom to those of us who had joined him upon the small stage. "'But we in it shall be remembered.'" The actor smiled. "'We few, we happy few, we band of brothers. For he today that sheds his blood with me shall be my brother, be he ne'er so vile, this day shall gentle his condition. And gentleman in England now a-bed shall think themselves accursed they were not here, and hold their manhoods cheap whiles any speaks that fought with us upon St. Crispin's day.'"

Booth raised his arms skyward as those final words rang throughout the ballroom. To this day, I don't know if it was clever acting or true passion on his part, but Booth's face had grown flushed and his eyes wild. It was if he had somehow carried himself back to the French countryside centuries ago on the eve of the Battle of Agincourt. For a moment, he was our sovereign, our beloved Henry, and we had no choice but to rally around him, ready to turn the world upside down at his plea. Alarmingly, I found that I had begun to tear up myself. Was this the same abandon and madness that had cut down my beloved uncle in battle? *It's only an illusion,* I repeated to myself, an illusion conjured up by an actor who was seemingly part magician, part madman. Looking about, I found that I wasn't alone. So stunned were we that witnessed Booth's portrayal at the Four Aces that it took us several moments to remember to applaud.

17

The next morning, I came up the steps to the Cataract House, looking for Mr. Douglas, only to find Captain Beall, sipping tea, in a wicker chair near the front entrance.

"What are you doing here?" I asked. "It's not safe."

"I can slip away like a shadow, my dear," he smiled. "Especially now that I know the secret way down to the river."

I couldn't believe how reckless this man could be.

"Besides, somehow I knew you'd be up and about," he said. "You seem to have a connection with this foolish place. It was better to find you here than Wreet's gallery of deceit."

I reminded myself to better cover my tracks. The man seemed to know my routine too well.

"Here, please join me," said Beall, and I reluctantly settled into a chair across from him on the wide veranda that overlooked the rapids and the Falls beyond.

"What did you think of last night's performance?" Beall asked. "John Wilkes Booth's rendition of the Bard?"

"It heartened me."

"Interesting." He took another sip of his tea and then asked, "How so?"

"I lost an uncle to this war," I told him, letting the truth spin out to encompass as many lies and tangents as possible.

"Yes, your Mrs. Thayer mentioned that the other night."

"I barely knew Wreet until a week or so ago," I said, and that much was true. "She's a distant relative, but I hadn't laid eyes on her since I was a child."

"And why did you come to the Falls? To finally meet her?"

I paused, uncertain of which lie to follow.

"My heart was broken after my uncle's death," I told Beall. "His name was Frank, Franklin Hawes. He lived on a farm outside of Baltimore," I said, testing this lie out. "In northern Maryland."

I pictured that part of the world in my mind. I had seen it once before, riding the train from Auburn to Washington in the company of Fanny Seward.

"He was a fine man. Loved the land," I added. "We often visited him at his farm. Near the village of Westminster. Do you know it?"

Beall shook his head thoughtfully.

As I spoke, I conjured up the names of the towns and hamlets as they flashed by the train window that day with Fanny.

"There was a skirmish with Union cavalry," I continued, letting the lie take root and grow. "And the authorities rounded up those who they decreed were responsible. One of them was my Uncle Frank."

Captain Beall took a sip of his tea and nodded for me to continue.

"Friends gathered around the jail, where they had been taken. It's what has happened all across the land. Harsh words were spoken, and events took a turn for the worst. The soldiers stepped in, and shots were fired. In the chaos, my uncle was shot. He died the next morning."

That's where I stopped, knowing that my tale couldn't hold a candle to John Wilkes Booth's performance from the previous evening. Still, I liked to believe that it might win over Beall.

"A tragic tale indeed," the rebel commander said. "I'm sorry for you and your family."

"You don't need to be." I saw how his eyes flared briefly in surprise. "As we've discussed, it's the world we live in now."

Beall nodded. "That's what led you here, Miss Chase? So far from home?"

"My home doesn't exist anymore. My mother is dead, my father long gone, and now my remaining uncle is dead, too. Such events propel a person off, sometimes in unexpected directions. Like leading them to one of the ends of the earth. Say, a curious place like Niagara Falls."

"Yes, it is certainly a curious place," the captain agreed. "If it hadn't been for you, I could have been locked away here."

"I doubt it," I said. "You seem too resourceful for that to happen, at least not for long."

"So do you, Miss Chase."

Beall then paused, as if he was weighing a major decision.

"I told Mr. Burley that I believe you can help us in our endeavor," he said. "He agrees. Deep down, he respects you."

"I find that hard to believe."

"Yes, he's said so, several times."

"And where is Mr. Burley?"

"Gone for the day on an important errand. We're about to put matters in motion, and I cannot help thinking that you could be a part of it, Miss Chase. Would you have a moment to accompany me? There is some material I'd like to show you."

We got up from the table, with Beall sliding several bills underneath his saucer. Up a flight of stairs, the rebel captain unlocked a door to a suite with a long table.

"But this isn't your room," I said. "You're staying on the other side of the border."

"It doesn't matter. Arrangements can always be made. Even in such a devilish place."

He nodded for me to have a chair and unrolled a map, placing several long-stemmed glasses and a decanter of amber liquid to hold down the corners. Immediately, I was struck by the similarities with the map Secretary Seward had shown Fanny and me.

"Behold Lake Erie," Beall said. "It's the smallest and shallowest of the Great Lakes and perfectly located for what we have planned."

He ran his index finger across the map until it tapped on a string of islands near the western end of the lake. The closest town was Sandusky, Ohio, with the larger city of Toledo forty miles or so to the west. Looking closer at the map, I saw that the islands to the north were called Isle St. George, Middle Bass, Put-in-Bay, and Kelleys.

"We're specifically interested in one of those specks of land," Captain Beall said. "Johnson's Island."

I cast a glance at the map, not sure how to respond.

"Few know of it, but it's become one of the largest prisoner-of-war camps north of the Mason-Dixon Line," he added. "The camp has swelled to more than three thousand since Gettysburg and the disasters along the Mississippi. Some of the South's best fighting men are now held there. Just think if they were somehow freed. The havoc they could rain down upon Ohio, Indiana, and Pennsylvania. Well, it would turn this war, once and for all."

To me, it sounded like a nightmare.

"I see the skepticism in your face," the captain said. "You're wondering how this happens without the wave of a wizard's wand."

He reached across the table and from a stack of papers pulled out a detailed drawing of a large warship.

"And here's the magic wand."

The two of us looked upon the drawing and map.

"If Mr. Burley was here, he would undoubtedly tell you that the USS Michigan was the first iron-hulled ship in the Federal Navy," he said. "How it is a side-wheel steamer also rigged for sail. It sports fourteen guns, including a thirty-pound Parrot rifle, five twenty-pounders, a half-dozen smoothbores, and a pair of howitzers."

Captain Beall smiled at me. "Yes, that's what our Mr. Burley would tell you. For his expertise is weaponry. And too often that's where matters end with him."

"I'm sorry," I interrupted. "But I don't understand how one ship, no matter how much firepower it may have, can be so important."

"Remember the riots in New York City after the last draft edict?" Beall asked. "How they went on for a week, leaving hundreds dead?"

"What does that have to do with this ship?"

"With the right prompting, the same thing could happen in Detroit, Cleveland, or Buffalo. So many in the North have grown weary of this long, hard war. They're like you. They've had enough."

As have many in the South, I thought. Yet I stayed quiet, letting him talk.

"The cities in the North have become tinderboxes of opposition to Old Abe and his epic struggle, especially now that he has decreed that the slaves should somehow be freed. Did you know that after the riots in New York, Detroit was on the verge of widespread demonstrations, too? It's true. But then this warship, the *USS Michigan*, appeared offshore, casting its long shadow, and any opposition soon dissolved. A week later, the warship made its way east to quell a similar situation in Buffalo."

I asked, "So what's to be done?"

"You are a quick study," he said. "I told Mr. Burley as much. That's why I'm contemplating some way you could help us. As our friend, John Wilkes Booth, would say, it's St. Crispin's Day. Time to make our move upon the field of history. We are due to leave soon, and I cannot help thinking that you may be of service to us. But how? What can you offer this band of brothers, Miss Chase?"

"I can help record the event," I told him. "For posterity."

"For posterity?" He repeated, a note of skepticism in his voice.

I nodded, now realizing how I might convince him.

"The newspapers, with their illustrations, have rallied support time and again here in the North," I continued. "Surely, the same is done in the South? If so, I'd imagine you'll need the necessary pictures to fully convey the importance of the ship's capture."

Beall shrugged. "Indeed, in this day and age memorable images are the new currency. We live within an onslaught of new methods and manipulations. That said, I don't see how it's done in this case. What's fashioned in your auntie's shop has to be completed within such an establishment. As you can imagine, our plan will happen under the cover of darkness, with as few onlookers who can sound the alarm as possible."

"But I can memorialize the event for you."

"How? I'm not following you at all, fine lady."

"I pride myself on being an artist," I told him. "I have much practice with a sketchbook in the wild. Put me there, allow me to draw what I can, and soon enough I'll give you a painting, a lasting vision of your conquest."

Beall grew quiet, surprised by this, until he said, "You claim to be an artist? Well, let's put it to the test."

With that, he stood up and hobbled out the door. Soon he returned, holding several sheets of paper and a pencil. He must have gotten them from the front desk.

"Granted, not the best of drawing instruments," he said. "But if you can work with these, you'll excel with the real goods, which we can provide for you."

He held out the paper and stub-nosed pencil, which was in need of sharpening.

"I'll try my best," I told him.

"Please do," Beall replied. He was becoming more animated, now gazing out the second-story window at the mist rising from the Falls. Considering our location, I expected him to order me to draw Niagara Falls itself, but he must have determined that to be too predictable because in the next breath he said, "The famed Suspension Bridge. The bane of my existence here. Let's see what you can do with that."

He turned, and I saw that he was serious. So, I had little choice but to make my way to the window as he stepped politely aside. How I longed for a quality sketchbook, with a fine writing instrument. Yet when I saw that he was waiting for me, I did my best to begin in earnest. Mother once told me that the key to succeeding under such circumstances, whether it was in art or music or even writing, was to somehow move inside the task at hand. Fall into what made up the very subject in question. In this case, it had to be the arches of the bridge, the way it flowed, almost beyond comprehension, from one side of the Niagara gorge to the other. How the two levels, the top one for the trains, where one was now moving to the Canadian side, and the bottom level for carriages and pedestrians, somehow supported and strengthened each other. Without thinking any more about it, I allowed the pencil to move across the paper, and with each new stroke of the pencil I let myself be carried deeper and deeper into what I saw and what I wanted to convey.

I'm not sure how long I worked in this fashion. Certainly not as long as I had back in Secretary Seward's study. Still, after a time, I stopped and handed my effort to Beall.

The rebel leader took up my rendering and then looked out the window at the Suspension Bridge itself. He was the one now lost in thought—seemingly uncertain of his next move.

Had I won over the rebel leader? I wasn't sure—not at all. A part of me wanted to carry the day. To be as worthy an actor as John Wilkes Booth. But if I did succeed in convincing Captain Beall of my loyalty to the Southern cause, I knew that I had put myself in grave danger.

As the rebel continued to study my sketch, still lost in thought, I again felt as if I was alone on a trestle, far too high above the ground, while behind me came the first moan of an approaching train. Either way I was at the crossroads in my dealings with the Confederates. And, as I soon discovered, it wouldn't be the last time.

18

"He told me the overall purpose, and it does dovetail with the glimmers Secretary Seward saw back in Auburn."

"But what of the particulars?" Wreet asked. "When and how do they plan to strike?"

"That I don't know," I told her. "It was like he opened the door and then closed it when I was about to walk through."

"And what did you tell him?" Wreet added.

"That I wanted nothing more than to help his side, do whatever I could. I even sketched a drawing for him. I did everything I could to prove myself to him, to their cause."

Wreet shook her head, "And how did he leave it with you?"

I said, "Captain Beall said he would talk it over with Bennet Burley. But then it was like he began to second-guess himself. Everything between us slowed to a crawl, and I realized that the Scotsman does have Beall's ear. At least some of the time he does. That the rebel captain trusts Burley, and here I thought he was just a henchman, a bit of a bumbler."

"So did I, child. So did I."

The two of us fell into silence, sitting across from each other in the backroom of Wreet's shop.

"Whatever is about to happen, it's going to happen soon," she said.

I agreed. "But what else can we do?"

"If something is afoot, our Mr. Douglas will have heard of it. C'mon, we need to pay him another visit."

Once again, we hurried the few blocks to the Cataract House. It was approaching the dinner hour as we walked along the wide porch, past where Beall and I had talked only hours before, and pushed through the double doors to the dining room. In the far corner stood Mr. Douglas, observing how his cadre of waiters moved like a military regiment, setting down the next round of dishes for the evening meal. When he saw us, Mr. Douglas nodded to one of the Black waiters, and the younger one took his place. If Mr. Douglas was annoyed by our appearance, he didn't show it.

"I'm sorry to disturb you at work," Wreet said. "But it couldn't wait."

"It's fine," Mr. Douglas replied. "As soon as I saw you two together, I knew it had to be of the utmost urgency."

"Rory has learned that the two rebels are leaving town. To move on the warship anchored off Ohio. But we don't know anything more than that."

Mr. Douglas turned to me. "The Reb didn't take you into his full confidence? Even after our dog-and-pony show the other day?"

"No, I'm afraid not."

"But you believe they are about to act?"

"Yes, Beall said it would happen as soon as the other one, Burley, returned from a short errand he's on."

Mr. Douglas looked up at the clock on his wall. "The next train from Buffalo is due in an hour. I'll send one of my men over to see if he's on it."

"We will be nearby," Wreet said.

Mr. Douglas nodded. "If matters are coming together, we'll soon find out."

Wreet and I passed back through the hotel's main entrance, and she suggested that we take a walk along the river. Side by side, we gazed across the small park to witness the raging river in the fading light of dusk.

"Those waters are the only constant in this part of the world," Wreet said. "Everything else lurches ahead or falls behind with the inconsistency of the breezes off the lake. But that river and the Falls itself are always there. It's only been in recent times that I've come to realize how much I've come to count on such blessings."

Mr. Douglas was back at his post in the grand dining room when we returned, not long after we left. After he gathered up another round of dishes, he motioned for us to join him in his room on the basement level.

"Sometimes God is good," he said as we sat down. "Burley was on that train. He's already back across the border, meeting with the other one, I'd imagine."

Wreet said, "Then they are about to act."

"And here's the rest," Mr. Douglas smiled. "They both have reservations on the nine o'clock train tomorrow morning for points west."

"Points west?" Wreet said. "That's Ohio, for sure."

"I believe so," Mr. Douglas added. "It does appear that they are making their move."

"What can we do about it?" I asked.

Wreet and Mr. Douglas looked at each other and then back to me.

"We can get you on that train, dear," Wreet said. "The rest will be up to you."

19

"I don't see them anywhere," I said.

"They'll be here," Wreet replied. "Our Mr. Douglas is rarely wrong."

The two of us sat aboard Wreet's buckboard wagon, around the corner from the main rail station in the Falls. Together we watched the people come and go from the station as the locomotive was readied on the track, the black smoke from its stack carrying up into the air, where it temporarily clouded the sky.

"There they are," Wreet said as the two Confederates exited a carriage and hurried along the platform. Beall leaned on his cane, and Burley carried a pair of valises. A moment later, the conductor blew his whistle—last call.

"Off you go, my dear."

I briefly hugged Wreet and then stepped down, striding along the platform toward the same railroad carriage Captain Beall and Bennet Burley had disappeared into. With a helping hand from the conductor, I stepped aboard just as the train lurched ahead and began to gain speed. Collecting myself, I smoothed down my long skirt. In one hand was a small bag of my own and in the other a white parasol, which Wreet had pointed out could make for a fine weapon, if needed. Mr. Douglas had learned that Captain Beall and Mr. Burley had reservations in one of the first-class compartments. After much discussion, he and Wreet had decided to book me in the same car.

Taking a deep breath, I made my way up the aisle until I reached the door. Sliding it open, I sat down across from them. Captain Beall was reading the Niagara Falls newspaper, and Mr. Burley gazed out the window as the train moved south along the river.

"Gentlemen," I said, with as much confidence as I could muster.

Beall gazed over the top of the paper. "Miss Chase?" he said with surprise.

"What are you doing here, lass?" Burley asked.

"I was given the impression that you wanted help in documenting your grand adventure," I told them. "Then to receive no word, to even hear rumors of your departure? Well, it can hurt a lady's self-esteem, don't you think? So, I decided to ferret things out."

Captain Beall smiled. "You are a determined one, aren't you?"

"I can put her off at the next station," Burley added.

The leader shook his head. "That would not look very good, now would it, kind sir? Undoubtedly, Miss Chase has a ticket. The conductor would not appreciate such a disturbance. Ugly scene, don't you think? No, instead, we can talk. At least until Buffalo."

By the time we reached Buffalo, we had reached an agreement. At least John Yates Beall and I had. I would accompany them into Ohio, where I would record the proceedings, something for the newspapers, even the history books. And the rebel leader had decided that I might be of help with someone named Cole, who had been in Sandusky for several months.

As for Mr. Bennet Burley? I don't believe he thought much of the arrangement.

Passing out of Buffalo aboard the Lake Shore Limited, the miles began to click along. After a stop in Fredonia, with the town of Erie and after that Cleveland still to come, I felt myself relax despite my determination to stay alert and ever vigilant. Resting my forehead against the cool pane of the window, I closed my eyes for a moment and then quickly reopened them. That brief respite had felt so glorious. Deep down in my bones, I was tired. The rocking motion of the railroad drew me in, like a wide, slow-moving river where I could think of nothing better to do than to lie back and float, letting the current carry me along, around another long, sweeping turn.

When I awoke, I was startled to find that John Yates Beall was no longer in our compartment. Only Burley was still with me.

"Hush now," he said in a low voice.

"Where did the captain go?"

"Disembarked. He has business elsewhere, and it was decided you could be better served by helping me with my part of the plan."

"And where are we?"

"We'll be there soon," he said.

"Cleveland?"

"No, we're well past it."

I couldn't believe it. "How long have I been sleeping?" I asked.

"Long enough," he said. "Time to gather your wits about you, lass. The stakes are rising, I'm afraid. For both of us."

Burley stood up and retrieved the remaining valise from the overhead rack. The train slowed, and out the window I saw a small platform and a placard that read SANDUSKY. Beyond it stood the beginnings of a town, and past that the shimmering blue waters of Lake Erie.

"With me," Burley said, gripping the remaining satchel in his right hand. Before the train came to a full stop, he was already heading down the aisle to the exit, and I hurried to keep up with him.

20

The small bell above the door to the Thayer Studio announced the arrival of a visitor.

"Just a minute," Wreet shouted from the darkroom. She grabbed a rag, then wiped her hands, brushing aside one dark curtain and then another. Her friend John Douglas stood just inside the room.

"Our Miss Rory got off?" Mr. Douglas asked.

"She was aboard when the train left the station," answered Wreet. "I was about to come by the Cataract House and tell you. But I thought you'd be busy, John, with the dinner hour coming."

"I am busy," Mr. Douglas agreed. "But I found that my mind was racing away from me."

"I'm worried, too," Wreet said. "What have we gotten her into?"

She gestured for her old friend to join her at the small table by the dark curtain. But Mr. Douglas shook his head.

"I do need to get back," he said. "I brought you something, though." He held out a small white envelope.

"Ah, another poem," Wreet said, taking the envelope from him. "Those always cheer me up."

"I find such practice helps," Mr. Douglas said. "Especially when all we can do is wait and try to determine what's next."

"John, this is different from any other operation we've done," Wreet said. "Rory is well away from the Falls, the Cataract House."

Mr. Douglas nodded. "Still, the principles remain the same. We back up our couriers in the field. Support them if things fall into disarray."

"As this will? Fall into disarray?"

"I suspect so."

As soon as Mr. Douglas left, the bell atop the door ringing again, Wreet opened the envelope he had given her.

From the wide porch of
The Cataract House
I've watched her down there,
Along the river,
Gazing upon the
Raging waters
And the edge
Of our world here.
Standing near the tourists

In their long coats,
Top hats, and useless parasols.
Her mother nicknamed her
For an Old Irish king, I'm told.
Let's pray a measure of
Such high station holds fast.

JOHN DOUGLAS

PART 3

Among the Rebels

The towering flames had now surmounted every obstruction,
and rose to the evening skies one huge and burning beacon,
seen far and wide through the adjacent country. Tower
after tower crashed down, with blazing roof and rafter; and
combatants were driven from the courtyard.

—WALTER SCOTT, *IVANHOE*

21

Charles Cole spoke in a dizzying swirl, the words rolling over us like the cries of the seagulls overhead.

"I was led to believe that you'd be here yesterday," he said to Burley. "And by yourself."

"Then you were mistaken," my traveling companion replied. It was Tuesday afternoon, in mid-September, and we had just arrived in Sandusky, Ohio.

Cole began again, but Burley waved him off. "Whatever it is, it can wait," Burley said as he strode ahead. "Where's your carriage, Cole?"

Behind us, the train blew its whistle, and the conductor shouted, "All aboard."

Faced with the reality of the task I'd taken on, I was tempted to run as fast as I could for the departing train. But I somehow stayed put, almost frozen in place, and allowed Cole's eyes to settle on me.

"My, my, you're certainly a beanpole topped by a lovely enough face," he said. "Nearly as lanky as our grumpy Scottish friend, aren't you?"

"Let's go, Cole," Burley said over his shoulder. "Time's a'wasting."

Cole directed us to his carriage, which sported a driver. The rig was regal black with an off-white trim pulled by two fierce-looking horses. Rarely did one see such fine mounts these days, four years into the war. So many horses had gone south, to the front lines, and I saw Burley eyeing the pair, undoubtedly arriving at the same conclusion: it must have cost a pretty penny to find such horses in these hard times.

As soon as we were aboard the carriage, Cole tapped on the inside of the roof with his cane, and we were off. Peering out the small window, I saw that we were on the outskirts of the small town. Despite the dust rising from the road, one could smell the humid air of Lake Erie ahead of us.

"Have you ever been to this part of the country, lovely lady?" Cole asked.

"No, sir."

He smiled at my use of the word "sir."

"I've found it to my liking," he said. "The people are hardworking and keep to themselves, which leaves plenty of room for mischief."

Soon we pulled up in front of the West House, a five-story establishment that stood on the corner of Columbus Avenue and Water Street, only a few blocks from the docks along Lake Erie. Promoted as one of the finest hotels between New York and Chicago, it had been built by W. T. West, who I later learned had helped construct the Johnson's Island Confederate Prison compound.

"It's fashionable enough," Cole said, nodding at the stately white-stone building. "Its chief asset is that one can see the islands and the ship from the top floors. From here, it is all laid out for us, pretty as a picture."

"Good to hear," Burley answered.

A bellhop appeared to take our bags. He picked up my small valise, but Burley wouldn't part with his tattered satchel.

"Well, your luggage at least fits the story I've been conjuring up," Cole said. "For those with any questions."

"Do I dare ask what you have in mind?" Burley asked.

"That my long-lost cousin from the old country has somehow found his way here," Cole said. He considered me. "And from there the story only gets better. Granted, it's what I'm coming up with at the spur of the moment, but somewhere between New York and Buffalo he came upon the love of his life and, lo and behold, promptly married her. That they deserve each other. Both being as poor as church mice."

He smiled at Burley, who shook his head in disgust.

"Best watch your tongue," he cautioned Cole, "or I'm of a mind to throttle you."

Upstairs we entered a suite with chandeliers and a generous parlor that would have belonged to any prestigious hotel. "This is my humble abode," Cole said as the bellhop waited in the doorway.

"If this is yours, why are we lingering here?" Burley asked.

"For the view, my good man. Haven't you been listening to a word I've said? You just have to take a look. It is simply majestic."

Snaking his arm around my elbow, he steered me toward the bay window. Burley reluctantly followed.

"For there lies the fabled Lake Erie," Cole said loud enough for the bellhop to overhear. "It may be the shallowest of the Great Lakes, but because of its configuration, how it sits at the very center of the largest freshwater drainage system in the world, it can also foster the most fearsome storms. The lads down at the docks tell me that the winds can whip it into a froth just like that," he said, snapping his fingers.

Then in a lower voice, he added, "Over to the left lies Johnson Island, and fresh by the breakwater you'll recognize the *USS Michigan*."

Burley's eyes had already settled on the prize. "And that's where she's at anchor?" he asked.

"That's right," Cole said. "Of course, she will move about some. In my short time here, I've seen her sail out past the islands there. She might be gone for days at time, but this is where she always comes home to roost."

"Let's make sure she's here when the captain is ready."

"My dear Mr. Burley, what do you think I have been slaving away at? Prepping for that very occasion."

With that, Cole pivoted back toward the door and to the bellhop, who was still waiting.

"Lead on, my good man," Cole said, and we followed the bellhop down the hall, where he opened the door to a much smaller room.

"Believe it or not, it's the next best suite in the entire establishment," Cole said. I saw the bellhop almost correct him before thinking better of it. "When two visitors arrive out of the blue instead of one, plans must be made on the fly, right?"

The suite began with an impressive enough parlor—a pair of chairs, a rocker and a straight-back, and a hardwood floor partially covered by a Persian rug with fraying edges. From here, it was only a few more steps to either of the bedrooms, whose doors opened to reveal much smaller confines, each with a bed and a lone window, which also looked out upon Sandusky's bustling harbor and the inland sea beyond.

"Dinner is at seven, my country cousins," Cole said, turning to leave. "Please come by and knock on my door a half-hour earlier. We will have a drink and then head down together."

With a thin smile, Cole left us, returning down the hall to his grand suite. The bellhop dutifully set my valise at the foot of one of the canopy beds as Burley dug into his pocket and retrieved a coin to tip him. The bellhop nodded his thanks and closed the door behind him.

Burley settled into the lone straight-back chair, while I walked over to the window.

"I apologize for that pompous fool," he began.

"No need," I replied. To be honest, I didn't know what to make of the curious exchange between the two of them. To me, they appeared to be more at loggerheads than on the same page.

"And these living arrangements," Burley added. "I'll see about getting you a proper room as soon as I can."

"It's fine," I told him, remembering my time with the 138th. "I can take care of myself."

"Indeed," Burley sighed and closed his tired eyes. "And, believe it or not, I can be a gentleman."

My traveling companion appeared to sorely miss his "secesh" friend, the rebel captain. As far as I could tell, their plan all along had been to go their separate ways at Cleveland: Burley to set up in Sandusky and Beall to make his way west, where he would carry on that part of their grand plan. There and then, I decided that this had to be my first task: to uncover as much as I could about what they were up to and send word back to Wreet and Mr. Douglas at the Falls.

"So, the captain says you're to document our epic adventure, our grand victory?" Burley began again.

"That's what I've been told."

"And what will you need for that?"

"Prayer and occasionally divine intervention."

Burley gave me a surprised look and then couldn't help but smile. "You are a sharp one, Miss Rory," he said. "I see I must never forget that. But all kidding aside, what do you need to perform your duties? Tell me straight, and I will do my best to procure it for you."

He shook his head and smiled again, as if something had reached out to him from the past. "Procure," he added, almost to himself. "That's one of Captain Beall's favorite words."

I waited until he returned his attention to me. "A sketchbook and drawing pencils. Maybe some pastels," I said, unable to believe that I had fled the Falls without any such tools on my person. "I'm sure I can find them on my own," I added. "There's no need for you to worry about it."

Burley shook his head as if he still couldn't believe he had ended up in this predicament. "No, you stay put, like a good lass," he replied. "I'll see what I can find for you."

"I can fend for myself."

"I'm not arguing that, Miss Rory. You've demonstrated that you're more than capable in a dustup. It's just that I doubt that this situation is going to be as easy as our little friend Cole believes it will be. I need to see to some things first."

I waited for him to say more. His longish frame hunched over, his elbows resting on his thighs, his eyes on the Persian rug, as if the design of that beleaguered fabric somehow held answers for him. In the next breath, though, he snapped out of his doldrums. Burley clapped his hands softly together and stood up.

"Come along," he said. "It's time you and I got some air."

Downstairs, I trailed Burley across the lobby, the desk clerks momentarily stopping their tasks to look us over. Only when we reached the street did Burley slow enough for me to draw alongside. I knew I should thank him, be contrite and demure, but his manner annoyed me.

"Why are you acting this way?" I asked.

"Because if it'd been up to me," he snapped, "we would have left you on the platform back in Buffalo."

"But it wasn't up to you, was it?"

Burley glanced over, as if he couldn't believe that I had dared push back at him. "Aren't you a brassy one?"

More than you can imagine, I thought.

With a sigh, Burley slowed some more, and the two of us made our way down the crowded street outside the West House. Tempting fate, I hooked my arm through his as he gave me another stern look. Yet he didn't shy away from me. Instead, he peered up at the sky with a keen eye, as if he was trying to predict the approaching weather by studying the ratio of sun and cloud. It was a glorious day, with plenty of blue sky overhead, but I could tell by his face, the way his eyes shifted to the west, the direction of the gusting wind, that he wasn't entirely pleased by what he was seeing in the heavens above. As we came down the block, approaching the harbor itself, he slowed even more, seemingly surprised by the number of boats and general activity on and off the water, especially near the Sandusky public wharf.

"Busy port of call," I suggested, and Burley only nodded before we soon turned toward the hotel.

"You appear taken aback?" I asked, wanting to know more of what he thought of it all.

Still, Burley was a cagey one, and he half-shrugged. "There are always stunners to be found, isn't that right, Miss Rory?"

"You tell me."

Burley nodded again and then reluctantly added, "The lake out there is as vast as any of the seven seas. And we will need to hope and pray that these waters lie down like a tired dog come our time. You combine that concern with what I make of our Mr. Cole? And, well, it soon becomes a package rich with many surprises, doesn't it?"

"Charles Cole may be a hindrance," I agreed.

"I fear it is more than that, lass. If first strokes mean anything, the man's ego runs deeper than the lake out yonder. And that doesn't bode well for either one of us."

That evening we dined on pheasant with champagne at Cole's table in the hotel dining room. Even here, one was afforded a fine view of the water and off in the distance, outlined against the horizon, the *Michigan* warship resting at anchor. Cole regaled us with stories about how he was already so popular and well known in Sandusky. He was playing the role of an oil baron from western Pennsylvania. A man with deep pockets, the country squire come to town, who could think of nothing better to do with his money than to wine and dine the Union's men in uniform. Demonstrate undaunting support when such enthusiasm was waning elsewhere in the North.

"And now that my beautiful cousin, or cousin-in-law, or whatever story we have, has joined me," he said, nodding in my direction. "Our job will be that much easier. I'm sure of it."

Before dessert, Mr. Burley excused himself for the evening. Cole was so relieved to see him depart that he ordered another bottle of champagne.

"That man is such a boor." He giggled conspiratorially. "I met him in Richmond soon after he came to the country, wound so tight and full of talk about his foolish torpedoes and weaponry. I would have sent him packing, but our Captain Beall saw something in him. I hope we're all not disappointed with the final results."

I nursed my champagne, while Cole did his best to drain the bottle.

Later, the two of us took the wide staircase up from the lobby to our rooms. By then, Cole was unsteady on his feet, leaning against my shoulder as we approached his door.

"I'm sure our Mr. Burley will be gone much of the night," Cole smiled, his eyes dancing with possibilities. "Would you like to come inside, darling?"

"Perhaps another time," I told him.

Cole leaned in closer and gave me a peck on the cheek.

"My kissing cousin." He chuckled. "I so like the sound of that. So much better. Yes, so much."

Cole fumbled with the key, and I helped him open the door.

"You're so lovely," Cole said, leaning in closer. "In a backwoods kind of way."

I pushed him inside and hurried down the hallway to my room.

22

When the assailant caught him with a lucky blow, it was all Burley could do to stay on his feet. He knew if he went down, it would mean real trouble, as the taller one was eager to pepper him about the ribs and head. This one had already bragged, back at the tavern, about how he enjoyed watching a bloke suffer.

Burley might have escaped the situation with nary a nick if the little one, a real weasel he was, hadn't come out with a knife. In the alley's half-light that weapon shone like Excalibur itself. What men packed on their person in this country to do damage to other human beings sometimes boggled Burley's mind. All of them had been carrying on like blood brothers back at the bar until the conversation took a hop, skip, and drop to the war and the upcoming presidential election. That was when the locals decided they didn't think much of Burley at all—not his accent, his dress, the way he could carry on. With that, the trouble began in earnest.

In the alley, around the corner from the tavern, the weasel stuck Burley with the blade between the left elbow and shoulder. There the keen edge caught plenty of flesh, and Burley was lucky to spin away and make a run for the main street. All he wanted to do was get away as fast as he could, back to the West House. What had begun as a simple reconnaissance mission, a quick prowl around the Sandusky docks, getting a better vantage point on the warship, had gone to tatters. At such times, Burley missed the captain. John Yates Beall could have gotten them out of that bar like smoke flowing under the door, without anything serious happening. But Captain Beall was miles away, settling into Detroit to put the next phase of their plan into motion.

23

The streets surrounding the West House soon fell silent our first night in Sandusky, and I thought I wouldn't have any trouble drifting off to sleep. Yet by ten o'clock, I found myself wide awake. Bennet Burley still hadn't returned.

Downstairs, the desk clerk said he had seen the Scottish rebel turn to the right out the front doors earlier in the evening—heading to the docks, he imagined.

"Only action at this hour is to be found there," the clerk told me. "The rest of town follows the sun during the week—early to bed, early to rise."

"I see."

"But be careful, ma'am. That part of town near the docks can turn rough in a hurry."

Except for an occasional light from the homes that lined Water Street, the hotel clerk had been right: the rest of Sandusky wouldn't be stirring until dawn. Closer to the harbor, there were a few more lights, but I hung back in the shadows, getting a better read on the situation. There were several taverns open along the main street here. Past them lay the dark waters of the harbor and the silhouette of the USS Michigan, and beyond that the vast lake itself.

That's where I stayed for a long while—in the darkness. A chilly wind was beginning to blow off the lake, hurrying the clouds along, and the evening stars began to disappear from view. There would be rain by morning.

My father didn't teach me much at all. He left Mother for California, agog with gold fever, when I was a little girl, and we were officially notified years later that he had died out there. Yet he did instruct me about the weather. This must have been early in my childhood because such notions were no more than whispers and ghosts in my mind now. Still, they included how to read the sky and to know the difference in the clouds and what they may foretell. He had also told me to breast my cards, hold them close, and let the rest of the world be the first to reveal itself. That's why I kept back in the shadows that first night in Sandusky, keeping an eye on the sky and the street out front. I did so until I heard a commotion—shouts and yelling—coming from the alleyway further up the block. Curious, I edged to the corner of the building and peered around, and there was Bennet Burley, half-surrounded by three men. One of them had a knife, which glistened in the streetlight as he shifted it gingerly from one hand to the other.

Crouching down, staying out of sight, I scrambled closer. The shortest of the three, the one with the knife, was closing in on my traveling companion, while the other two carried on like jackals. Burley looked from one side to the other, but there was no escape. The alleyway ended at a high wall, and the three men had cut him off from fleeing to the main street. Soon their threats and yelling tapered off, and the trio moved ever closer, while the short one brought the knife down, now close to his side, ready to do real damage.

When he made his first thrust, Burley dodged it easily enough, but the move brought him too close to one of the other men, who pushed him back toward the one with the knife. Before Burley could gather himself, the hooligan caught him with a well-placed strike to the upper arm.

Through it all, I moved closer, hiding behind a stack of wooden crates. They had once been filled with onions and carrots and the like, vittles for the nearby tavern. Most contained some straw, and I grabbed one, raising it high. After taking a few steps closer, I brought it down hard atop the nearest attacker's head. When I went to yank it free, I let the jagged pieces crawl up his face. The man's cries of pain drew the attention of the others, and I swung what was left of the shattered crate toward the one closer to me. The mess of wood and straw caught him across the chest, and Burley then punched him in the face.

Seeing that I had nothing else that could serve as a weapon, the man with the knife decided to come for me, a cruel look on his face. Thankfully, Burley had made quick work of the second villain, and before the shorter fellow was any wiser, Burley dove for the back of his legs, bringing him down at the knees. In the ensuing confusion, Burley was able to slip past and come alongside me. He took me by the hand, and we turned and ran as fast as we could.

As we headed along Water Street, the men's taunts soon faded. We slowed, but we didn't stop running until we reached the West House. Together we hurried through the lobby and upstairs to our rooms.

Once we were there, Burley couldn't stop pacing back and forth in the parlor, holding his left arm and trying to patch himself together as best he could. He kept on until I convinced him to let me have a look.

"You're badly hurt," I said. The gash was nearly to the bone and extended for several inches. While he had tried to remedy the situation himself with a bath towel, the dressing wasn't nearly enough. The wound was too deep.

"Just a moment," I told him and hurried back to my room.

Returning with a petticoat, I looked around for something to cut it with. "You must have a blade about you, too? Some kind of knife?"

He nodded and rummaged inside his bag until he found a small switchblade.

"Where was that marvel when you needed it tonight?" I asked.

"Forgotten in the rush to survey the situation," Burley replied. "The story of my life, I'm afraid."

With a flick of his wrist, the blade's gleaming edge revealed itself.

"You practice that parlor trick much?"

He grinned, "More than you can imagine, Miss Rory. I find it's popular with the ladies."

"Hush now," I said. "Let's see if we can bind you back together."

With the razor-sharp edge, I cut the petticoat into long swaths. Bringing over the wash basin, I cleaned the wound as best I could. After that, I stretched one length of cloth and then another, tightly binding his arm. He gasped as I pulled the ribbons of fabric taut, finally tying the last stretch of cloth with a snug knot.

"You still need a doctor," I advised.

"Not now," he replied. "I'll get some rest, and we'll see where it sits in the morning."

Deciding not to argue with him, I found a decanter of amber liquor and poured him a glassful.

"Have this," I urged and watched him down it in short order.

"Once a Scotsman, always a Scotsman," he joked. I found myself heartened to see a smile come to his face.

"What happened?"

He shook his head. "I need to learn when to keep my big geggie shut."

"Your mouth?"

"Aye, Miss Rory. I got into it with a few of the locals about the war. Just a jolly good show of words until this demented gent pulls out a blade and begins swinging it about. Caught me before I ever saw it coming. The whole place became a real pagger, and I was lucky to get out of there with only this nick."

"It's more than a nick. You've lost a lot of blood."

"Your fine bandaging job will last me until the morning. Right now, I just need some shuteye."

Bracing himself with his one good arm, he arose from the chair and staggered to his room. Lying down on the bed, he cradled his wounded limb with his good arm. He took a deep breath and then another, trying to calm himself.

But then he blinked open his eyes, staring up at me.

"Why'd you help?" he asked. "Binding my wounds and all. Another Florence Nightingale, aren't you?"

"I don't like to see a person outnumbered," I replied. "It's not fair."

He smiled at this. Taking another deep breath, he closed his eyes again.

"I should have taken you with me," he said, his voice beginning to trail off. "You would have shown those jokers the back of your hand."

I returned to the parlor, keeping his door open. My petticoat wraps had done an adequate enough job—for now. Out the window, I gazed down upon the town of Sandusky, which had grown as still as my traveling companion.

Settling into the armchair, I decided to rest there for a spell, where I could keep a better watch on him. Before closing my eyes, I glanced at the side table, where I discovered several notebooks, drawing pencils held together by ribbon, as well as a box of pastels. Almost in disbelief, I stepped closer to the bay window, holding the pencils up to the moonlight. The materials were of top quality—Ball, Dixon, Holden & Cutter. The poor man didn't know what I preferred, so he must have ordered anything and everything and had the front desk bring them up to the room.

Finding a blanket, I tiptoed back into Burley's room and covered him to the waist. He barely stirred, still cradling his wounded limb with the hand of his good arm.

A pair of slender books lay on his dresser—*Poems of Thomas Gray* and *Shakespeare's Sonnets*—and I realized I had left my dog-eared copy of *Ivanhoe* back at Wreet's shop. That's how much of a hurry I had been in to catch the train heading west. How I wished I had something to read—something to slow my racing mind.

Taking *Shakespeare's Sonnets*, I returned to the chair in the parlor. There, in the dim glow of the whale oil lamp, I slowly turned the pages until my eyes grew heavy.

24

The sounds of cursing awoke me the next morning. Sitting up in the parlor chair, I saw that Burley was trying to shave himself. The process wasn't going well, and he became more and more agitated as he nicked himself again, this time under the chin.

"Wait," I told him, and he paused, studying my reflection in the mirror as I entered his room.

"It's the blasted arm," he said. "I've grown accustomed to using this hand for such chores. Now that's been done in but good. I've decided that you're right, Miss Rory. I better go for stitches this morning."

"Before that, let me help," I said.

"You've already done enough. Being my bed nurse. Watching out for me through the night. Ye didn't need to coorie me."

"Coorie?"

"Watch out for me. Cuddle me like I was some kind of homesick schoolboy."

"Consider me your guardian angel." I held out my hand for the razor. "Don't worry. I know my way around such devices."

Reluctantly, he turned the blade about, offering me the handle. I took it and nodded for him to sit in the straight-back chair. I brought over the soap and wash pan, then told him to hold still. He closed his eyes, almost in prayer, and I couldn't help but laugh at his apprehension.

"If I'd wanted to inflict such damage upon your person, don't you think I would have done it last night?"

His dark eyes fluttered open. "Aye, you're right."

Still, he couldn't help but close his eyes again as I took the first pass, running the blade delicately down the right side of his face. For a moment, we both held our breath, but I hadn't drawn any blood. After rinsing off the blade, I began a series of short strokes right under the chin, scrapping away the stubble. Burley had a pencil-thin mustache, and I worked at the bottom edges, leaving the rest of it alone, wetting my fingers in the basin and running them down the hair atop and on either side of his mouth.

From a distance, he exhibited such a stern countenance. Yet when one drew closer, when he closed his eyes, holding his breath with trepidation, his was a face that many might be intrigued with. When he sighed after another passing of the blade, seemingly relieved that he would somehow survive this ordeal, too, I shook my head at this new-found vulnerability. Finishing up, I couldn't help but run my fingertips lightly across his forehead, brushing back a strand of his black hair.

"There," I said. "We're done."

He turned to his reflection in the wall mirror. "Thank you," he said with a measure of true gratitude. "Maybe the captain was right about you. Maybe you can help us with this bizarre mission of ours."

Then Burley glanced at my reflection in the mirror.

"You don't strike me as a follower of the Bard," he said.

"Likewise, kind sir."

"Kind sir? There's some Shakespeare talking. How did you come to him and his works?"

"Like you, I'd suspect," I replied. "As a child. A good friend of mine growing up—" and here I told myself to tread lightly. No mention of Auburn and certainly not Fanny or the Sewards. "She and I both read him."

"Me, too," Burley said, eager to turn talk back to himself. "When life knocks one about, nothing better to get a person back on his feet. The Shake's words tumble ahead, taking you with them."

"I cannot disagree, kind sir."

A few blocks away from the West House, Dr. Jeffrey Parsons's office was open, but the good doctor wasn't in. "He's on rounds this morning," the nurse told us.

She was a heavy-set woman, an efficient matron dressed in a white frock, looking like a giant cloud that had plummeted to earth to frighten all comers.

Deciding that he couldn't wait, Burley asked if she could piece him back together. Take care of what he called a scratch.

"That's hardly a scratch, mister," she said as she peeled away my petticoat wrap. "If I didn't know better, I'd say you were on the losing end of a quarrel of some sort. A knife fight from the looks of it."

Burley didn't rise to the bait and simply asked, "You can take care of it then?"

"I cannot promise that I'll do as neat a job as Doc Parsons. But it will hold together, good and proper. I'll make sure of it."

"Thank you, ma'am."

She shrugged at his change in tone, dismissing it for the insincerity that it was. "And if anyone ever asks about the scar you'll surely have, just tell them that Madge Morris put your poor arm back together again. Half the ruffians in these parts can make the same claim."

After that declaration, Madge Morris went to work, laying out a scalpel, scissors, and more wraps on the small table. The office cupboard was littered with bandages, jars, and the like, and I couldn't help wondering if Dr. Parsons went about his business in such a slipshod way.

"I'll need more cleanser," she said, turning to me. "Fetch me another vial, young one. It's there on the top shelf."

In gazing up at the shelves of bottles and ointments, trying to determine what Madge Morris was referring to, I inadvertently knocked over a larger jug, spilling its contents onto the floor.

"Fumes," Madge cried out, reaching for wraps in the front pocket of her apron. She put one over her face and tossed another to Burley. Then she hustled past me and flung open the window. The spill was chloroform, and with no way to protect myself, I quickly began to lose consciousness, feeling myself go down in a heap.

Madge Morris must have dragged me away from the liquid pooling on the floor and then cleaned up the mess. Yet that is only guesswork on my part, as I was long gone from this world. It was only after she waved smelling salts under my nose that I began to come around.

"None the worse for wear," Madge Morris pronounced, eager to finish stitching up Burley. But he continued to kneel over me with real concern on his face. Blinking my eyes several times, I came back to him, rising from the rabbit hole filled with ghosts and shades where I'd found myself.

"That's it, luv," Burley was telling me. I could see Madge Morris just over his shoulder—both of them gazing down at me. "Deep breaths now. You'll be all right in a jiff."

25

During my bout with the fumes, I'd pictured myself back at the Niagara overlook, once again high above the Falls and the narrow gorge below. Off to one side was the familiar sight of the Suspension Bridge. A thunderstorm was moving in from the northwest, from across the far edge of Lake Ontario, and the air was hot and sticky, seemingly ready to erupt. Yet as I turned away from the overlook, the winds rushed over me, and the air turned somehow colder and colder until snowflakes began to fall.

Before me stood the Cataract House, with many of its windows aglow despite the frost quickly building up on their panes. Then, in a growing number of the windows, faces appeared—Wreet, Cesar, Sissy, Aran, and, finally, Mr. Douglas. I waved to them, motioning for someone to open the door. To let me in. But either they didn't see me, or they refused to acknowledge me, for one by one they turned away and soon faded from view.

I was trying to make sense of this while I sketched the Sandusky harbor, with the *USS Michigan* at anchor inside the breakwater, from our hotel window that afternoon. I was determined to lose myself in my work when Cole knocked on our door.

Burley promptly opened it, and for an instant the two men simply eyed each other, the contempt they felt clearly visible. Finally, Burley held the door open, and Cole entered.

"Ah, the country cousins are together," Cole smiled. "And the pretty beanpole so lost in her labors."

"She's doing her job," Burley said. "Let her be."

"Easy, my Scottish friend. I've received another telegram from Beall. He's asking about the ship's exact location, even its whereabouts for early next week."

"And what did you tell him?"

Cole gazed out the window upon the harbor below us. "To be frank, I haven't replied yet."

Burley grinned at this. "In other words, you don't know what to say, do you?"

Cole shrugged.

"Don't you worry your sweet little head," continued Burley, enjoying the moment. "I'll see what I can find out."

Relieved, Cole soon left us, and I saw Burley's face cloud over. "That man is the fly in the ointment," he muttered to himself. Then he turned his attention to me. "I trust the sketching materials are adequate."

"They certainly are," I replied. "More than adequate."

"At least something's falling my way," Burley said. "My gut tells me that matters here are as loose as the buttons on my grandmother's frock after a night dancing on the town. You do good work with the sketchbook, Miss Rory. There's no doubt about it. But landscape views won't carry the day. I need to know the particulars of this harbor and even out on the breakwater, to the water's edge. That's why I need to check out the docks again tonight. Determine exactly what's where and who's who. Perhaps even hear what the majestic *Michigan* is up to in the days ahead. Because it appears that the captain is once again racing ahead of any semblance of a plan. For that I'm going to need your help."

I nodded in agreement.

"We'll sneak away an hour or so after dinner," he said. "Cole doesn't need to know."

"I'll be ready." I turned back to the window, looking out on the peaceful harbor, the array of ships and boats at anchor and nestled in their dock spaces. I tried to sketch it again, fall under the spell that I enjoy when the work is going well. Yet my hand, perhaps gripping the pencil too tightly now, didn't move as fast or as surely as it had moments before.

26

Once more we strode through the shadows near the West House, along the alleyways as the chatter and music of the taverns rose toward the heavens. There was hardly any breeze here, in the harbor, but out past the pier and shelter rocks the waves of Lake Erie were rough, with plenty of choppy water. Back in the shadows, we tried our best to stay out of sight. Burley wasn't interested in getting into any confrontations this evening. He didn't even try to hide it with bluster or boast. Time and again, we stopped, and he ordered me to sketch this row of storefronts or network of docks or views of the harbor entranceway. His curiosity about how the Sandusky harbor fit together seemingly had no end, and I did my best to keep up with his requests.

We had been at it for several hours and had reached the breakwater, only a stone's throw from the USS *Michigan* itself, when our situation turned dire indeed. The rocks were wet from the building waves. Despite the approaching darkness, we drew the attention of several sailors aboard the *Michigan*. They shouted for us to halt—stop where we were.

"C'mon, let's go," said Burley, and we began to scamper along the jagged rocks back toward the harbor and the streets at the docks.

We made good time, easily putting distance between ourselves and the interested parties out on the water. We wouldn't have had any trouble getting away if Burley, well ahead of me, hadn't tripped and fallen headlong into the water.

"Help," he gasped as he resurfaced. Out past him, I saw a small rowboat from the *Michigan* swing toward us, coming across the expanse of harbor water. A sailor crouched in the vessel's bow shone a lantern in our direction, while two others pulled hard on the long oars.

As I set my sketchbook down, Burley ordered for me to wedge it between several large rocks so it wouldn't blow away in the rising breeze. After doing so, I leaned down, and he clasped hold of my forearm. At first, I feared he would pull me in, right on top of him. Yet I somehow held steady, and he began to climb upward. With only one good arm, Burley made poor progress. By then dripping wet, he didn't manage to scramble to his feet until the Union rowboat was almost upon us.

It would have been easy to delay a few more minutes and let them seize us. I could have told them everything, shown them my sketches of the harbor, let them take Bennet Burley away. Then it came to me that such action wouldn't accomplish much of anything. Even though I had had my fill of this nightmare assignment to the shores of Lake Erie, I felt as overmatched here as I did at the Falls. I would be returned to Wreet and Mr. Douglas and the rest at the Cataract House with little in hand. A bunch of crazy tales about rebel pirates and a warship that appeared as formidable and steadfast as anything upon the Great Lakes. I needed to know more. So much more. As a result, I continued to play my part and helped the Scotsman escape.

As fast as we could, we ran along the harbor breakwater until we reached Sandusky's streets and alleyways, where we once again hung in the shadows, staying out of sight, until we finally reached the West House. Burley looked like a drowned rat when we arrived in the lobby, but he glared at the desk clerk, and the poor man didn't dare say a word. Once again, we stole up the stairs until we reached our suite.

"What a debacle." Burley sighed as he closed the door behind us.

"You're freezing," I said, feeling the coldness in his fingertips, seeing his face grow pale. "Sit down. I'll fetch you some hot water for a bath."

"Once we evaded the Yanks," he continued, "my mind began to run away with me. I feared we would run into the switchblade gent from the other night."

"I would have taken care of him," I lied.

Downstairs, at the front desk, I gained the services of a bellhop who soon delivered the steaming water and helped Burley out of his wet clothes, wringing them out in the sink before tossing them to me. I draped them about the room to dry.

"Miss Rory," he called out from the bathroom, and I peered around the half-open door.

"Your sketchbook?"

"It's here," I said.

"Pull out the best images," he replied. "I'll get them to Captain Beall."

"Yes, sir," I told him. Even though I wasn't about to hand him all of my best renderings. Some I would hang on to for myself.

"You succeeded when it was required of you, and few can truly say that," he added, sinking further into the water. "I was wrong about you, Miss Rory. You've proved to be a valuable addition."

"Thank you."

"Let's make a pact, you and I," he said as the bellhop closed the door, eager to leave us. "That someday we'll return to these parts and instead of prowling about in the darkness, we'll walk down to the harbor in the light of day in our finest garb. I'll hold out my elbow to you and you'll take it, and side by side we'll reach the water's edge and gaze upon it all as proper people do."

"Whatever you say, Mr. Burley."

27

Early the next morning, Cole was at the door. "Where's the Scottish fool?" he demanded when I opened it for him.

"What's the ruckus, Cole?" asked Burley, coming out of his room. "And at this hour. It's barely seven."

"You need to get away quick, man," Cole said. "Flee while there's still time."

"What in the name of heaven are you blathering on about?"

"This," Cole answered, holding out a wanted poster. "I saw it on my morning walk. There're sprouting up all over town."

As we peered closer, I saw it was a sketch, a poor one if I say so myself, of Burley with a brief description—six feet, two inches; solidly built—and a $1,000 reward.

"That doesn't look anything like me." Burley said.

"It's enough," Cole said. "Enough to derail the entire operation."

"Nonsense," Burley retorted.

"Take that up with Captain Beall," Cole said. "I alerted him this morning, and he agrees with me. Time for you to join him in Detroit."

"And how am I supposed to simply fly away?" Burley asked. "If this is already all over town?"

"By heading to the next station to the west—Port Clinton," Cole told us. He was a good step ahead of my traveling companion. "But we need to leave—now."

When we arrived at the Port Clinton station, the train was just pulling in. Cole handed Burley several tickets.

"This is the secondary line that runs to Toledo," he said. "From there you switch to the northbound, which will take you to Detroit proper. Captain Beall will meet you at the station."

As the conductor's whistle blew, Cole held out his hand, and Burley reluctantly shook it. Then Burley turned and briefly embraced me. "Watch yourself, lass," he whispered in my ear. "He's a bad farthing if I've ever seen one."

From the railway station, Cole's carriage didn't slow as we approached our hotel. Instead, it passed by at a good clip, and we headed toward the waterfront. Here we stopped, and Cole's driver jumped down to open the carriage door.

The sky was heavy closer to the shore, with dark clouds, the threat of a thunderstorm, riding the horizon over Lake Erie. When Cole moved beside me, I had little choice but to take his elbow as we fell into the crowd of vendors calling out their wares and the seamen hurrying along the docks. On the far side, like a silent sentry above the fray, lay the USS Michigan at anchor. While nobody else paid it any mind, it certainly held Cole's attention.

"I know what Mr. Burley was up to, down by the docks," he said. "Trying to work out every possible angle for his captain. But he can be too much of a bumbler, don't you think?"

"Is that why you cooked up that scheme to send him away?" I replied. "I didn't see any wanted posters for him as we were coming back through town this morning."

"You are more than a pretty face." Cole smiled. "Let's just say I decided that your Mr. Burley and I are too much like oil and water. Always at loggerheads. He should be with Captain Beall, and if so, I can better run operations here. As for the wanted poster? A bit of fiction when needed. Something to grease the skids."

We entered a small tea shop, the ringing bell above the door reminding me of Wreet's place back in Niagara Falls. Cole motioned to a table looking out on the bustling waterfront.

"Believe it or not, they have fine blends here," Cole said. "What would you like?"

"You choose for me," I told him.

Cole nodded, and soon he returned to the table with a pair of steaming mugs.

"It's from the Orient," he said, setting one of them down in front of me. It smelled of wheat with a faint glimmer of cinnamon. "In this country, I've only found it in New York."

"You've traveled a great deal?"

Cole blew faintly on the steaming cup. "More than you can imagine, Miss Chase," he replied.

He paused, as if he was expecting more questions. Instead, I returned my gaze to the harbor and the people who were busy with their lives.

"All right then," Cole said, as if he was starting over. "What to do with you? Especially with Burley out of the way."

I returned my attention to him, trying to determine what this man was about. Years ago, back in school in Auburn, when Fanny Seward and I read many of the plays by Shakespeare—*Romeo and Juliet*, the Henrys, *Macbeth*—Fanny had a miniature stage with figurines that her father had brought back from one of his trips around the world. As I listened to Cole, I remembered scenes from *Julius*

Caesar one winter afternoon back home, and I realized that Cole was like Cassius in that Shakespeare tragedy. Arrogant, willful, with a way of getting people to do his bidding. I knew I had to listen hard to what he was proposing and then find a way out of the spider's web I was becoming ensnared in.

"As you may know by now, the locals are holding a masked ball tomorrow," he was saying. "We'll both be going, with different roles but a common purpose. . . .. Are you following me so far?"

Although I nodded, Cole wasn't convinced.

"Your attention seems to wander sometimes, my lovely. That troubles me."

As Cole sat there, a smug look on his face, I had little choice but to recite nearly everything he had said to that point back to him. How an extravagant party was scheduled for tomorrow. How the upper crust of the town would attend, including the officers aboard the *USS Michigan*. How Cole had worked so hard to earn their trust.

His self-assured manner faded by time I was finished.

"Precisely," he stammered. "I must remind myself never to under-estimate you. For you are as much brains as beauty."

"What are we trying to accomplish at this masked ball?"

The question brought him up short.

"Well," he began. "You see, it's complicated, Miss Chase. While I've tried to worm my way into every nook and cranny of this god-forsaken town, I fear that I haven't found enough able hands. Not yet anyway. The North is so tired of the war. But one can always use the help of more kindred spirits in endeavors such as ours. Even in a burg like lovely Sandusky, Ohio."

"How does that matter?" I asked. "From what I know of Captain Beall, he hasn't grown tired of the war."

Cole nodded at this. "Indeed, he hasn't."

"And now with Mr. Burley rejoining him, I'd imagine he'll be even more determined to accomplish his ends."

Cole turned to look upon the harbor and the *USS Michigan* at anchor. "But they need my help to make it all work," he said. "They know that as well as anyone."

"Help with what?"

Cole shook his head at my ignorance. "My dear, I'm the spark that lights the candle," he said. "None of this here, absolutely none of it, goes into motion without my signal, my say-so."

"Your signal?"

"Ah, Miss Chase," he grumbled, now focused on me. "So many questions. If it was up to me, I'd cook up a wanted poster with your likeness on it, too. Find some way to send you fleeing from Sandusky. And something tells me you'd like nothing better. That you've been pulled into a scenario where you'd rather not be. At times, you have the look of a very reluctant heroine, my dear. Someone caught in so many crosscurrents."

I must admit I didn't know what to say to any of this. That such a duplicitous man could somehow see right through me was downright terrifying.

"Don't you fret, Miss Rory," Cole said. "Follow my lead. Perhaps you can be of help to our effort yet."

It was midday by the time Cole dropped me at the West House as he hurried off on another of his many errands. I knew I needed to get word back to Wreet and Mr. Douglas in the Falls. But what to tell them, especially without Cole being the wiser?

Back upstairs, entering my room off the parlor, I saw the abridged volume of Shakespeare's sonnets. One of Burley's books. As I picked it up, a note fell to the floor.

It was on West House stationary, done in a hasty scrawl. "Something to help in the wee hours," it read. "BB."

28

When Mr. Douglas came downstairs after the dining room closed, well after nine o'clock, he found Wreet waiting outside his room.

"News?" he asked, opening the door.

Wreet held the telegram out for him. "Maybe, maybe not."

Puzzled, Mr. Douglas read aloud: "MR. B. LEFT TO JOIN CAPTAIN STOP CC RUNNING THINGS HERE NOW STOP."

"Who's CC?" Mr. Douglas asked.

"I have no idea," Wreet replied. "I was hoping you'd have a clue."

Mr. Douglas shook his head. "Well, I'll reach out to what's left of our network in northern Ohio. I haven't heard anything from them to this point. This came to you, Wreet?"

She nodded. "From the West House in Sandusky, which I remember as being a pretty fancy operation. But we don't have anyone at the hotel proper?"

"I'm afraid not," Mr. Douglas said. "They don't hire our kind."

Wreet sighed. "We sent her off blind, didn't we? No code words, protocol?"

"We didn't have any choice," he reminded her. "We didn't even realize she was going with the rebels until the last minute. Whether she knows it or not, Miss Rory is our lone courier on the scene."

The two of them sat there for a time, uncertain what else to say or do.

"I was looking through Rory's belongings when the gram arrived," Wreet said. "Nothing mischievous or anything. Just putting things together, and I found a copy of *Ivanhoe*. Stamp on the title page says it's from the Seward Library."

"'*Ivanhoe*,'" said Mr. Douglas. "I don't know that story."

"It is about knights in England. The dark times after the Norman conquest, and they're at odds with the Saxons."

Mr. Douglas chuckled. "Sounds like it could be from today."

"Oh, it's much more romantic than what we have now. King Richard was captured coming home from the Crusades, but he's eventually rescued and joins up with Robin Hood and his merry men."

"A tale with a happy ending?" Mr. Douglas asked.

"It certainly is," Wreet told him. "Miss Rory must find solace in such books. Perhaps her friend Fanny Seward does as well."

Soon it grew late, and Wreet prepared to go home.

"I'll check the railroad schedule," Mr. Douglas said, "even the ferries from Buffalo. We'll be ready."

"Ready for what, John?"

Mr. Douglas shrugged. "I don't rightly know."

Later that evening, when Mr. Douglas couldn't fall asleep, he sat down at his small desk and began to compose another poem. One that he planned to drop off at Wreet's in the morning. An excuse to see if any more word had arrived from Sandusky.

Despite his insomnia, the pen flowed well across the paper, almost as fast as the river waters flowing past the Cataract House.

> *In the shadow of the Falls.*
> *That's where I do my best work.*
> *While the few pictures taken of me*
> *Were in my black coat and white shirt*
> *And crease-ironed pants at the Cataract House,*
> *Where I directed my men who needed little*
> *If any helping hand by the time another*
> *Dinner hour arrived and those delivering*
> *The morsels for the night were as much*
> *A part of the show as what hit the plate.*

> *No, it was down those two hundred and ninety stairs*
> *To the Niagara itself. That's where I did my best work.*
> *For there, in the mist and shadow, with the*
> *River roiling and carrying on so much*
> *That one could barely hear one's self think.*
> *That was the arena where I took up my long oars*
> *More times than I can remember now, being like*
> *Charon, the ferryman upon the Styx, as I stole*
> *Another soul across to promise and freedom.*

> JOHN DOUGLAS

29

As Burley came off the train in Detroit, he knew to look for Captain Beall in the shadows, near the far exit.

"The news from Sandusky?" Beall asked as he approached.

"I have sketches of the harbor and the whole of the waterfront. They're in my bag."

"And the overall situation?"

"Cole claims to have it under control, and Miss Chase will duly record it, as you requested."

"So, she has been an asset." Beall smiled. "You didn't think so highly of her last week."

"A man can change his mind, can't he?" Burley replied, slowing his gait a tad to fall into step alongside the rebel leader. "Besides, I trust her more than that show pony John Wilkes Booth."

"As I've told you, Booth's a bagman. No more, no less," Beall said as they emerged from the station and onto Woodward Avenue. There the captain hailed a carriage.

"Booth has delusions of grandeur."

"Enough," the captain warned. "He is of no matter to us anymore."

Minutes later, the hack pulled up in front of the Russell House, Detroit's finest hotel. As Burley took up his satchel, the two of them paused to listen to the latest reports from the battlefields far to the south. None of it was good news for the Confederacy.

"Sherman has fully secured Atlanta," the crier told a growing crowd outside the hotel's main doors. "Rebel forces are in retreat."

The stentor was dressed in a dark suit, reading from a clipboard of papers, detailing how General William Tecumseh Sherman had outflanked the Confederate force one last time. With Atlanta under Union control, rumor had it that Sherman would now begin to march across Georgia to the sea. As the crowd cheered, Burley remembered the farmer he'd met on his first foray to the south. *The one who told me how there were always more bluecoats coming down his road.*

"They never should have replaced Johnson with Hood," Captain Beall muttered. "Johnson didn't have the numbers, but he knew how best to use them. How to keep his troops out of harm's way and able to fight another day."

"That only leaves Lee at Richmond," Burley said.

Beall nodded. "That's why we have to complete our task, and do it soon. Conjure up a fresh nightmare to keep Old Abe and his brethren awake at night."

When they entered Captain Beall's suite, the rebel leader gestured for Burley to join him on the balcony, where the clamor of the streetcars, horses and buggies, even snippets of the crier's news drifted up to them.

"I don't trust our surroundings," Beall said when Burley gave him a curious look. "The Russell may be the top establishment in Detroit, but there are too many nooks and crannies. Too many places to eavesdrop on us. So, indulge me, please."

Although Burley nodded in reply, he was alarmed by the captain's manner and even his appearance. The poor man was in an agitated state and didn't seem to have slept since Niagara Falls.

"The mission has been pushed up," Beall announced. "We'll commence in a few days. And you'll be with me."

"But I thought I could return to Sandusky? To make sure Cole does his bit."

Beall shook his head. "I need you here. I've learned it's easier for you, as a British citizen, to do our business across the border here, in the Windsor area."

"All right then," Burley said. "But what's the hurry, sir? Aren't we working ourselves into a lather?"

When the captain didn't answer, Burley knew not to argue with him. For this was how Maxwell and the others often felt: thrown for a loop because plans with Captain Beall could change with the wind.

"We've found a suitable vessel," Beall continued. "Sufficient funds have changed hands so the skipper will indulge us. I'll need you to tie up the loose ends there."

"Easily done," Burley replied.

"Good, we cannot dither any longer. As you heard from the town crier, time isn't on our side. We need to push ahead here and pray that Cole holds up his end in Sandusky."

30

The night of Sandusky's Merchants and Craftsmen Ball, I came down the wide staircase at the West House to find Charles Cole waiting for me in the lobby. The bellhops and desk clerk paused to look me over, too, and that was somewhat embarrassing even if I had to admit that the off-white evening gown that Cole had selected suited me perfectly. He had also insisted that I do something about my hair, with a local dresser visiting me in my room earlier in the afternoon, edging the short locks back from my face and lacquering it all down.

"Miss Rory Chase?" Cole called out. "Is that you? My goodness gracious, you sparkle like something from a sailor's dream."

I pursed my lips and tried not to smile, which only caused Cole to clap his hands with glee. "Admit it, you are Cinderella come to life. Like it or not, you're going to be the belle of our ball."

Cole took my arm, leading me out to his carriage, and I saw that every piece of metal on the rig, from the horses' harnesses to the brass latch on the door, had been polished.

"Our destination is the Bellevue Mansion," Cole said as we departed the West House. "It's a mile or so outside of town and offers grand views of the town and the harbor."

"And what's our purpose?" I asked.

"Purpose?" Cole chuckled. "Oh, Rory, you are too curious for your own good sometimes. Where are your manners, my country cousin? Tonight is a reconnaissance outing, just a look-see, to take a gander. Win over some more hearts and minds if the opportunity presents itself."

Burley was right: Cole loved to talk in riddles, determined to tie the listener in knots. I knew the rebels would soon try to seize the USS Michigan. But when and how—the particulars of their plan—remained hidden from me. I knew I needed to send more news back to Wreet and the others at the Cataract House, but as of now I had no idea what to tell them.

The party was well underway when we pulled through the gates to the Bellevue Mansion and came up the white-stone walkway. Every window in the two-story palace of fieldstone was aglow, including an observation deck erected at the center of the grounds. The women wore long gowns and sparkling jewelry, and the men strutted about in tailored suits or tuxedos. With few exceptions, everyone's face was shielded by some kind of mask.

Cole held out a light-colored face disguise attached to a wooden stick, which matched my gown. With that, we fell in with the others, moving up the sweeping walk to the front entranceway. Somewhere, far in the background, came the sound of violins and cellos. Inside the entranceway, Cole handed a card to a servant dressed in black tails. He announced our names in a rich baritone voice.

"Now mingle, my dear," Cole said. "There are important folks here I need to buttonhole. But promise me that you'll tell me anything and everything that you hear."

I tried to smile as his hand gripped my forearm. "Promise," I replied.

Once we parted, I made my way into the larger ballroom. Indeed, much of the town seemed to be there, dressed in their finest, wholeheartedly sporting masks for the evening. Most of the men had tied theirs around their heads, with the women holding up their disguises with long wooden handles. Sometimes I raised mine, even though it seemed absurd to do so in a place where I was a complete stranger.

Looking about, I moved farther into the cluster of people near the dance floor. Here the dance music grew louder with each new step, and I felt myself becoming captivated by simply being in the midst of it all. I had rarely attended such events in Auburn. There was the annual Christmas party at the Sewards, where I watched from the shadows, always the wallflower. So unlike my friend Fanny, who would nod in my direction, beckon for me to come on to the dance floor. She was shy by nature, too, but much better at rising to the occasion, especially if her dear father urged her to do so. Still, I always had difficulty in following Fanny's example. Who wanted to be with that tallest girl standing like a post in the middle of the dance floor in another ill-fitting dress?

"Rory Chase?"

Someone was calling my name here? Amid the conversation and music?

"Rory, is it really you?"

I turned to see Alden Gilbert gazing up at me like a starstruck schoolboy, easily seeing past my mask. Alden had been one of the first from Auburn to enlist in the war, and now here he stood in a blue uniform with polished buttons and a few bars and braids that signified that he had been heroic in the confrontation.

"Yes, it is," he said, almost laughing at the absurdity of it all. "I just knew it had to be you."

Alden was as disbelieving as me at how I had been transformed from a tomboy from the wrong side of the tracks to this spectacle of high society.

"The last I heard," Alden continued, "was about your uncle. Passing so soon after your mother. I'm so sorry."

"Thank you," I told him. "It's fine."

Looking past Alden, I saw Cole at the far end of the ballroom, speaking with several Union officers. My childhood friend followed my eyes. "That's the top brass," he said. "Captain Everett and the rest of his command from the *Michigan*."

"The warship?"

"Yes, the one that takes up half the harbor."

"You serve aboard the *Michigan*?"

"No, not at all," Alden answered. "I'm with what's left of the garrison at the docks. Not many of us there now with the war winding down."

Cole saw that I was also talking to someone in Yankee blue and smiled in my direction.

"But I don't know that chap," Alden said. "The civilian dressed to the nines."

"I do," I said, taking Alden by the elbow. "He's an old family friend. You should meet him."

Perhaps by forcing my way into Cole's conversation with the *Michigan* command I could find out more about what was afoot.

"No, that's all right, Rory," Alden said.

"No, you should meet him," I replied. "His name's Cole, and he's a regular rapscallion."

The most direct path to Cole and the Union leaders was across the dance floor. So, against Alden's protestations, the two of us waded into the swirl of swaying bodies, battling our way like fish against the current until we reached the far side of the ballroom. With a bemused look, Cole watched us approach while carrying on his conversation with the officers from the *USS Michigan*.

"And here she is now," he declared as I approached them with Alden in tow. My guess was that my hometown friend rarely, if ever, interacted with those in the high command. Once more, Alden tried to hang back, but I took him by the arm, bringing him with me.

"Gentlemen, may I present Miss Rory Chase," Cole said. "A cousin, once removed, on my mother's side."

Everett and the two others in blue dress uniforms nodded in my direction. Then they turned their attention to poor Alden, who was growing more flummoxed by the minute.

"Sirs," Alden said, snapping off a crisp salute.

"And who are you with, soldier?" Everett asked. "There's been so many comings and goings in recent months that I've lost track."

"With the garrison in town—" Alden began.

"I thought they were all gone by this point," said Everett as his subordinates snickered. "Furloughed or sent south to help Grant finish the job against Lee."

"Almost," Alden replied good-naturedly. "There are about a half-dozen of us left."

"Well, is it all right if they're invited, too?" Everett said to Cole. "I don't want to overburden any of your preparations. You've been so kind so far."

"What's the occasion?" I chimed in, and Cole gave me a hard look.

"The celebratory dinner Mr. Cole is throwing the boys from the *Michigan* the day after tomorrow," Everett said.

"It's been tailored for your men aboard the *Michigan*," Cole said.

Everett nodded before adding, "I must admit that I completely forgot that there were still a few boys left with the garrison down by the docks. Certainly, we can bring them under the night's festive umbrella as well."

Cole shrugged in agreement, but he wasn't happy I'd brought Alden over. "I'm sure it can be arranged," he muttered.

"Will Miss Chase be there?" Alden asked, smiling at me.

"Certainly, she will," Cole told them. "As well as a few other lovelies. Wine, women, and song, as they say."

"It sounds like a crackerjack evening," Everett said. "Charles, I cannot thank you enough for doing this for our boys in uniform. I'll grant as many furloughs for the evening as possible."

"You won't be disappointed," Cole replied.

"And on that note, lady and gentlemen," Everett said, giving a slight bow. "I'm afraid my officers and I need to call it an evening. Much to be done before our gathering, Charles."

"I understand, sir."

As the men from the *Michigan* took their leave, I had a feeling that I should slip away, too. Before Cole had time to quiz me and poor Alden.

"Why, I'd love to dance," I said, turning to Alden.

"You never did before," he replied.

Before he could say another word, though, I had him by the hand, pulling him onto the dance floor. Out there, among the swell of people, I did my best to follow Alden's lead. Yet I would never be much of a dancer.

"Perhaps we should have something to drink," Alden said after I'd stepped on his toes one too many times. "Give us both a chance to catch our breath."

Soon we were both nursing crystal cups of reddish punch at the far end of the ballroom.

"Thanks for getting me invited to the party," said Alden, downing his punch. "The *Michigan* crew usually doesn't want anything to do with us from the garrison. They think we're a half-step above cannon fodder."

He set his cup down and looked at me. "I cannot believe you're here. In godforsaken Sandusky. We have so much to catch up on, Rory Chase."

Thankfully, horns at the far end of the room broke into the opening notes to "The Battle Hymn of the Republic," and everyone dutifully paused in what they were doing to sing along. As what had become the anthem of Union unity drew to a close, Alden located another glass of punch, this one with a broader hint of bourbon, and he raised it high with the others.

The rebels would strike in two nights' time. With Cole wining and dining as many boys in blue as he could, I was now sure of that. But how to stop them?

31

The final meeting in Detroit was held across the river, in Windsor, at the home of Colonel Eliot Steele. Captain Beall and Mr. Burley took a ferry across the Detroit River, where they were joined by John Maxwell and Jacob Thompson. A former US secretary of the interior,

Thompson had been sent to British Canada by those in Richmond months before most of the rebel spies had crossed the border. Burley had never met him, but he knew that Thompson and the captain got along famously.

"The captain of the *Philo Parsons* has agreed to the additional stops?" Thompson asked after they had settled around the table in Steele's parlor.

"Yes, Mr. Burley reached a final agreement with him this afternoon," the captain replied. "Your funds have once again done the trick."

"That's what they're there for," Thompson said. "Apply the grease when needed."

Thompson's base of operations was in Toronto, and he sometimes shifted to Halifax to usher in people and money for the Confederate cause. So much was riding on this operation that he'd ridden the train from Toronto to meet with Beall, taking a final temperature of the situation before giving the go-ahead. Thompson sported a salt-and-pepper beard that reached his collar line. The way his eyes could lock on a person would make anyone uneasy.

"Let's go through it one last time," he said, and Captain Beall dutifully did so.

"As I said, Mr. Burley here has gotten the necessary stops scheduled."

Thompson nodded in Burley's direction, and Burley saw that this would be the only recognition he'd receive for a job well done.

"The *Philo Parsons* will begin its regular run from Detroit to Sandusky in the morning," the captain continued. "Mr. Burley will be aboard and assure that the vessel stops at Sandwich, on the Canadian side of the border. That's where myself and two more of our men will join him. A few miles farther down the river, before reaching Lake Erie proper, the *Philo Parsons* will make a final unscheduled stop at Malden, where the bulk of our force, sixteen raiders in total, will come on board with the necessary ordnance."

Thompson asked, "And what does that include?"

The captain turned to Maxwell, for this had been his assignment.

"A dozen Navy Colts, three dozen hatchets, and four grappling hooks," Maxwell said quietly. The poor man was as skittish as a black cat caught out in the rain. Yet much to Burley's disappointment the poor sod held himself together in such high company. As Maxwell finished, Burley realized that the two of them had always been placed in opposition to each other. The two outsiders: Scot versus Scot. That's how Thompson and the rebel command had arranged things.

"I wish it was more firepower," Thompson said, and for a moment Maxwell's face clouded over. Yet when John Yates Beall interceded, reassuring Thompson, Burley recognized that the rebel captain was eager to move ahead with his mission. He wanted no more delays or deliberations.

"It will be enough," he finished saying to Thompson.

Thompson leaned back in his chair, considering this. "All right then," he finally said. "If you're that sure."

"And what of Cole?" Beall asked.

"I received another telegram from him this morning," Thompson said. "He says everything will be ready in Sandusky. As we agreed, he'll signal you by a lone red flare. That's the nod to go ahead and seize the warship."

"We'll be ready as well," Beall said confidently.

"As will our brothers imprisoned on Johnson's Island," Thompson added. "Cole says he has somehow gotten word to them about the operation. They'll arm themselves as best they can, with clubs and the like. At the signal, the single red flare sent aloft, they will create whatever ruckus they can."

"Then we need to move ahead as planned," Beall told him.

Thompson nodded and then glanced around the table, focusing briefly on each of them. "Gentlemen, I don't need to tell you that much is riding upon this endeavor," he said. "It may be our last chance to stem the North's fast-rising tide."

32

In the early morning hours, I headed downstairs to the front desk. The towering timepiece in the hotel lobby read just past five o'clock, and only a sleepy clerk manned his post.

"I'd like to send another telegram," I told him.

"The office doesn't open until seven, ma'am."

"But if I gave you the particulars, you could send one for me as soon as it opens?"

He gazed back at me with dull eyes, and only after determining that I wasn't some kind of apparition about to dissolve into the night did he slide a pad of paper and a pencil across the desk.

"Kindly fill this out," he said.

"And you'll see that it's sent?"

"Yes, ma'am," he sighed. "At the end of my shift."

"And your name," I said, taking up the pencil.

"Richards, ma'am. I'll be working again tonight, and you can check with me then, if you'd like."

I nodded and wrote down the particulars to Wreet's shop in Niagara Falls.

"You've been stuck manning the store, while the rest of the town carried on into the evening?" I asked.

"Afraid so, ma'am."

As he waited, I tried to distill what I could to a few words. Plans were racing ahead. The way Cole carried on, like a man with the world by the tail, said as much. On the carriage ride home from the ball he had babbled about letting loose the hounds of hell. How he was the master who would set everything in motion.

As the night clerk waited, the lobby grew so quiet we could hear the ticking of the grandfather clock across the lobby.

"I'm not sure what to say," I told him. "I'm trying to use as few words as I can."

The clerk nodded at this. "They do add up, ma'am," he said.

I nodded and began the message to Wreet again.

FEASTING TO BEGIN SOON STOP MUCH TO DO STOP MUCH TO REJOICE STOP

I handed the paper back to Richards, who read it over. "A bit of a puzzle," he said. "Even for a gram."

"They'll understand," I replied, praying that those back in the Falls could somehow make sense of it all. That, hopefully, they knew as much or more than I did about how the rebel operation was to be executed.

"All right then," Richards replied.

"Could you send it first thing?" I asked, sliding a few more of the bills from Secretary Seward across the desktop. "And, please, let's keep this between us?"

Richards nodded. "Of course, ma'am. Not that Mr. Cole is likely to notice. He receives plenty of grams every day. From Buffalo, Cleveland, Detroit, even from across the border."

He pointed to a cubby hole, one of the largest in the wall of keys and messages and mail rising up behind him.

"I can take those to him," I offered.

"I appreciate it, ma'am," the clerk said. "But it's best that I hang onto them. Hotel policy and all. If anything, I love to see the look on Mr. Cole's face when he reads through them. Sometimes he gets so excited. He may try to hide it, but you can see it in his eyes."

"Thank you."

"My pleasure, ma'am," he smiled and glanced at the grandfather clock that stood directly across the lobby. "Little Benny, that's what we call that beautiful piece of machinery over there. Well, Little Benny says I only have a few more hours. You've helped me make it through another night shift."

After nodding for the clerk to send the gram, I paused, knowing this wasn't enough.

"Do you have a likeness shop nearby?" I wondered.

"Of course," Richards replied. "It does the latest in such work, tintypes to the fancy *cartes de visites*."

Thankfully, the establishment was around the corner and had no other customers when it opened later that morning.

"Three separate portraits?" the owner asked. "*Cartes de visites*?"

"Yes, sir."

"It would be far cheaper to do copies of the same pose."

"I realize that," I told Mr. Higgins, who had made a point of introducing himself as soon as I opened his door. "But I'd like them to be different. Regardless of the cost."

"Oh, we can do that," Mr. Higgins said. "Yes, ma'am, we can do whatever you'd like."

"And we can change the background? Just slightly for each one."

"Indeed, we can."

An hour later, when I returned to the West House, Richards was gone. As I approached the front desk, I didn't notice Cole off to one side, looking through his stack of telegrams.

"Miss Chase," he said, and I had no choice but to stop and chat.

"Mr. Cole."

"I hear you've been all about this morning," said Cole as he stacked his telegrams into a single pile and tapped them lightly on the desktop. "Chatting with the good lads here at the West House and then off to have your portrait done. Come, let's see how they turned out."

Reluctantly, I held the three *cartes de visites* out to him.

"How adorable," Cole said, leafing through them. "And you're sending them to your aunt, too?"

"Yes, in the Falls," I said.

"The same one you sent the gram?" said the clerk, who was too interested in making small talk for my taste.

"A gram?" Cole asked. "You have been busy, my dear. Can I see it, my good man?"

"Certainly, sir," the clerk said, giving me an apologetic look. Obviously, Cole spent so much money here that no one could tell him no, regardless of hotel policy.

The clerk handed the form I had written out for Wreet's telegram. Cole read it and reread it, and then turned to me with a quizzical look on his face. "Kind of a mishmash, isn't it?" he said. "Still, good to see that you're more excited with our event than I realized, Miss Rory. So precious."

He looked through the three *cartes de visites* again before returning them to me.

"And these are going to your Mrs. Thayer, too?"

"Yes, with extra copies for family."

"How good of you," Cole said.

"I can have them on the next train," the clerk offered.

"Splendid idea," Cole decided. "Speediest way possible. And please put it on my tab, my good man."

33

Wreet and Mr. Douglas sat at the small table in his room at the Cataract House, trying to decipher Rory's latest telegram.

"Feasting?" Mr. Douglas shook his head. "Much to rejoice?"

"She's trying to tell us something, but I don't have a clue what it may be," Wreet said. "Maybe she's using phrasing from her beloved *Ivanhoe*. Or perhaps someone was looking over her shoulder."

Mr. Douglas shook his head. "And so few words."

"I know."

"We should have prepared her better. Given her code words, ways to hide things in a gram."

"John, we didn't have time. We've gone over this."

Mr. Douglas stood and paced back and forth in his small room below the Cataract House's dining room. Above them they heard footsteps and the occasional voice, the growing swell of noise and activity marking the start of another day at the hotel.

"I need to go to her," Mr. Douglas said. "Something is unfolding fast."

"That's ridiculous," snapped Wreet, holding up the telegram. "She'll send along more information, and we can act accordingly then."

"How can she?" the head waiter said. "She has no idea what she's doing, what she's up against."

"She's figuring it out," Wreet told him. "I bet we'll receive another gram in a few hours."

"We're running out of time."

"John, how do we know that?"

Mr. Douglas paused midstep and turned to face his old friend. "Something's tugging at me, tugging at me good, Wreet. It's like when I'm out on the river sometimes. When you shove off from the dock, the plan may be to head at things from one angle, but then the current and the weather edge you away and you need to correct course. Do it in a hurry because events are speeding up."

"I don't see how you can be so certain," Wreet said. "As you said, all we have here is a few words."

"I don't know what to do," said Mr. Douglas, his voice becoming more resigned. "How best to help her."

Moments later, someone knocked on Mr. Douglas's door.

"Yes," he said, collecting himself, and Sissy poked her head inside.

"The noon sitting is nearly ready, sir," she said.

Mr. Douglas nodded, momentarily lost in thought. Then he said, "Tell Mr. Chapman that I'm under the weather, Sissy. Charles Templeton can direct the next shift."

"John, you don't need to do this," Wreet said. "Let's wait for more information from Rory."

"All right," Mr. Douglas decided. "We'll wait."

An hour later, dressed in pressed trousers, white shirt, dark cravat, vest, and suit coat, Mr. Douglas came up the stairs to the majestic foyer at the Cataract House. In front of him, he saw his men already prepping to deliver another meal in the high fashion that had been maintained for decades at this famous hotel. The place he took so much pride in. Mr. Douglas was about to step into the dining room when he heard a commotion behind him. Turning around, he saw Wreet coming through the main doors, out of breath.

"What's the bother, old bird?" Mr. Douglas asked.

"These just arrived from the train station," she said. "By special messenger."

Mr. Douglas took the three *cartes de visites*, not much larger than playing cards, and fanned them across a small table outside the dining room.

"They're all of Miss Chase," he said.

"In the same frock," added Wreet. "But look at the lower right-hand corner. See how it changes. Ever so slightly. She's trying to tell us something."

"The evening upon?" he said, reading one of the *cartes de visites*. He shook his head and raised another closer to the light.

"And this one says, 'Upon the thane's castle,'" he added.

"When I saw the word 'thane,'" Wreet said, "I snatched her copy of *Ivanhoe*."

"'*Ivanhoe*?'"

"As I told you, Rory loves this book," Wreet said, flipping through the pages with her thumb. "See how dog-eared it is."

"'Dark sits' says this one," Mr. Douglas said. "Here, let's get them in the proper order," he continued, shifting around the *cartes de visites*. "How about this—Dark sits the evening upon the thane's castle."

"That sounds like our *Ivanhoe*," Wreet said.

"But what does it mean?"

"It has to be somewhere in here," Wreet answered. "I'll bet it's one of the folded-down pages. A passage that she must know by heart."

Mr. Douglas looked over Wreet's shoulder as she flipped through the pages. "Oh, this book is too long," he said.

"We'll find it," she said, and before too long she did. Near the end of chapter 31 was a poem that extended for a good page and a half.

"Let me see," Mr. Douglas said. She handed the worn volume to him, and the leader of the Cataract House wait staff began to read aloud:

> *Dark sits the evening upon the thane's castle*
> *The black clouds gather round;*
> *Soon shall they be red as the blood of the valiant!*
> *The destroyer of forest shall shake his red crest against them.*

Then he paused, and Wreet shook her head. "What in God's name is she trying to tell us?" the old woman said.

"And what's this?" Mr. Douglas asked. "There's a bit more on the last one. Here, come with me."

Downstairs, in Mr. Douglas's room, he fished a magnifying glass out of his desk drawer.

"It's a mess of numbers," he said, leaning in closer.

Then he held the glass out to Wreet, who stole a look. "John, I can barely make out anything at all."

Mr. Douglas took the tool from her and looked again. "It reads, 19–09–64."

"Today's date?"

"No, Wreet, that's tomorrow's date. Whatever Rory has stumbled upon is occurring tomorrow. The black clouds are gathering, and she needs our help."

Mr. Douglas turned to go back upstairs. "I'll find Sissy and tell her to locate Mr. Chapman. It's like I said before—I'm under the weather. And Wreet—"

"Yes, John."

"Find Cesar and Aran. Have them meet me in my room. Tell them to hurry."

"Cesar and Aran?"

"They're not feeling well, either," Mr. Douglas said.

"But I saw Cesar as I was coming back in," Wreet questioned. "He looked good and rosy, ready for another day."

Mr. Douglas shook his head. "He's sick, I tell ya. He just doesn't know it yet."

34

I had fallen asleep, taking a short nap, when I awoke to Cole again hammering on my door.

"Arise, arise, my lovely lady," he sang out. "Open up, I know you're in there."

I cracked the door.

"My goodness, time's fleeing the day," Cole exclaimed. "Please let's find that radiant face of yours and be ready to shine it for the rest of the world to see."

"What's this about?" I grumbled.

"We've been invited aboard the USS Michigan," Cole replied. "Fruits of last night's reconnaissance and glad-handing. A prelude for my reception for the boys in blue. So, let's dress with a touch of eloquence and an eye for comfort. It appears the winds are up again on Lake Erie."

"The Michigan?"

"Aye, me matey. Now, c'mon, please get a move on. We need to be down at the dock within an hour."

A rising breeze speckled the water between the docks and the short stretch out to where the USS Michigan lay at anchor. With one hand on my hat, I reached out to grasp the sailor's hand as he guided me into the longboat. As soon as Cole and I were settled, side by side in the stern, we pushed off with a pair of sailors pulling hard on the oars, swinging us about and into open water. Once again, the wind tugged at my hat, and I decided to hold it in my lap, atop my sketchpad, and allow the wind to take the wisps of hair away from my face.

While my hair remained far shorter than the fashion, much of it had grown since my attempt to join the 138th Regiment. Dressed in my black traveling dress, with the small ruffles at the neck and cuffs, I tried to play the part of a woman of fine upbringing. The side glances, the way the sailors' eyes lingered on me as they took another long pull in unison on the oars, told me the illusion was working well enough.

The first swell of the water caused my stomach to jump, and the officer who had been chatting with Cole sensed my distress.

"Don't worry, miss," he said. "It won't be long. Just thank your lucky stars we're not out on the big lake today. It's really blowing out there."

Past the breakwater, which marked the entrance to the Sandusky harbor, whitecaps billowed like clouds torn from the sky above. As we ventured farther from the shore, a sliver of beach appeared off to our right. The town sat on the slight rise of the headlands, gazing down upon it all.

Soon we came alongside the side-wheel steamer, the oars rising as one to be stowed away. The building chop pushed us alongside the iron hull, and a rope ladder tumbled down from above.

"No ladylike way to do this, I'm afraid," the young officer said as he nodded at the hands reaching down for me. "Here we go."

He took me by the elbow, leading me to the rope ladder. I reached for the hands above while taking a step upward on the swaying rope lattice. Behind me, the officer reluctantly grasped me first by the waist and then pushed upward at the buttocks, and an awkward instant later I was above the rocking longboat, being borne aloft until I came down upon the deck.

"Welcome aboard, ma'am," said Captain Everett. "Did you enjoy yourself at the ball?"

"Yes, sir."

Moments later, Cole joined us on deck.

"Captain Everett," Cole said, extending his right hand, but the naval officer snapped off a brisk salute before they shook.

"How is our chief booster this morning?" Everett asked. "Our honorary seadog?"

"Fit as a fiddle, believe it or not," Cole replied, peering up at the vessel's three masts and taking in the *Michigan's* impressive armament— the Parrot guns and rifles, the twenty-four-pound smoothbores, and a gleaming pair of howitzers. "Somehow I survived one too many champagne cocktails last night."

Everett followed Cole's eyes as he surveyed the battleship. "It can pack a wallop, Mr. Cole. It's a shame that it didn't have a true role in this war. I'm sure it would have represented itself well in any such skirmishes."

"No doubt," Cole agreed.

"It's also unfortunate that we cannot have our gathering aboard the ship itself," Everett added. "But once again I'm reminded that orders are orders. No soirees on government property."

"The West House will be a fine host for our purposes," Cole replied. "I've reserved the grand ballroom, with plenty of food and more French champagne."

"How did you accomplish that, kind sir?"

Cole shrugged. "Pull a string here and another there. It promises to be a glorious evening. It will put that two-bit costume party at the Bellevue to shame."

"Now, now, that was a grand time," Everett said. "The lads enjoyed it. While the *Michigan* herself hasn't seen any action, many of those currently serving aboard her certainly have. Most of my crew has been rotated from the more intense theaters of the war to finish their service here, upon the more placid Lake Erie."

"And that's why I'm determined to make sure that they have a good time," Cole said, "even if it is only the backwoods of Sandusky."

"Mr. Cole, it could be Broadway or the Champs Élysées the way you dress it up to the nines."

"Captain Everett, you're embarrassing me."

"We will be happy to celebrate with you, my friend. Together we will raise a glass to the dear Union and our beloved President Lincoln."

"And your entire crew will be able to make it?"

"Almost all of them," Everett answered. "I'll leave a few unfortunates here. Such sticks and carrots make for better discipline. Now, allow me to give you a proper tour before the lake grows too rough."

By the afternoon, the weather had taken a turn for the worst, with the waves building even in the small inlet separating the *USS Michigan* at anchor from the Sandusky waterfront. Rain was beginning to fall by the time we returned in the longboat back to shore.

"I must be a sight," Cole muttered as we climbed into his carriage for the West House. "At least that's settled. The grand evening is on, even if it did destroy this fine suit I'm wearing."

I brushed back my wet hair. "Why go to so much trouble?" I asked. "Champagne and all?"

"It has to be a grand evening, my dear. I need to draw as many as I can off the ship."

"So Beall can act?"

In an instant, the excitement faded from his face.

"No more such talk," he ordered. "You understand?"

At my side, I clenched a fist. Ready if he went to strike me. Instead, Cole pursed his lips, intent on collecting himself.

"Play your part, Miss Rory," he said in a low voice. "If not, I swear you'll rue the day."

35

Thanks to Thompson's funds, the *Philo Parsons* made an unscheduled stop at the hamlet of Sandwich on the opposite side of the river in British Canada. There Captain Beall and several others came up the gangplank while Mr. Burley watched from the deck above. After that brief docking, the paddle-wheel steamer made for Grosse Ile and the smaller Crystal and Bois Blanc islands, heading for its next stop—the town of Malden on the Canadian side. At this point, sixteen more rebels came aboard with a large trunk in tow. Nothing was said among them. Everyone knew the plan. From here, the *Philo Parsons* soon left the narrow confines of the Detroit River and headed into the larger waters of Lake Erie, bound for the necklace of islands on the far side, just offshore from Sandusky.

"We appear to be in good stead," Captain Beall told Burley.

The two of them were dressed in three-piece suits and trench coats, taking in the air along the starboard rail. The day had begun with plenty of cloud, but now the sun was breaking through as the waters faded from dark green to a deeper blue.

On schedule, the steamer reached Middle Bass Island, twelve miles north of Sandusky, at four that afternoon. As was his custom, the ship's captain, Sylvester Atwood, disembarked here, where he had a small home a short walk from the public pier. Atwood often spent the night at home and rejoined the *Philo Parsons* the next morning for the return trip back across Lake Erie to Detroit. Captain Beall was happy to see Atwood go. "One fewer man to deal with," he told Burley.

After the brief stop for Atwood and three other passengers to disembark, the *Philo Parsons* edged away from the small harbor and began the last leg of the journey, heading toward Sandusky itself. As the steamer reached open water once again, Captain Beall nodded to the men standing next to the large trunk, which still sat in the rear cargo area. Soon they were joined by others from the foredeck. The trunk was opened, and its contents—the Colt pistols and the half-dozen rifles—distributed as planned. The taking of the *Philo Parsons* had begun.

"Mr. Burley, to the wheelhouse," Captain Beall said. "I will be along shortly."

As planned, three others fell in behind Burley and moved along the starboard side, concealing firearms under their long coats. At the wheelhouse, Burley put a shoulder to the door and pushed it open.

"Hey," a sailor at the navigation table said. "No passengers in here."

Burley leveled his pistol at him, and the man stepped back, raising his arms.

"No more talk, and be smart about yourselves," he ordered and nodded for the sailor at the wheel to keep steering straight ahead.

Soon Captain Beall entered the wheelhouse. "This vessel has been seized in the name of the Confederate States of America," he told them in a measured voice.

"You're Rebs?" one of the sailors exclaimed.

Beall smiled. "In the flesh and blood."

36

The next morning, Cole arrived with another gown for me, which he wanted me to wear that evening for the gathering in honor of the Union sailors. It sported a lower neckline than the previous one, as well as shorter sleeves. It came with white gloves. It was yellow with faint tannish flower images, all billowing out from the waist down, thanks to a hoop skirt. God, how I despised those cage-like undergarments.

"As you remember, Miss Rory, our affair begins at eight sharp. One cannot be late for it. I just won't allow it."

His eyes lingered on me; then he leaned in and gave me a peck on the cheek.

"Apologies for my outburst yesterday," he whispered. "You and I need to find time to celebrate once this over. Revel in a job well done."

After he left, I took the sketchpad and headed downstairs. Anything to get as far away from him as I could and try to clear my head. A few blocks from the West House, the streets of Sandusky gave way to green fields and, beyond that, stands of second-growth trees. It was as if the town had simply run out of purpose and surrendered to the larger, more natural world that will overwhelm us all someday. At least that is what Mother would say.

In the shadow of a set of bluffs, which stood like dwarf sentinels before everything rolled downhill to the white-sand beaches that ran along Lake Erie, a group of schoolboys, little tykes, were playing baseball. I didn't know much about the game myself, but I had seen the boys back in Auburn play it.

Opening my sketchbook, I sat on the grass and watched the players take turns with the so-called bat, which appeared to be little more than a varnished branch with a handle that had been sanded down for a better grip. Several good paces out in front of the batter stood another player with a ball of stuffed leather in his hand. He lobbed the sphere toward the batter underhanded, as if he was trying his best to put it out there on an easy trajectory, so the batter could strike it. That happened time and again, with the ball sent flying at various angles and speeds into the field and the boys scampering after it like puppies fetching a stick.

At one point, the ball was sent high into the air near to where I was sitting, and I leaned out, letting the sketchpad roll off my lap. Somehow, I snatched it with one hand, which brought whistles and cheers from the boys. After that unexpected performance, they begged for me to take a turn at bat. And how could I refuse their smiling faces and attentive charms?

That's how I ended up at the plate, as they said, swinging the bat stick myself. I soon learned it wasn't as easy as it looked. I swung mightily at the first offering, only to miss badly.

"Keep your eye on the ball," one of the little ones shouted, and I had no idea what he was talking about.

He held up a finger and then moved it past his face, with his eyes tracking it like a hawk flying high above. The next time around, I was so intent on watching the ball as it came toward me that I nearly forgot to swing. At the last second, though, I flashed on why I was standing there and pulled that bat as fast as I could through the air, feeling the exertion in my arms and back. Surprising myself, I connected and sent the ball high in the air toward the players standing the farthest away.

"Run, run," one of the boys yelled out, but I had no idea what to do.

"To first base," another said, pointing off to the right, where another piece of wood had been laid on the ground.

Raising my skirts, laughing at the silliness of it all, I headed in that direction and promptly stopped at the specific station in the game. The boys out in the field were still retrieving the ball, throwing it from one to the other until it soared closer to the plate, toward the area that reminded me of a stage set inside a theater.

"You should have made it farther," the boy standing closest to me said, and I could only smile. I didn't have the heart to tell him that I had no idea how to play this game. That I was making up much of everything as I went along.

"Someday we'll be as good as the ones on Johnson's," said another boy.

"Listen to you, Riggs," said one of them. "Those are grown men, hardened soldiers, locked up in that place."

"I'm only saying that we're getting better," Riggs replied. He was a strapping boy with an enthusiastic look about him. He nodded for the ball, and one of the boys tossed it to him.

I asked, "They play this game at Johnson's Island?"

"Yes, ma'am," Riggs replied. "The prisoners and the guards sometimes take up sides."

"Says you," said one of the boys.

"And I would know, wouldn't I?" Riggs said, refusing to back down. "Seeing my pa is a guard there."

That quelled the debate for now.

"So, they get along that well," I continued. "That they can play ball together?"

"It ain't all warm and cozy like that, ma'am," Riggs replied, flipping the ball from one hand to the other. "Papa says it's another way to keep such dangerous men at bay. Keep them soft in the head. The

Rebs locked up on Johnson are as bad as they come. If given half a chance, they'd slit your throat and not think twice about it. That's what my papa says."

37

When I entered the lobby, the desk clerk said, "Miss Chase, you have a message."

Yet when I held out my hand for it, he continued, "And the darkie refuses to fork it over."

He nodded to the corner of the lobby, near the front entrance. There, seemingly ready to bolt if need be, stood Mr. Douglas. I couldn't believe he was here. Actually standing in front of me. For the first time in days, I felt the weight of the world briefly lift from my shoulders.

As I approached him, he raised a small white envelope. "Let's talk outside, Miss Rory," he said. "These men need to learn to be more polite about such matters."

Back on the street, I again held out my hand for the envelope, but Mr. Douglas only smiled. "There's nothing in it," he said. "Only a ruse. A way for me to find my way to you."

As we walked toward the docks, Mr. Douglas asked, "You believe the attack will be tonight?"

I nodded. "It makes the most sense. Cole is throwing a party here, at the West House, for the Union men. Nearly every sailor from the *Michigan* will be there."

"But that's only a stone's throw from the waterfront," Mr. Douglas replied. "They could easily hustle back."

"That may be. But Cole's all full of himself. Acting like he's got the world on a string."

"What did he tell you again? His exact words, please."

As we neared the docks, I saw that they were alive with activity. A ferryboat, this one from Cleveland, was preparing to dock, while several freighters unloaded their cargo. Workers lined the public pier, and off in the distance, riding at anchor, stood the USS *Michigan*, the massive sentry taking it all in.

"Mr. Douglas, you have to remember that Cole was in his cups when he was telling me much of this. The way he can carry on. God, he makes my skin crawl."

"Miss Rory, please tell me what he said. Word for word if you can."

I nodded, determined to do my best. "The other night, after the ball, he was going on about how nothing begins without his say-so. How he's the spark that lights the candle."

"The spark?" Mr. Douglas repeated.

"Yes, those were his exact words."

Mr. Douglas pointed to the left, away from the public pier, where a small steamer I'd never seen before was berthed. When we reached it, he rapped several times atop the vessel's squat cabin. Two long and one short—some kind of code—and shortly thereafter the hatch opened and Cesar, from the Cataract House, poked his head out.

"What are you doing here?" I asked, catching a glimpse of Aran smiling behind him.

"C'mon," Mr. Douglas said. "Let's get out of sight before anyone is the wiser."

With that, we headed below, and Cesar closed the hatch behind us.

"I came by train," Mr. Douglas explained as we huddled around the vessel's lone table. "I wanted to make sure I got here in time. Aran and Cesar came by sea and just arrived, right?"

Cesar nodded. "Not too rough a passage."

"Speak for yourself," Aran told him. "I'd rather have come by train."

I looked from one familiar face to another and was truly heartened to have them here, so ready to help. Still, unless more were en route, I didn't see how we would stop the rebels.

"From what I can guess, Beall will have at least a dozen men with him," I said. "And Bennet Burley's with him now, too."

"Steep odds," Mr. Douglas agreed. "Especially if Cole's party goes off without a hitch."

"So, what can we do?" I asked.

Mr. Douglas tried to put a brave face on things, but Cesar and Aran were clearly frustrated. We all knew this pint-sized vessel would be no match for what Beall and his men were bringing to bear upon the Sandusky harbor.

"Maybe the trick is to derail things," Mr. Douglas began. "Somehow stop their operation before it gets started."

"And how to do that?" said Cesar, looking at his boss with questioning eyes.

Mr. Douglas smiled. "With befuddlement and confusion."

"Well, that pretty much sums up our state of things, doesn't it, sir?"

Mr. Douglas refused to fall into an argument with his younger associate. Instead, he turned to me, saying, "Cole called himself the spark? The one who gets this operation rolling?"

I nodded. "But the man thinks very highly of himself. Especially after he's tipped back a few."

"There must be some truth to it," Aran added. "He thinks of himself as some kind of spark, setting things off. That could be a signal of some kind."

Mr. Douglas began to tap a few fingers atop the small tabletop. "And if that's the case, we could confuse them. Perhaps there's no signal. Then the Rebs won't know what to think. Or perhaps there's too much of a signal?"

"Too much of a signal?" I asked.

"Either might do," Aran agreed.

Unsure of what they were talking about, I asked, "But what should I do?"

"Miss Rory, you need to be at this party Cole's throwing," Mr. Douglas said.

"Oh, I'd rather be anywhere else," I complained. "That man—"

"And you've been invited?"

"Yes, I'm supposed to accompany him."

Mr. Douglas nodded. "Then that's where you need to be. We cannot do anything now to alarm them. Not this late in the proceedings."

"But what are you going to do?"

"Me and my men from the Cataract House are going to play a hunch I have," he said. "Let's pray that it works."

38

That evening, Cole ordered me to join him at the head table with Captain Everett and two of his subordinates. The other dozen tables were filled with men in Union blue, and I saw that Alden Gilbert was among them.

In between the front dais and the other tables, room had been cleared for a fair-sized dance floor, with a band of trumpet, clarinet, and upright bass off to one side. Music filled the room, and there were a dozen women that I surmised were whores from the waterfront. They were available to dance with any sailor who summoned the nerve, and as the evening gathered momentum and the champagne flowed, more of them did just that.

Cole had begun things with a champagne toast to the men in blue. "My respect, dare I say my love, for your courage knows no bounds," he said with a raised glass. From there the glasses were refilled time and again as the merriment continued into the night.

In time, I made my way down from the front, through the crowded dance floor, to Alden's table.

"What a time," Alden said when I sat down beside him. "Your friend knows how to throw a party."

"Yes, he does," I replied.

"Here, you need a drink," Alden said, signaling to the waiter to bring one. "Word has it that your Mr. Cole has convinced Captain Everett to push back curfew for the night, too. For all of us."

I accepted the champagne glass and took a sip. There was something about this gathering, the way it had taken off, already roaring down the tracks like a runaway train, that I found rather bewildering.

"It looks like everyone is enjoying themselves," I said to Alden.

"Oh, you don't know the half of it," he said, leaning in so he could make himself heard over the rising din of talk, laughter, and music. "Most of the boys have been on that warship for days at a stretch. And the rest? After what they've been through down south . . . Well, words don't do it justice."

He took another long draw of his drink, and the two of us watched the excitement going on in all corners.

"Oh, where are my manners?" Alden stammered. "Miss Rory, would you indulge me in a dance?"

I agreed, figuring we had to do a better job of it than our last effort, and the two of us made our way to the packed dance floor. This time, though, it was Alden who was badly out of step with the music. He lumbered about like a sleepy bear.

"Alden, we should sit down."

"No, no, I haven't felt this happy in God knows when," he exclaimed. "And I've never seen a woman as beautiful as you are tonight."

"That's the liquor talking now."

"No, it's true. I know you've been through a lot. The whispers back in Auburn say as much. But to see you here, looking so lovely—well, it can make a person believe that one day this horrible war will be over and we'll make it through. Somehow."

"Hush now," I told him. "Of course, we will."

When we returned to the table, Alden plopped down in his chair and rested his elbows on the table. Then his head nestled atop his hands.

"Are you all right, Alden?"

"Never felt better," he replied, but the words were becoming increasingly slurred.

"You're drunk."

"Nonsense, sweet Rory of Auburn. I've had what? Two or three glasses of champagne?"

He yawned and briefly closed his eyes.

Up at the front table, I saw Cole raise another toast with Everett and his officers. Throughout the ballroom, as the band played on, more and more of the sailors returned to their tables. While some briefly held hands with one of the women paid to dance with them, many more moved in a clumsy, disjointed fashion. Back at the front table, Cole had somehow disappeared, leaving Everett and others to enjoy another full bottle of champagne. Frantically, I looked about, but he was nowhere to be found.

Turning toward Alden, I kissed him on the cheek. Then I hurried toward the rear door to the ballroom, determined to find Cole.

39

Now under Captain Beall's command, the *Philo Parsons* slowly neared the entrance to the Sandusky harbor. It was dusk, and inside the breakwater the rebels saw the *USS Michigan* riding regally at anchor. All was quiet aboard the magnificent war machine, and Beall gazed upon the prize with a small spyglass. Burley saw several longboats pull away from the warship, ferrying more uniformed men ashore.

"Cole's party is drawing them like pilgrims to the chapel," Beall said with approval. Yes, everything was going according to plan until one of the rebels approached Beall and Burley.

"Begging your pardon, kind sirs."

"What is it, Kurbs?" Beall said.

"There's been talk up in the wheelhouse. Among the captives."

"Tell them to clam up," Burley said, "or we'll gag the lot of them."

"No, it's a good thing we caught them talking among themselves," Kurbs said. "They say that we're low on firewood. The boilers will die down to nothing if we don't do something about it."

"Can't it wait?" Captain Beall asked.

"Not the way they're talking, sir."

Beall and Burley headed to the wheelhouse, and the crew grew silent as they entered.

"Tell the truth," Beall said, nodding at the one who stood at the wheel, "or you're going over the side. What's the situation with the wood?"

The three sailors looked at each other, not sure how to answer.

"Out with it." Burley stepped closer to the one at the wheel, grasping him about the collar. "Methinks, it's time to feed the fishes."

"No, wait," said another sailor, the one at the navigation table. "It's true."

"What's true?" Burley demanded as he continued to push the first mate toward the door.

"Cochrane, I'm warning ya," the first mate shouted as Burley twisted this one's arm behind him. "You ain't got to tell them nothing. Not a word."

"Better talk, Mr. Cochrane," Captain Beall urged. "Or you know what's going to happen to your friend."

"We usually refuel in Sandusky," Cochrane stammered. "There or back at Middle Bass. It's the end of the line after all."

Captain Beall stepped closer and drew his pistol. "Do we have enough wood to last until morning? No lies now."

"I'm no engine man," Cochrane answered.

"But you're an experienced hand aboard the *Philo Parsons*. What would you advise us to do?"

Cochrane glanced at the pistol trained on him and closed his eyes.

"Answer me, Mr. Cochrane. Or we'll send the whole lot of you over the side."

Cochrane blinked as the rebel commander edged closer.

"We need more wood," the sailor said.

"Cochrane, you coward," the first mate said.

"It cannot be here, at Sandusky proper," Beall decided. "The authorities will be on us in no time."

He stared down Cochrane. "You said there's wood available on Middle Bass?"

Cochrane nodded. "Aye, sir."

"Then we need to double back," Beall said. "No chatter, you hear me? A quick stopover should do it."

If only it had been that easy for the Confederates. Minutes after the *Philo Parsons* docked at Middle Bass Island, another vessel, the *Island Queen*, came alongside. The rebels soon learned the second steamer was making its scheduled late-day run from the mainland to the islands off Sandusky. There didn't appear to be any reason for concern until Burley saw about thirty blue-uniformed soldiers on the deck of the *Island Queen*. The men were from the 130th Ohio Volunteer Infantry, returning to their families and homes on furlough.

"What do we do now?" Burley asked Captain Beall.

"Slip into the shadows before anyone is the wiser."

"Too late," Burley replied. "Look at them sizing us up. And here comes one of their officers. Too curious for his own damn good."

The rebel leader shook his head. "Then they leave us no choice."

Minutes later, Beall's men took the initiative, with a dozen shots breaking the early evening calm on Middle Bass Island. Even with the rebels' element of surprise, hand-to-hand fighting ensued, extending for a half-hour, during which the *Island Queen*'s engineer was shot in the face. In the end, no one died in the capture of the Union troops. Years later, it would be determined that the men of the 130th were the northernmost captives of the South during the Civil War.

As Beall's men took command of this second vessel, the disturbance brought several townspeople down to the dock, including the skipper Sylvester Atwood.

"What are you doing to my boat?" he shouted.

"Go away, old man," Beall warned.

Yet Atwood was already coming up the gangplank, and the rebels had no choice but to take him prisoner, too. In the wheelhouse of the *Philo Parsons*, Beall held a parley with Lieutenant Benjamin White, the top-ranking officer for the men of the 130th. Atwood was there too, thoroughly enjoying the predicament Beall and Burley found themselves in.

"Two steamers and a flock of prisoners of war." The skipper cackled. "Sounds like you boys have bit off more than you can chew."

"I'm warning you, old man," Burley muttered.

"Or what, you Johnny Reb with your Scottish tongue? Seems to me that you're up to your chin in all kinds of complications."

"Quiet," Beall ordered, and his command briefly checked everyone. "Here's what I propose," he said, focusing on Lieutenant White. "We'll parole everyone under your command, as well as the remaining passengers, here to Middle Bass Island. For that you need to agree that you'll do nothing, no alarm, for twenty-four hours."

Lieutenant White turned to Atwood, "The next scheduled ferry isn't until tomorrow?"

"Late morning from Cleveland," Atwood confirmed. "Mine makes the first daily stop, but that won't happen now. Not with these jackals in charge."

Lieutenant White nodded. "Then I have no choice but to accept your terms," he said.

"We can take on both vessels?" Beall asked.

Burley didn't see why not. "We have enough men and remaining crew to do so," he said.

"The two of you are making this up as you go along, ain't ya?" Atwood interrupted.

"Enough," Beall said. "Get these two back down to the dock. We're pushing off."

As Atwood and Lieutenant White watched them from the public wharf, the *Philo Parsons*, followed by the *Island Queen*, pulled away from Middle Bass Island. Out in the deeper water, Captain Beall ordered the *Island Queen* to come alongside the *Philo Parsons*. After the remaining crew was shifted to the larger steamer, Burley and Maxwell dropped to the *Island Queen*, axes in hand. In short order, they went below deck and bashed in several hull planks and released the bailing corks. The water, still warm from the long summer, surged through the newfound openings and within minutes the *Island Queen* began to sink, so fast in fact that several of the men had to pull Burley and Maxwell back aboard the *Philo Parsons*.

As the smaller steamer fell below the glassy surface of Lake Erie, the rebels again moved into position, putting down anchor just inside the Sandusky breakwater. There they waited for Charles Cole's signal that all was ready for them to storm the *USS Michigan*.

40

The offshore breeze began to slacken as night settled over Lake Erie. The long silhouette of the *USS Michigan* still stood guard over the Sandusky harbor. Yet as I gazed upon it, I saw that another vessel had drawn closer to the Union warship in the lengthening shadows.

Outside the hotel's back door, away from the short blocks leading down to the Sandusky waterfront, Cole had nearly reached a white staircase leading to the beach. It wasn't far from where I had played ball with the young ones. Stepping out of my heels and raising my long skirt, I ran in his direction. When I reached the top of the staircase, I descended as fast as I could, briefly imagining I was back at the Falls, hurrying down the Ferry Landing steps, in the shadow of the roaring cataract. I didn't stop moving until I reached the beach.

Despite my haste, I somehow lost sight of Cole. I stood there in the newfound darkness, looking in one direction and then the other until I saw a pinprick of light far down the beach. There it was, and then it was gone. That's when I realized Cole was trying to signal

Beall and his men, out there on the water. To alert them that the *Michigan* was ripe for the taking, with its sailors drunk on doctored champagne.

Running hard now, in the direction of the last flicker of light, I came upon Cole. He was huddled over, striking another long-stemmed match, about to ignite what appeared to be a fireworks-style flare, which was wedged far into the sand.

Without hesitation, I sprinted as fast I could until I collided with him. Both of us sprawled across the sand, trying to regain our bearings.

"You," Cole exclaimed as he scrambled to his feet. "I knew you were a viper in our den."

With that he kicked me hard once, twice, in the ribs and smacked me across the face with his fist. When I rolled over, dazed, face down in the sand, Cole hurried back to his signal flare. Thankfully, another gust of wind delayed him enough for me to regain my senses. On all fours, I slithered out of that damn hoop skirt and crawled in his direction. For a moment, all I could do was throw several handfuls of sand into the air, letting the wind take it toward Cole.

"You witch," he cried out, rubbing his eyes. "You Jezebel."

Before Cole could turn on me, I went at him, punching wildly at his face with all of my strength. I fought hard and dirty, as I had been taught when I was a soldier and wore Union blue. But it wasn't enough. With a loud grunt, Cole tossed me aside and scrambled to the flare, which was standing upright in the sand like a soldier at attention. Frantically he struck another match, and this time he successfully lit the short fuse. As I watched, it caught, and the flare soon came alive, hissing loudly for a moment before rocketing skyward into the pitch-black sky.

The signal had been sent aloft, and I peered at the deeper waters near the harbor wall. There I saw the other craft, the shadow vessel, begin to move closer to the *Michigan*. It was a ferry steamer. One that Captain Beall and Bennet Burley must have commandeered from somewhere on the far side of Lake Erie.

Behind me, Cole lay exhausted on his back on the beach. Still, he wasn't too tired to laugh. A low, mocking sound that so incensed me that I found a piece of driftwood and with both hands I struck Cole, time and again, until he finally fell quiet.

Back out on the water, Beall's steamer drew closer, and I wondered how many Union men had been left aboard the *Michigan*. Undoubtedly, it wasn't enough. The rebel plan was working to perfection, and all I could do was watch it unfold.

I walked back to Cole and stood over him. Even though he was now out cold, he wore an idiot's grin. I resisted the urge to smack him again for good measure. The damage had been done. There was nothing I could do to stop the rebels from advancing on the Union warship. I had failed at my attempt to spy along the northern border.

Flopping down on the sand, I simply sat there, my head in my hands, when another light appeared on the breakwater to the harbor itself. It had a whitish glow, like fireworks on the Fourth of July, and in short order it soared skyward, where it burst open. This was followed by another small explosion on the other side of the harbor, and then another was borne aloft in its wake. What insanity was this? It seemed that Cole's flare had torn open the lid to Pandora's box, and now all kinds of madness of light and thunder were raining down upon the world.

The display lasted for only a few minutes, but as I gazed upon the rebel waters, I saw that the commandeered steamer had slowed in its approach toward the *USS Michigan*. For a moment, its shadow hovered nearby. The additional flares sent aloft into the heavens must have confused those on board, because the rebel craft came to a complete standstill, drifting in the current, only a stone's throw away from the *USS Michigan*. There was no sign of life aboard the warship. Still, the new signals that had briefly lit the evening sky couldn't have been what Captain Beall and his crew were expecting. In the quiet lull that followed, I heard the faintest of conversations, angry voices, carrying across the water to me onshore. Yes, there was real division about what to do. I watched as the moment extended into an interminable period of hesitation. The steamer continued to drift just inside the breakwater, close to the Union warship. And then I couldn't believe my eyes. The rebel craft turned and began to bear away, heading for the open sea.

41

Another veil of cloud passed in front of the moon, briefly shading the black waters of the Sandusky harbor.

"The wind's shifting," Burley told Captain Beall. "Starting to build out of the northwest."

The two of them stood together along the starboard rail, gazing upon the harbor, which had grown eerily quiet in the hours they had been watching. For a time, nuggets of noise had been borne out to them by the offshore breeze. But now that the evening warmth had given way to a stronger, chillier wind from the lake, such clues had disappeared.

"The bells?" Burley asked.

Captain Beall stole a glance at his pocket watch. "Almost eleven."

"Ahh, where is he?" Burley replied.

"Patience, my friend. Let's not let the men hear your carrying on."

"They're as nervous as I am."

"We need to give Cole time to deliver," Beall said.

"And what if he doesn't?"

"To be honest, Mr. Burley, I haven't considered the notion."

That's when Maxwell and two others found their way to the two rebel leaders.

"Mr. Maxwell?" said Beall, and Burley knew what this was about.

"None of us have seen any hint of a signal."

"Nor I, Mr. Maxwell."

"So, what happens now, sir?"

"We shall remain in position."

"Until first light, when the *Michigan* can train its guns upon us?" replied Maxwell. "Until the whole town wises up to why the ferry from Detroit hasn't come into dock?"

Captain Beall smiled. "You've been doing a great deal of thinking, haven't you, Mr. Maxwell?"

"Aye, and the boys and I have been talking."

"Too much time on your hands," Burley said.

"Perhaps, Mr. Burley," Maxwell replied angrily. "But one would have to agree that things aren't going as planned."

"Excellent deduction," Captain Beall answered. "And after all that thinking, what do you believe we should do?"

"Set a curfew and stick to it," Maxwell said.

"And, pray tell, what's your deadline for it all, Maxwell?" Burley interrupted. How he wanted to take a swing at the coward!

"Till two bells," Maxwell replied. Those on either side of him nodded.

"And if nothing happens by then?" Burley asked.

"We pull back."

Burley couldn't help by laugh. "Retreat like cowardly schoolboys?"

"It beats being boarded or sunk come the morning, doesn't it, good sirs? That will still give us sufficient time to get away."

Even though it had only been a few minutes since he last looked, Captain Beall brought out his pocket watch and stole another glance.

"Mr. Maxwell, you have a good head on your shoulders," he said, gazing back upon the quiet dark shore, with the silhouette of the USS *Michigan* only a few hundred yards away. "We will take your suggestion under consideration."

Burley would never forget those words. *Under consideration.* Because as soon as the captain spoke them, a flash of light exploded off the starboard side. Yes, down along the beaches, a bright-red flare soared into the heavens. And there it was. The signal from Cole.

"Prepare to attack," Captain Beall ordered, and even Maxwell couldn't help but grin.

"Yes, sir," Maxwell replied. They began to glide through the darkness, making their way toward the *Michigan*.

Even in the shadows, Burley could make out several of the fourteen guns that the warship carried, and there was the thirty-pound Parrot gun sitting like a glorious beacon of possibility near the bow. My God, the mayhem they could rain down upon the Yankee lands with such a craft at their command!

Beall's men were closing in on the prize when the night skies above them suddenly erupted into more lightning and thunder. At first, Burley thought they were under attack and pulled the captain briefly below the gunwale. Then they both realized that no cannon fire or shrapnel was raining down. Not a single man had been hit. Instead, it was the most curious as well as the most terrifying thing to behold at that particular moment on that memorable night. No, they weren't under attack, but first over to the left of the harbor and then up from the city pier itself and from the highlands closer to the hotel soared flare upon flare. The whole lot of them skyrocketed in quick progression into the evening sky. If one didn't know the calendar, it could have been one of the Yankees' Fourth of July fireworks displays.

"What in hellfire?" Maxwell blurted out as they stared dumbfounded at the flares flashing above them.

Actually, there were only a few such disturbances. But the timing of it stopped the rebels in their tracks. Even though Captain Beall never voiced such an order, the *Philo Parsons* slowed, and someone shouted, "They're on to us."

"Now, now," the rebel captain replied, but the grand opportunity was already slipping away. His men were scurrying around like chickens in a thunderstorm, and soon Maxwell was back for another audience.

"Just a momentary disturbance," the captain told him. "Look at the *Michigan* over yonder. No activity at all. It is still ours if we move on it now."

Maxwell wasn't buying such reasoning. "No, good sir," he stammered. "I tell ya, they're on to us."

The coward's words soon spread through the rebels' ranks. The fireworks disturbance from out of the blue had them quaking in their boots, and fear overran the Confederates' ship. With Maxwell as the major instigator, many proclaimed they didn't have the stomach to attack, no matter how close they were to the *Michigan*. Some began to jabber about how there were shadows already moving about the warship, ready to train those big guns upon them. Of course, no such game was afoot. It was just the wind and the darkness playing with their minds. The mighty vessel remained as a quiet as a church after a funeral.

Burley soon realized there was no talking sense to the worthless collection of nilly-weeds. They had gone squirrelly in the head, and not even Beall's sweet words and reassurances could stem the tide this time.

Too soon, it was decided that they would turn tail and run. To assure that John Yates Beall wasn't blamed at some later date, that his resolve wasn't questioned in any way or fashion, Burley insisted that every man sign a hastily drawn together petition to that end. Every one of the rebels eagerly did so. That's how far gone they were.

With a pained expression, Captain Beall ordered the *Philo Parsons* to bear away from the Sandusky harbor and the *USS Michigan*. Within hours, the sun rose in blood-red hues, and by midmorning a driving rain was falling. Knowing the alarm had been sounded, the rebels disbanded near the entrance to the Detroit River. Several of them, including John Maxwell, were ordered ashore in the first of the rowboats.

"That man cost us any chance at success," said Beall as he and Burley watched them pull away.

"I could shoot him dead from here," Burley offered.

The rebel commander seemed to consider this for a moment and then smiled. "A coward like that isn't worth the bullet," he replied.

Further upstream, the others who had grown weak in the knees were ordered ashore. Perhaps in an attempt to be considered in a better light by the rebel command, several of them had ransacked the steamer, taking an ornate parlor chair and several landscape paintings with them. They were truly fools.

Captain Beall and Mr. Burley watched them go. Then, along with the ship's helmsman, engineer, and first mate, they continued toward Windsor, on the Canadian side. There they scuttled the *Philo Parsons* in shallow water and took the remaining rowboats to shore.

42

From the top of the steps, I looked back upon the harbor. Thankfully, the warship still lay at anchor. The shadow of the other craft, the attacking steamer, had disappeared from sight, heading toward open water.

I hurried across the lawn, holding my skirt up with both hands—happy to leave my hoop cage back at the beach. Inside the dining room, most of the men in uniform were sprawled across chairs or heads down, fast asleep, upon the tables. Cole's potion had drugged the lot of them. The local women had disappeared with the sudden flashes of light across the heavens, and on the small stage a lone musician played the upright bass, soft and slow. It sounded like raindrops falling against a pane of glass.

Captain Everett was one of the few barely mobile, and he stood gingerly in the back of the room, rocking from one leg to the other, as if he was trying to regain feeling in his limbs. He was speaking to Mr. Douglas.

As I drew closer, Everett asked me, "You summoned these good men?" His face was flush, and he seemed to be coming around from a bad dream.

"Yes, sir."

"Thank God you did, Miss Chase. If you hadn't done so? Well, I fear we would have lost the *Michigan*."

For a moment, none of us said a word. I told Everett that Cole could be found on the beach, but the other rebels had escaped across the lake.

"We'll go in pursuit," Everett said. "Once I can pull a crew together."

Cole was taken into custody on the beach, led away in handcuffs by several Union soldiers. Out in the harbor, activity was building aboard the *Michigan*. Still, it would be hours before they were ready to cast off. *The Union forces won't catch the rebels*, I thought. Captain Beall and Bennet Burley had escaped before, and undoubtedly, they had done so once again.

Mr. Douglas soon left, heading to the station to await the early morning train, while I returned to the West House. I was to meet him there in a few hours so that we could take the next train east together.

As I came downstairs with my lone valise and sketchbook, the night clerk, Mr. Richards, the one who had sent the telegram to the Falls, called to me.

"You're checking out, ma'am?" he asked, and I nodded, placing my key on the desk. "And what of Mr. Cole? I've yet to see him come in." He gazed across the room at the towering grandfather clock. "Me and Little Benny have been here again all night. And, my goodness, what a night it was, wasn't it? When we saw the fireworks, we thought the war was over. But I'm told that isn't true?"

"No, I'm afraid not. It was . . . ," And here I struggled with how much to tell him. "It was a part of Mr. Cole's celebration. Kind of a closing fanfare."

"Now that must have been some party he threw."

"It surely was."

Mr. Douglas was waiting for me at the train station with a first-class ticket. Yet once I saw that he was heading toward the rear coach, relegated to second class, I decided to follow him. We didn't say a word as we sat down together and the train pulled out of the station.

Sandusky, Ohio. I wouldn't forget this place as long as I lived, and I knew it would be some time before I told the entire story of what had transpired here. I was still trying to sort it all out in my mind as the train picked up speed, heading toward Cleveland and beyond.

"That Union man back there," Mr. Douglas said.

"Captain Everett?"

"He seems to think that the worst is over. But I fear it isn't."

Outside our window, the land faded to fields, pocketed by the occasional farmhouse and barn. It was fast becoming autumn, and the harvest would soon be at hand for the folks who lived in these parts. We barreled along the southern edge of Lake Erie, heading for Cleveland and beginning the long sweep up toward Buffalo.

"What Captain Everett doesn't understand," Mr. Douglas continued, "is that last night didn't solve much of anything. Beall got away, and from what I hear he's as devious and as calculating as they come. The rebel devil escaped, so that means he'll lick his wounds, bide his time until he tries something else, something that's even more of a death blow to our side. A man like Beall doesn't simply go away, Miss Rory. Disappear into thin air because we wish it so."

How I wanted to believe Captain Everett's judgment of things. That our struggle was over or nearly so, and with it my role in it. I'd had my fill of playing spy in a war that seemingly had no end. Still, as Mother once told me, life comes down to the company you keep. Which people and groups you befriend and look to help and which ones you move against and try to stymie. Deep down, I knew that Mr. Douglas was right. John Yates Beall would strike again. He would do so until he was captured and caged, once and for all.

The explosions and excitement from the night before soon faded away as the miles rushed past. Had I been wrong all along? Thinking that being part of this great conflict would somehow lead me to a better place, a way to transform myself? Once more I felt lost—a wallflower at the gala ball who couldn't stay in step with the fevered melodies playing in her head, no matter how hard she tried.

As our train approached the terminal in Buffalo, I told Mr. Douglas that I would continue on with him to the Falls.

"Are you sure, Miss Rory?" he asked. For he knew, as well as the rest of them at the Cataract House, how the borderlands could haunt me. He would have understood if I'd told him I was taking my leave in Buffalo, continuing east to Auburn and what was left of home.

"Yes," I replied.

Late that afternoon, I opened the door to Wreet's shop, and the ring of the bell sounded like the greeting of an old friend.

"Be right out," Wreet shouted from the dark room at the rear of the building.

I set down my bag and waited until Wreet appeared from the shadows, wiping her hands on that familiar rag of hers.

"It's you?" she said. "But how?"

I half-shrugged, not sure how to explain myself.

"To be honest, Rory Chase, I wasn't sure I'd ever lay eyes on you again. Not after we sent you off to our strange war along the lakes."

"And strange it was."

Wreet came out from behind the counter and looked me over.

"I heard some of what they were trying to do there," she said. "You must have been very strong."

"I don't know about that. I'm still trying to decide."

Wreet motioned for me to sit down at the small table with her.

"It can be like that," the older woman said. "Not that I'm involved as much anymore. In the early days of the war, when those in Washington decided to open this store, I had so little help in such matters."

"When it comes right down it," I said. "I'm not sure what I really did back there, in Ohio."

"The warship, the last on the Great Lakes, still flies the Stars and Stripes. That's the important thing," Wreet said. "The Rebs were so certain that they were going to snatch her that their prisoners rushed the gates at Johnson's Island. That's what the reports say anyway. The prisoners thought a rescue attempt was imminent. Instead, I'm told they were met with significant force."

"The *Michigan* left Sandusky this morning," I said. "In pursuit of John Yates Beall and his pirates."

Wreet considered this before saying, "If I was going to wager on the outcome, I'd bet they got away."

I nodded in agreement.

The older woman paused. "And that's why you came back?"

"On the train from Sandusky," I said, taking a breath, "Mr. Douglas said this damn war isn't over. That we haven't heard the end of Captain Beall. And I found I couldn't disagree."

Wreet nodded. "I can't, either."

She turned on the kettle for tea, and we sipped it slowly, until our cups were cold and the sky outside her shop faded to dusk.

"What are you going to do now, child?" she eventually asked.

"I was going back to Auburn," I replied. "But I don't have any family or many friends there anymore. Only the Sewards, and they're mostly in Washington."

"Stay here," Wreet offered. "Until you get your bearings."

I shook my head. "No, I wouldn't want to impose."

"Impose, my eye. I can always use an extra hand around here. There's too much for one able body to do."

"I don't know."

"Stop it now. Something told you to come back here. Between the two of us, I'm sure we can puzzle it out. I've got the spare room. You set yourself up there until life presents itself again."

PART 4

At the Precipice

He comes to me sometimes, I wrote. He comes and sits with me at my table or stands in my doorway after I've had one of my bad dreams or goes walking out on some business across the yard. I try to talk to him but he will not talk to me. Only sits or stands there. Not all things disappear quickly.

—LAIRD HUNT, *NEVERHOME*

43

Rebel Raiders Cross Border into Vermont

Special to the *Buffalo Courier*

St. Albans, Vt., Oct. 19, 1864—Between 20 and 25 armed desper-
adoes, supposed to be in the rebel employ, attacked several banks
here this afternoon.

The National Bank was robbed of $70,000 to $90,000 in bills.
Nearly $80,000 was taken from the St. Albans Bank and an undis-
closed but considerable amount from the Franklin County Bank.

The rebels rode into town brandishing pistols and rifles. At
least three citizens were shot, one fatally. One of the roughs briefly
stepped onto the porch of the Ethan Allen Hotel and announced,
"In the name of the Confederate states, I take possession of
St. Albans."

After a half-hour terrorizing the citizenry and robbing the
three local banks, the rebels fled in the direction of Canada. An
armed party of local militia followed soon afterward in pursuit.

"Look at this, child," Wreet said, holding up the morning paper.

I took it from her and read the front-page story. "Nothing about
John Yates Beall," I said. "Or Bennet Burley."

Wreet sighed. "I fear they're part of a larger scheme. Mr. Douglas
feels the same. Something to send everything to tatters before the
presidential election."

In letters I'd received from Fanny in Washington, nobody agreed
about President Lincoln's re-election chances. Fanny wrote that her
father, Secretary Seward, predicted that the final result would be
razor-thin, but that the president would secure a second term. Others in the capital were more pessimistic, she added. Although we were

finally winning the war, Lee's army continued to fight on, and the conflict seemingly had no end. That's why Lincoln, Fanny said, was far less confident than others in his cabinet—even his own family—about whether he would win a second term.

"I admire him greatly, as you know," Fanny wrote me. "But the man has a deep sense of melancholy. It troubles me. It troubles many of us here."

Until a few weeks ago, the contest was expected to be between three candidates—Lincoln for the Republicans, George McClellan for the Democratic Party, and John Fremont as the nominee for the Radical Democracy Party—a situation that many of us thought would greatly enhance the president's chances. Then Fremont, who had criticized Lincoln for a delay in offering freedom to the Blacks, dropped out of the race. That left McClellan, a man who made my blood boil, as the lone challenger. If McClellan had been more of a general, willing to take the fight to the rebels in the early years of the war, this awful conflict would have been over long ago. Through it all, the Copperheads, a growing faction of the Democratic Party, wanted to bargain with the Confederates for peace. While McClellan publicly disavowed the Copperheads' peace platform, few believed him. Fanny wrote that Daisy Conley and others like her in Auburn were backing McClellan.

Wreet, often the pessimist, believed that Lincoln could lose in a lopsided fashion. Her reasoning was "war fatigue" throughout the North. Too many people had been worn down by the summer's series of battles—Wilderness, Spotsylvania, Cold Harbor, and now the siege of St. Petersburg.

"This has been Lee's plan all along," Wreet said. "To make us so tired of this war that we'd give up the struggle. Try and go back to how things used to be, even though deep in our hearts we know that can never happen. Some hold Lee in such high esteem. They think he's such a gentleman warrior. But he's doing the devil's work."

Despite the state of our world, Wreet's shop was as busy as ever. While the North may have been worn down by war fatigue, there was also a growing hunger in the land, so many ready to step out of our shared nightmare, and the only remedy at times seemed to be securing another likeness or portrait from a shop like this one.

I had shown aptitude as a crayonist. I'd been pressed into service when the woman who had been doing the job eloped with her lover, who had somehow survived the war and found his way back to western New York. While the work wasn't as satisfying as my own drawing, I soon learned to be at peace with it. I let my intuition take me to what particular colors and highlights to add, especially with the larger prints that Wreet was able to produce with the new wet-plate process. She had brought a local man into the fold—a Mr. Sherk, who had the gift of the gab and was better than either of us at suggesting the best poses for the growing number of customers who came to the shop. Mr. Sherk could cajole them into holding such poses in the expanded second-story studio, which resulted in better images and higher prices charged.

Wreet fancied Mr. Sherk as well, and she would sometimes accompany him back to his flat a few blocks away when another workday was finished. Sometimes she didn't return right away. Of course, that was no business of mine.

I still walked along the rapids above the Falls—that sliver of land that fell downstream from the Cataract House to the Falls itself, where Leila Beth Kidder had once feared I was about to hurl myself into the raging waters and be carried over the edge as the seagulls mocked us overhead. Such bouts of uncertainty and melancholy had mostly left me since Sandusky. Mostly.

44

One-third of a mile
From my Cataract House
To the top of the bank.

Two hundred and ninety steps
From the top of the bank
Down to the river itself.

One-quarter of a mile
From the US to the Canada side
The width of the mighty Niagara,
At this point in the angry river.

Then the last quarter mile
Up the Canadian bank
To a freedom that is
Lasting, solid, and mostly good.

I hold tight to such numbers.
Such figuring and ciphering
Helps keep me sane.

JOHN DOUGLAS

"I worry about her, John."

Wreet and Mr. Douglas sat in rocking chairs on the porch at the Cataract House. It was early morning, and Wreet had been returning home from another evening at Mr. Sherk's flat when she saw Mr. Douglas taking in the dawn.

"I could stay home more," Wreet continued. "Make sure I'm there for her."

"Nonsense," Mr. Douglas replied. "Our Rory is finding her way. We just need to give her time."

"But, John, what if events won't allow it? Beall and his ilk are still out there. They'll strike again."

"No doubt."

"And in all likelihood, we'll need Rory to help stop him."

Mr. Douglas nodded and gazed across the strip of lawn to the rapids of the Niagara River.

"Wreet, you ever notice how the waters awake in the morning?" he asked. "Yes, they make their presence known at night. Hearing them in the darkness can calm one. Still, with the dawn, they seem to come more alive, ready for what the new day does bring. I cannot help thinking that it will be the same with Miss Rory. She surveys the river as much as any of us now. She does so from that favorite spot of hers—hard by the overlook. I've seen her there plenty of times. So, maybe the river and the Falls are schooling and leading her, too. Whispering to her what she needs to know. How to heal."

Wreet listened, slowly rocking in the chair next to Mr. Douglas. After a time when the two of them said little more, listening to the mighty river, she rose to leave.

"I pray you're right," she said before heading for home.

45

"They went ahead without us," Burley said, placing the front page of the *Toronto Examiner* on the table between them.

Captain Beall picked up the paper, which was a good week old, and read the main headline aloud, "Confederates Attack Vermont Town."

With a puzzled look, he glanced back at Burley. "The next raid was to be ours."

"Your Commander Thompson lied," Burley replied. "And I bet the bastard has plenty of practice at it, too."

"Then who led this attack?"

"Does it matter? All I know is the struggle is going ahead quite well without us."

"But we needed to go into hiding," said Beall, still looking puzzled. It was one of the few times Burley remembered his rebel partner being surprised by much of anything. "Everyone agreed that after the *Michigan* debacle, it was best to lie low."

"But for this long?" said Burley, nodding at the cabin's small window. Outside, snow flurries were in the air. "They've forgotten about us. And I for one am done with it. Captain, you are truly the best commander I've ever had the good fortune to serve with. But your Confederate friends? They've never respected your skills, let alone your service."

"No, it's not like that," Beall insisted.

"And when was the last time you heard from Thompson or anyone with him?"

"He said they were putting together more raids. A big one outside of Buffalo. Even another attempt on the *Michigan*."

Burley tried to laugh. "And when was that?"

The rebel leader fell silent as the wind shook the small cabin in the woods well north of Toronto, where the two of them had been holed up since fleeing the calamity on Lake Erie.

"Three weeks ago," Beall said.

"Almost a month," Burley added. "This isn't how an army treats its officers. Leaving them hanging out to dry like yesterday's laundry."

"But Lee's forces are in disarray. Grant is squeezing hard."

"That's no excuse," Burley said, his voice rising. "To totally cut us out."

"No, Burl, it's not like that."

"Isn't it, sir? Believe what tall tales you want to believe. I'm leaving this godforsaken place come the morn. I'm getting out before winter settles in and they look to dig us out in the spring."

"No, Burl."

"If Thompson remembers where he stowed us, tell him I'm plenty crabbit with the whole situation. Leaving us to rot in the middle of nowhere."

Three days later, Burley reached the home of Adam Robertson, a distant relative and a master mechanic specializing in the construction of torpedoes, gun carriages, and other such armaments. Even though the pair hadn't seen each other in years, back in Glasgow they'd shared an affinity for weaponry. After several rounds that evening, Robertson told him about his recent purchase of a fourteen-pound gun, which was to be fitted aboard a steamer, part of a new plan to finally seize the *Michigan*.

"It'll have three or four vessels in play," Robertson said as they huddled near the fire, tankards in hand. "One outfitted up right, with enough firepower to take a serious bite out of the Yankee beast. The others are to be diversions. Lure the *Michigan* out from the harbor at Sandusky."

"I've heard nothing of this," Burley said. "Neither has Captain Beall."

"Don't get your head out of sorts, lad," Robertson cautioned. "It's only come together in the last week or so. And where you've been at, out in the wilds north of Toronto, isn't exactly on the beaten trail."

"I could get back to Captain Beall. Tell him."

Robertson urged Burley to stay put. "From what little I know, Thompson has other plans for Beall," he said. "Perhaps they include you. I don't rightly know. But between us, you're better suited for this task. Water, boats, and weaponry. Ah, lad, it's right up your alley."

And so it seemed. In short order, a 350-ton steamer, the *Georgian*, was purchased with rebel money. It had been launched that summer on Lake Huron and was powered by the latest screw propeller. With time running out before winter closed the Great Lakes for shipping, it arrived at Port Colborne on the Canadian side of Lake Erie. From there it would have access to the Welland Canal and Buffalo, New York. Weapons were sent in boxes marked POTATOES, while the *Georgian*'s hull was reinforced with iron bars and a battering ram was attached, which could be deployed against the *Michigan*.

On November 2, 1864, the vessel headed for Sarnia in British Canada at the southern-most tip of Lake Huron. Its mission was to retrieve more weapons. Arm up good and proper. However, authorities on both sides of the border were keeping a keen eye on the new lake raider. When British authorities boarded at Port Maitland, Burley took his leave, returning to Guelph and the Robertson home. His goal was to return to hiding with Captain Beall. Thompson had been right: they had become wanted men. Too recognizable for their own good. Yet within days of his arrival back in Guelph, officials arrested Burley after some bootlicker tipped them off.

Ironically, the authorities at first thought they had apprehended John Yates Beall, and Burley decided not to correct them. Let them believe he was Beall. Perhaps that would give the captain time to make his next play.

46

Wreet and I were in her studio, putting the finishing touches on an Imperial print of Mr. Douglas. He'd posed for Wreet a few weeks earlier, striking a characteristically solemn pose in the upstairs studio. She had been working on the print ever since, developing the image that showed him from the starched collar up, his eyes peering straight at the camera. Wreet had labored so hard on his likeness that it appeared to glow, especially his eyes. Now it lay in a slim frame, ready to be hung on her wall.

"The man has been through so much," Wreet said. "But you wouldn't know it from talking to him. He plays his cards close to his vest. Has to, I'd imagine."

I agreed. "He could be a character from a Shakespeare play, couldn't he? The way he moves about the shadows."

"There you go with that Shakespeare again." Wreet smiled.

I had told her that Fanny Seward and I used to act out elaborate, make-believe stories when we were growing up, soon graduating to his plays.

Wreet surveyed the Imperial print of Mr. Douglas one last time and then lifted it to a place on the far wall, a few feet away from smaller images of Cesar and Sissy Morris. I helped her, and in short order, Mr. Douglas was there, amid so many other faces from the Falls.

"Ah, Miss Fanny Seward," Wreet said, her eyes still on the portrait. "She's one I'd like to do a likeness of. Hang it on my wall and see what it said to me."

"She's like Mr. Douglas," I said. "Another who's more than meets the eye."

Wreet agreed. "Since I got into this business with my dear departed husband, I've come to believe that the camera doesn't lie," she said. "While it doesn't take away our souls like the Indians out west may believe, it does allow one to truly contemplate and consider a person. Get to know them in a way that a painting doesn't allow."

With that Wreet gave me a long look, as if she was trying to figure me out. Thinking that having me pose in her studio on the top floor, bathed in sunlight, might do the trick.

"The way you're talking," I said, "reminds me never to sit for your camera."

"You're wise to steer clear of me sometimes, child. Still, I'm beginning to figure out what makes you tick."

"And what may that be?" I asked, trying to smile away such talk.

"Any person is a tangle of contradictions, of course. But I've never seen a package quite like you, Miss Rory Chase. Perhaps it's growing up in the shadow of a heroine mother. Maybe it's having no more direct kin. Whatever the reasons, you're all purpose and determination one minute and hesitation and indecision the next. Perhaps I need to read more Shakespeare to truly understand why you walk along the Niagara River and gaze upon it like a star-crossed character."

While I tried to say it wasn't so, Wreet shrugged and turned back to Mr. Douglas's portrait.

"No, I don't need to do an Imperial of you to get an angle on such things," she continued. "I've spent enough time working with you, watching you from afar, to know you're at some kind of crossroads. Trying to decide if you're going to hang back in the shadows through all of this or come out into the light. Are you truly going to act upon what you've carried for so long in your heart?"

47

At Mr. Douglas's invitation, we sometimes sailed from the village of Youngstown, about ten miles downriver from the Falls. Mr. Douglas seemed to have boats at his disposal all along the Niagara River, and with him at the helm we would fly across those shimmering waters, soon reaching the inland sea of Lake Ontario. From the Youngstown dock, we passed by the two forts, the wooden stockade on the Canadian side and the white-stone fortress on the American side, which dated back to the French and Indian War. After that, the vista opened up to the horizon, with nothing but green-blue waters as far as the eye could see. There the three of us would fall silent for a moment, as if to pay homage to the wider world around us. Then we'd drift back to the affairs of the day. That afternoon, the topic of conversation soon turned to Bennet Burley.

After being arrested in British Canada, on the far side of the lake, his true identity had been determined. In recent days he'd run out of appeals in a Toronto court and been sent back across the border to stand trial in northern Ohio, not far from where the USS *Michigan* was still anchored.

"His father has been lobbying the politicians in London on his behalf," Wreet said.

Our craft heeled gently over to one side as we left the wind shadow of the river.

"They could hang him soon," Wreet added. "Rush everything along."

"Maybe," Mr. Douglas said, steering us away from shore. "But I doubt it."

His eyes shifted between the sails and the lake's surface, and I followed his gaze, seeing how the freshening wind roughed the waters. Cat's paws. That's what Mr. Douglas called the condition, and it was a sure omen that more wind was heading our way.

"Where they're holding him ain't much of a jail," Mr. Douglas replied, almost as an aside. "Not for a man like him."

"I can't help thinking he's still tied to John Yates Beall," Wreet said. "Two birds of a feather."

"They weren't together when Burley was captured," Mr. Douglas said. "Word has it they're no longer partners."

"I find that hard to believe," said Wreet, facing the wind and letting the breeze blow back her gray mane. "I wonder what he's thinking, that mangy mutt of a man."

That's when I realized the conversation, at least Wreet's side of it, was for my benefit. A way to possibly nudge me along.

"Where exactly are they holding him?" I asked.

Mr. Douglas didn't reply, concentrating on the next shift in the wind. Instead, he glanced at Wreet as the sailboat sped away from shore. We had caught a good puff of air, and we were moving well across the water now.

"I'm serious," I told them.

"There's no need," Mr. Douglas. "Others are in play."

"No, tell me."

"A local jail," he said. "Some backwater between Cleveland and Sandusky."

"Let me go to him," I told them. "Ben Burley and I had a good rapport."

Wreet smiled at me, the wind still rustling her hair. Out here, on the water, she looked like a warrior from bygone times. A witch right out of Shakespeare or *Ivanhoe*.

"That might be of help, child," she said, but as soon as she said those words, Mr. Douglas brought our craft too far up into the wind, and the sails briefly flapped furiously.

"Damn it," he muttered, and I realized that I had never heard him curse before.

Moments later, Mr. Douglas had the boat back in good form as he gazed over his shoulder at the American shore.

"We need to go home," he announced. Then in a softer voice, his words nearly borne away by the lake breeze, he added. "You don't need to do this, Rory. As you can tell, Mrs. Thayer and I disagree about this matter, and we haven't disagreed about much over the years. Bennet Burley's a young fool. Not worth our time or attention. Not so close to the possible end of the war."

"But, John, any such information is worth the effort," Wreet insisted, "especially if he's still in cahoots with that Captain Beall."

"I don't see it," Mr. Douglas replied. "Our people tell me that Beall and Burley are no longer in league. That they had a serious quarrel."

"But, John, wouldn't it be good to be sure?"

"Enough," Mr. Douglas said. "It's time and resources that might be better spent."

Wreet and I watched as he steered the boat across the wind and the waves slapped against the boat's glistening hull, with the sails fluttering in protest until we secured them again. As quick as that, we were heading back to shore.

48

When I entered the rail station, I was surprised to see Mr. Douglas sitting on one of the long benches, waiting for me. He knew that my train, the one arriving from Lockport and continuing on to Buffalo, where I could transfer to the Lake Shore Limited heading west, was a few minutes away. I had little choice but to join him on the bench.

Not knowing what to say, I looked up at the huge clock overhead, which witnessed everything and everyone that passed through these corridors. Mr. Douglas followed my gaze.

"That old bird of a woman and I go way back," he said. "Her husband used to work at the Cataract House before he opened his likeness shop."

"I had no idea."

Mr. Douglas smiled, as if there was much that I didn't know about these parts. "As I've said, Wreet and I have a history."

I glanced over at him, wondering where this was leading.

"I'm not here to try and stop you," he said. "Or even warn you."

"Then why are you here? You must be missed back at the hotel."

Mr. Douglas shook his head. "That establishment runs well enough without me. I'm now little more than a figurehead."

It was my turn to smile at the absurdity of it all. "I find that hard to believe," I said.

"Wreet doesn't know I'm here," he added.

"So why—"

"Because when I heard what you'd decided, it seemed important that I speak with you."

I was expecting to hear the reasons why I shouldn't visit Bennet Burley. How he had been seemingly forgotten by both sides in this war. Certainly, people like Wreet would be curious about what he was up to next. But in the grand scheme of things did it really matter?

"If I've learned anything in my life," Mr. Douglas said, "it's that one cannot be filled with vengeance. It's a fire that hollows you from the inside out. Wreet and I have debated this at times. It's a reason why I worry about her."

I wasn't sure what he was telling me. "If anyone should be filled with vengeance, filled with revenge, it's you," I said. "And Wreet, too. After what you've seen and battled against. I have done so little compared to the two of you."

"Hardly," he grunted.

"It's true," I told him. "If it hadn't been for you, arriving with Cesar and Aran at the last minute, Beall would have seized the *Michigan*."

"And that's the key, isn't it?" Mr. Douglas said.

"What do you mean?"

"That this Captain Beall is one of the puppet masters pulling the strings. Between you and me, Miss Rory, he's the rebel spy that keeps me up at night."

"You're just saying that on my account," I said. "Because of why I'm here and what I'm doing."

"No, Miss Rory, I'm privy to much information, even more than our Wreet is. And from what I've heard about Bennet Burley, he wants nothing more than to go home now, and who can blame him? He was never a slaver. A voice saying that one kind of people should serve another. He was just a young buck on the make. Keen for adventure and got more than he bargained for. Do I forgive his kind? No, I don't. But I am able to forget. It appears that this war may actually be drawing to a close, and when it does the only ones who are going to be comfortable in the light of a new day are the ones who have been able to forget and, most importantly, forgive."

"But he may know what Beall will be up to next."

"That may be, Miss Rory. But it's like what I was trying to say the other day, out on the boat. Perhaps we've reached a point with this awful war where we don't have to be so hellbent, so desperate about everything and every foe anymore. Yes, stay determined when it comes to the likes of John Yates Beall. The sooner we put him in a cage and throw away the key, the better off our world will be. Keep his kind behind bars forever. Yet that doesn't mean we have to treat all of our enemies as we would Captain Beall. Perhaps we need to regain a sliver of sanity in our lives. Not be chasing after so many shadows and ghosts."

The two of us looked back at the clock overhead.

"Mr. Douglas, I need to go," I said, standing up.

"Yes, Miss Rory, or you will miss your train."

49

From the second floor, where Bennet Burley was being held, he couldn't see me in the clearing down below and I couldn't see him.

The situation we found ourselves in reminded me of the balcony scene in *Romeo and Juliet*, with me craning my neck for a better view.

"This isn't much of a jail," I called up to him. "And your Sheriff Lattimore is away?"

"Until tomorrow sometime," Burley said. "He took his sorry excuse for a wife and his two brats with him, too. When he does, he often gives me the run of the place. It's a fine arrangement—until they hang me."

Above me, I saw his shadow in the window frame.

"It seems to me that you could walk out of this jail anytime you wish," I said. "From what I understand, you have the good sheriff wrapped around your little finger."

Burley laughed this away. "And what if I do? It doesn't do me much good, Miss Rory."

"I'm just telling you what I see, good sir."

"You can be real trouble, can't you? Always whispering in men's ears. Is that what happened to poor Cole in Sandusky? Did you lead him down the garden path?"

"I have no idea what you're talking about, kind sir."

"You don't, do you, Rory? The good captain and I talked at length about this, when we were holed up in that stinking cabin in the Canadian wilderness. So far off the beaten track we could have been on the far side of the moon. How we did our jobs on that grand lake, but when it came time for Cole to deliver? Well, the heavens themselves erupted into fire and light."

"And that was enough for you to stop taking the *Michigan*?" I asked.

"That's because the men themselves went stark raving mad," he replied. "There was no talking any sense to them after that ungodly display."

"It was quite the fireworks show."

"Ah, Rory Chase, listen to you. Playing the innocent bystander with your sketchbook and fancy pencils. All I know is that you were there, on shore, where everything went sideways."

"So, I'm somehow to blame?"

"I didn't say that, lass. Frankly, if we'd had you aboard the *Philo Parsons*, I'd wager that between the three of us we could have held the rest of those jackals in line."

I had to smile at how Burley left the situation open for me to rewrite my part in all of this.

"Cole failed you," I told him after a time.

"But how?"

"He was too caught up in the moment. So full of himself."

"Anyone could see that," Burley said. "So, what happened on shore? When we were making our move on the warship?"

"We saw your vessel in the shadows," I told him. "You were closing in."

"Within a stone's throw."

"Yes, you were," I agreed.

"So, what happened then, Miss Rory? If they hang me for this, at least send me to my grave a happy man. Tell me what transpired there on land."

And for a time, I didn't know what to say. What lie to tell the poor man.

"Rory, are you still there? Or did my question drive you away?"

So, it was time again to lie. Lie with abandon.

"Cole had a whole box of flares and Roman candles," I began.

"But why? We were only waiting for one to rise into the sky. That was the plan."

"Once you seized the *Michigan*, Cole had decided we needed to celebrate."

"Celebrate?"

"Light the sky so much that anyone and everyone within a twenty-mile radius would know. So that the prisoners on Johnson's Island would rise up."

"The prisoners on Johnson's?"

"That's right, Mr. Burley. But his celebratory lights were lit too soon. Maybe by mistake?"

Above me, I heard Burley muttering to himself. "The man made as much sense as giggles after midnight. Crazier than Captain Beall and I ever could have imagined," he finally said. "I mean if you light up the sky, that only draws the attention of the bluecoats. It only agitates a situation when you're better served by laying low, staying quiet, doing the dirty work, and then sailing for the horizon."

For a long time, he continued to mutter to himself.

"What's that, Ben?" I called up to him.

"I was saying, Rory, that if it's become that much of a circus, they will hang me for sure."

Somehow my lie about Cole had shaken him. In an instant, his normal bravado vanished.

"I wish I could see your face," he said. "This conversation is getting the better of me. I didn't realize how much you can read from a person's countenance, how they conduct themselves while they're saying something. We're operating too much in the fog here, don't you think? You and me? Not really knowing where we stand."

"You won't hang, Ben Burley."

"What makes you so sure, Miss Rory?"

"Your Captain Beall, some part of the rebel operation, will arrive at the eleventh hour and save your hide."

My comment was greeted with another round of silence.

"You still there, Mr. Burley?"

"Yes, I am, my dear. Nowhere to hide from such conjecture, no matter how misguided it may be. For I fear you've fallen into the same trap as the Union authorities, my friend. Putting too much credence in the Northwest Conspiracy. This enterprise that supposedly extends from the Maritimes to north of Superior. If only it was so. Then I could truly believe that this might play out in my favor."

"But you and Captain Beall are as thick as thieves. I've seen it with my own eyes."

"I'm done with the good captain."

"I find that hard to believe, Ben Burley."

"And he's done with me," said the voice from the window. "Not that it matters to you or anyone else, but we had a bad row about the St. Albans raid. I left him soon afterward."

"Only to reunite at some point in the future."

"There you go again, Rory. That's one of your fairy-tale endings talking. My times have become more bittersweet, more desperate."

"But it's rumored that Captain Beall will make another raid. Even another attempt on the *Michigan* warship."

"That's a ridiculous notion, and you know it."

"It's all the buzz about the Falls."

"At that damned Cataract hotel? Now there's a place full of fun-house mirrors."

"But Beall, your captain—"

"He's not my captain any longer," Burley snapped. "My God, he's become like the ghost on the moors, haunting everyone's story. The rumors run rampant, don't they? John Yates Beall making another attempt on the *Michigan*, robbing more banks along the border, raiding trains running from Detroit to Buffalo."

"I heard that, too," I said, wanting him to tell me more.

"Listen to us, Rory. Carrying on like a pair of washerwomen over the clothesline."

"And you'd be with him for any of those adventures?"

Burley laughed at this. "Sure, if it got me out of here. Yet it doesn't matter. They'll catch the whole lot of us before too long, and when they do, they better chuck the good captain in prison and throw away the key. Not hang him like they're intent on doing with me."

"Why is that?"

"You hang Captain Beall, and you make him a martyr, Rory. His memory becomes something too many can rally around. That's a scenario that doesn't do anyone any good. Not either side."

For a time, the two of us fell quiet as darkness began to creep across the surrounding streets. The sheriff's residence, which doubled as the jail, was a few blocks from the small downtown. A short carriage ride from the rail station.

"Why not slip away from here?" I said again. "You yourself say they are barely watching you. That you get along well with the sheriff, so he doesn't pay you much mind."

"That may be," he replied. "But I wouldn't get very far, would I? Not without money, a train ticket. They would light up the skies around here again looking for me and they would find me—considering the situation I'm in."

I realized Ben Burley was asking me for help. That he was too proud, too unsure of what might exist between us, to come out and simply say so.

Later that evening, I returned to the local jail. Burley had told me that the sheriff only locked the front door when he left. How it would be easy enough to slip out his upstairs window and climb down the fat limbs of the red oak tree to the front yard, where I again stood.

I had taken my leave around dinnertime, walking around town, eating at the counter of the local diner, stopping by the rail station, deciding what to do next. Had the world become such a cruel place that a misfit like Bennet Burley deserved to hang?

"Mr. Burley," I called up to his cell window.

"You did return, Miss Rory," he answered. "Is your train running late?"

"No, good sir. Still on time. I have a few more minutes."

"How nice of you to call on me again."

"That night aboard the *Philo Parsons*? As you were moving on the *Michigan*. We could see it onshore."

"I bet you could. You know what runs through my mind when I think of that evening, Miss Rory? Our adventures upon the Chesapeake, earlier in the war. We tied the Union warships in knots on those waters. If we'd stayed there," he declared, "we would have been legends."

"But you were captured there, too," I said.

"A technicality."

"A technicality? Mr. Burley, from what I know they rounded up the whole lot of you. Sent you off to prison."

"If the good captain hadn't been so loyal, the two of us could have slipped away well before the bluecoats appeared. I'll go to my grave believing that. Beall too often plays out a bad hand. He refuses to push away from the table when he knows he should."

"Is that what happened at Sandusky?"

"Oh, darling, what a bolloxed mess that became."

"How so?"

"You know the story, Rory. The men turned against Captain Beall. The only time I've seen it happen in the years I've been with him. You know what a charmer he can be. Able to sweet-talk a widow out of her last tuppence. Starting with our time on the bay, right on up to that night near here, he's always somehow carried the day. But not then, not with that crew of pirates."

"And why not?"

He didn't reply.

"The men, your crew?" I asked. "They were no good?"

"No, the men were fine enough," he replied.

"But they deserted you," I said. "Wouldn't go through with your plan."

"It was the captain's plan. I'm just a lackey."

"Then what happened?" I said, pressing him. "How did a few of Cole's celebratory fireworks turn it all upside-down?"

Above me, Mr. Burley fell silent once again, before saying, "It's the times."

"The times?" I repeated.

"Aye, Rory, I cannot help thinking that this world has been at war for so long that too many of its people have become crazed in the head. No matter how sincere the orders, how precise and truthful they may be, people on both sides are refusing to follow. To arguably do what's best. And, frankly, Rory, who can blame them? I'll admit it, I'm as much of a scoundrel as any of them. I came to America looking for fortune and adventure, slipping away from a fresh marriage already gone bad. Those reasons don't count for much. Not after so many bodies have fallen. No, I don't blame the men aboard the steamer, the *Philo Parsons*. Not anymore. They'd witnessed so much they couldn't hear or believe in any of it anymore.

They couldn't carry on like good and proper soldiers. There are no more good soldiers left in these lands. And perhaps that's how it should be."

As Burley's words rained down upon me, echoing through the clearing, I realized I had never heard a better assessment of our conflict and what it had done to us as a nation, as a people. Perhaps it took an outsider, such as Burley, to truly understand the damage that the long war had inflicted across the country and to warn about the scars we would be left to deal with.

"So, if I returned in an hour or so," I asked, "you'd be ready?"

"Ready for what?" Burley blurted out. "A kiss on the cheek? A dance under the half-moon beneath a cloudless sky?"

"No, to get away."

"Away?"

"Yes, with the necessary provisions and precautions."

After a few moments of silence, Burley said, "As you know, Miss Chase, I can be down that tree in three shakes of a monkey's tail."

Later I heard that search parties with bloodhounds fanned out in all directions from the sheriff's jail that evening and well into the next morning. If Bennet Burley had been on foot, they would have captured him for sure. I sometimes wonder if Sheriff Lattimore left his jail door ajar so Burley would try to escape. So they could gin up the charges against him with the new trial pending.

They never got the chance, of course. For when Bennet Burley stepped out of the open window and climbed down from the tree, I was waiting with a rented buggy. In short order, we reached the station as the westbound train pulled into the station. There I handed him an envelope with a ticket and monies, and then I kissed him on the cheek.

"Hurry now," I whispered, "before it's too late. For both of us."

And like a good lad Bennet Burley did as he was told. As the train pulled out of the station, he was safely aboard, peering out the window back at me.

50

A few days later, Fanny Seward entered Wreet's shop. Neither of us knew she was coming. Fanny claimed that she had been in Auburn, visiting her mother, and decided, spur of the moment, to take the train the few hours west to visit me, to see the Niagara Falls courier operation. But I've known Fanny Seward since we were girls, and she's much like her father: little is ever done on a whim.

"What's she doing here?" Wreet whispered to me as she came out of the darkroom.

"Fanny is here to see me," I replied.

"Why?"

I shrugged, but I knew my childhood friend had heard what had happened in Ohio, about Bennet Burley's escape.

Bundled up against the chill, Fanny and I left Wreet's shop together and walked toward the roar of the Falls.

"Bennet Burley," Fanny soon began. "What's he become to you?"

"He's nobody."

"Really? And now he's escaped."

"Has he?"

"Rory, you know he has," Fanny said. She was walking faster, heading toward the river.

"So what if he has?" I asked in a louder voice, trying to sound strong and calm, determined to keep up with her.

Eventually, Fanny waited for me. As I drew closer, she shot me that knowing smile of hers. "Reports from Ohio say that he had help," she said. "A tall, fetching woman with short-cropped hair."

I couldn't hold her gaze.

"Oh, Rory, what are you caught up in now?" Fanny continued. "Bennet Burley is a small fish who was smart enough to swim away when he saw what was good for him. It's the other one, this Captain Beall, who's still very much in play. That's why I decided I'd better pay you a visit."

"I know all about John Yates Beall."

Fanny shook her head. "I doubt it. What you don't realize is the election is next week."

"We know about the election here, too."

"And do you appreciate that President Lincoln could very well lose? The newspapers say that McClellan has now pulled even with Lincoln. People are so tired of this war that they could turn out the man who saved the Union. Many in the cabinet are convinced it is going to happen, and Father is worried sick about it all."

While Fanny tried to collect herself, together we reached the overlook and gazed down upon the raging Niagara River.

"It all just makes me so mad," she said in a softer voice. "You see, Rory, it's like this. Beall and too many of his kind are still out there. One ugly incident between now and next week, the wrong kind of headlines, and the election is lost. The voters will go against Abraham Lincoln, no matter how much good he's done for the country. Remember, dear one, the war isn't over. Not by a long shot. That's why the border needs to be secured. All of you at the ready."

For a while, we remained at the overlook, pulling our coats tight against the cold breeze.

"Did you tell Wreet or Mr. Douglas about Ben?" I asked.

"Ben is it now?"

"Did you, Fanny?"

"No, this is between the two of us. Do they even know Burley got away?"

I shook my head.

"When they do, they'll put two and two together, if they have half a mind to. But, as I said, there are bigger things in play now. That's why I need you to stay a trusted sentry on the border, the avenging angel you once desired to be. The reason Father sent you here in the first place."

"I will."

"Please make it so."

Satisfied that I had been properly chastened, Fanny left by train early that afternoon, heading home to Auburn. After an evening in our hometown, she was scheduled to return to Washington, the center of it all.

51

To our relief and delight, President Lincoln was re-elected, defeating George McClellan by the stunning margin of 212 to 21 in the Electoral College. There had been no attacks, no ugly headlines from our part of the world, and enough people voted with courage and hope.

Early the following afternoon, Mr. Douglas took Wreet and me sailing on Lake Ontario. All of us were fuzzy-headed, bundled against the winds building out of the northwest. Like much of the town on the American side of the Falls, we had gathered outside the telegraph station as the crier gave us the early results, which were almost all in Lincoln's favor, and such good news only built throughout the evening until we retired in the wee hours. Our beloved leader would serve a second term. Right then and there, I decided to visit Fanny in Washington, eager to attend the president's second inaugural.

"If I was able to, I'd join you, child," Wreet said as Mr. Douglas steered closer into the wind. "But the shop will be busy throughout. After so long it appears to be over, doesn't it? President Lincoln has won, and soon this damnable war will be finished as well. I can feel it in my bones."

I stole a glance at Mr. Douglas after Wreet's pronouncement, and a flicker of concern clouded his face before he returned his gaze aloft. Behind us, the shoreline and the entrance to that mighty river, only a few miles downstream from the Cataract House and the Falls itself, blurred to hazy lines of blue and green.

"You don't agree, Mr. Douglas?" I asked. "That the war will soon be over with President Lincoln staying in the White House?"

He kept his eyes on the weathervane high atop the mast.

"I dearly hope so, Miss Chase," he said, still looking skyward. "I pray for it with all my heart."

Snowflakes began to fall at dusk, swirling with mist rising from the Falls. Before turning in, Wreet asked me to join her for a short walk. Outside, the old woman clung tight to my arm, sheltering her face from the cold.

We'd gone only a block or so before she announced, "Bennet Burley escaped."

I didn't reply.

"And isn't he a cheeky one?" Wreet continued. "He left a note in the sheriff's Bible saying 'I have gone out for a walk. Perhaps I will return shortly.' He didn't."

Of course, he didn't, I thought. I had made sure of that.

I'd like to think that I helped him escape because I was taking a stand, granted a private one, against the ongoing conflict that divided our nation. Perhaps I was suffering from my own version of war fatigue or self-delusion. No better than a Copperhead like Daisy Conley.

"He got himself to Detroit and crossed over to Windsor and made his way to Toronto," Wreet said. "And then he had the gall to reach out to the sheriff back in Ohio. Do you believe it?"

Oh, but I did.

"He asked the poor man to send along the books he had gathered in his cell. I'm told he'd bought some of those tomes and borrowed the rest. Claimed the whole lot was now his. He mailed the sheriff funds for the shipping, and Sheriff Lattimore was so happy to be rid of Bennet Burley that he did it."

I pinched my palm hard, between the thumb and forefinger, determined not to laugh. I knew that if I did Wreet would realize what I had done. Yet such antics had my heart soaring like the waters propelled over the Falls itself. Had I been beguiled by Bennet Burley?

I'd like to think not, but there was little doubt that I was thrilled that he had gotten away.

Rumor had it he would soon be returning home to Great Britain, Wreet said, and I was happy for him. Perhaps I wasn't much of a Union courier or Yankee spy, but I believed that I'd retained a degree of humanity. Which said something after what had happened.

52

"I thought Burley would be a part of this," Commissioner Thompson said. "But rumor has it that he's leaving for England soon. He's going home."

Beall nodded and sipped his tea. The two of them sat in a suite located on the top floor of the Queen's Hotel in Toronto.

"Mr. Burley has grown tired of our war," the captain said. "The St. Albans raid stuck in his craw. He felt that should have been our mission, and I cannot say that I disagree with him."

"That would have been impossible," Thompson said. "The two of you were the most wanted men in these parts at the time. Much too far away from the Vermont border."

"We could have gotten there," Beall protested.

"Not in time," Thompson replied. "As you know, we're desperate for any diversion along the northern borderlands. Besides, it didn't help matters when Burley got himself arrested near Guelph. He was lucky to get away, especially after getting extradited back to Ohio."

"But he did get away," the captain said, setting down his cup. "The man has more lives than a cat. That's something I'll miss about him. How he would laugh at the first sign of any trouble."

"From what I hear, he wouldn't have gotten far, certainly not to Detroit, without help."

Beall gave him a puzzled look. "Someone helped spring him from the sheriff's hometown cell?"

"Didn't you hear, John? There were reports of a woman, almost as tall as him, who drove him to the rail station in a buggy she had rented. She made sure he got on the train to Detroit and then she took the next one going in the opposite direction, heading east."

"Rory Chase?"

"Maybe so. Unlike our Mr. Burley, she isn't eager for center stage."

Beall smiled. "It's always good to have a guardian angel."

"Enough of this," Thompson grumbled. "Here's what's in play for us."

The next week, December 15, 1864, several Confederate generals were scheduled to be transferred from the Johnson's Island prisoner-of-war camp near Sandusky to Fort Lafayette in the New York harbor. Their ranks included major-generals and brigadier-generals, and all were members of the prisoners' secret organization, the Order of the Brotherhood of the Southern Cross.

"If we stop their train, help them to escape—" Thompson said.

"Our ranks would be strongly bolstered," Beall said, finishing the thought.

"And there's more," Thompson said. "It's our understanding that this same train regularly carries significant amounts of gold. We will make arrangements to ferry away whatever is found on board."

That afternoon Beall left by coach for Buffalo, and the next morning he gathered the other men Thompson had assembled to a meeting in his hotel room. Their ranks included such seasoned raiders as Lieutenant John Headley, who had served with Nathan Bedford Forrest, and Colonel Robert Martin, who had helped create unrest in New York City. Despite such experience, the ten-man unit was plenty green. As they gathered around the table in his suite, Captain Beall eyed Forney Holt and George Anderson, the two youngest members, and wondered how much help they would actually be.

The general plan of action had been outlined by Thompson, with Beall responsible for the specifics. They would stop the Lake Shore train coming from Cleveland south of Buffalo. With snow already on the ground, they would then make their way into Buffalo, with the rescued generals, by horse-drawn sleighs.

"That will also carry any gold we procure," Captain Beall said.

"Taking out a rail will be easy enough," Headley added. "With that gone, we can flag down the driver. And we'll look like so many good Samaritans."

"Until they see our guns," Martin replied.

The next morning, one of Beall's band was waiting for the rebel leader when he came down to the hotel lobby in Buffalo.

"Did you see the paper, sir?" Anderson asked.

"Whatever it is, it can wait," Beall said.

"No, it can't, sir. Please, look at this."

Beall took the copy of the *Buffalo Courier* from him as he summoned a hack.

"Railroad depot," he said, and Anderson scrambled into the seat next to him.

"Hemming, Holt, and I have all read it," Anderson said. "It's downright alarming. You'll see."

Beall read the orders issued by Major-General John Dix of the Union Army: "All military commanders on the frontier are therefore instructed, in case further actions of depredation and murder are attempted, whether by marauders or persons acting under commissions from rebel authorities at Richmond, to shoot down the perpetrators . . ."

Dix had to be reacting to the St. Albans raid, Beall decided, which had been a huge embarrassment to the Union command. Dix's proclamation went on to detail how federal and local authorities were to pursue any rebel agitators "wherever they may take refuge, and if captured, they are to be sent to these headquarters for trial and punishment by martial law."

"It's bad, isn't it?" Anderson said.

Beall handed back the newspaper. "We won't let it stop us," he told his underling.

At the Buffalo rail station, Beall ordered Martin to board the west-bound train to Erie, Pennsylvania. There Martin would learn which train the generals were scheduled to be on. As soon as he departed, Beall rented a double-seated sleigh to survey the countryside along the railroad tracks south of the city. He left Hemming and Headley at the station, awaiting Martin's return. He took Holt and Anderson, the two younger members of the strike team—an effort to calm their nerves after Dix's public announcement.

About four miles south of Buffalo, they found a desolate area where the main road crossed the railroad tracks. Beall stepped down from the sleigh and surveyed the terrain. It reminded him of the land back near his home in Virginia. There the small forces under his command had ambushed a Yankee regiment. In the grand scale of things, the overall scope of the war, it was a very minor event. Yet John Yates Beall would never forget it. How they had surprised the Union troops and carried the day, back when the war was young and the South *was* carrying the day.

"What do you think?" he called out to the other two still sitting in the sleigh.

When no answer came, Beall replied for them, "It will do handsomely."

53

"The Reb commander has been sighted in Buffalo," Mr. Douglas said. The three of us were gathered in his room below the dining room at the Cataract House.

"What's to be done?" I asked.

"It's more what can't we do," Mr. Douglas said, turning to Wreet with a resigned look.

"You see, Rory, Mr. Douglas and I are now under strict orders to stay here—at the Falls," Wreet said. "Until the war is officially over."

"Somehow Lee holds on at Petersburg, and Richmond still stands," Mr. Douglas added. "Until he surrenders, we've been told to stay in place."

I couldn't believe what I was hearing. "But if it wasn't for you coming to Sandusky, Mr. Douglas, they would have seized the *Michigan*. Besides, Buffalo is only a short train ride away."

Mr. Douglas shook his head. "The folk in Washington are adamant. They're convinced more raids are coming, like the one at St. Albans. Dix has them all riled up. As a result, everyone is to remain at their posts. Be ever vigilant, we're told."

"By order of Secretary Seward himself," Wreet added.

I considered this and saw that I didn't have any choice.

"Well, I'll go to Buffalo then."

Both of them exchanged glances.

"We were hoping you would," Wreet said. "But I was wondering . . ."

I waited for her to continue, realizing that rumors of what had occurred in Ohio, with Bennet Burley's escape, must have gotten back to them.

"Where was John Yates Beall last seen?" I asked, eager to move ahead.

"Word has it that he's at the American Hotel, with a number of men," Mr. Douglas replied.

"That man always has a mob about him, doesn't he?" Wreet said.

"The American is where President Lincoln stayed on his way from Illinois to Washington to be sworn in," Mr. Douglas said, as if he was remembering a precious moment from a long time ago. "He worshipped at the Unitarian church down the block. Me and several others watched him enter and waited for him to come out."

"I doubt that Beall cares about that," Wreet said.

"Yet I can take solace in it, can't I, kind lady?" Mr. Douglas replied, and Wreet grew quiet, likely in embarrassment.

Mr. Douglas turned his attention back to me. "I'll secure you a room at the American," he said. "Ask for a gent named Finley. He works in the kitchen, but he used to be here with us. He knows the drill."

Buffalo had done well for itself during the war. Many of its richer citizens had been able to avoid military service, paying others to take their places in the Union Army. The city itself had profited greatly, its population growing from eighty thousand to nearly a hundred thousand because there was plenty of good work to be found as its reputation and ranking as a top shipping port rose in stature. The streets were crowded as I made my way from the train station to the American. I didn't know what Beall was up to or how to stop his operation. Still, I found Finley soon enough. He was helping prepare the evening meal, which would be served buffet style in the dining room.

"He's here," Finley told me. We were standing in the hallway outside the kitchen. "And he's assembling a number of brutes."

"That's his way."

"He got himself a suite, the biggest in the hotel, up on the top floor. I went by once I got word from Mr. Douglas that you were coming. No way to listen in there, but it may not matter. Beall and his like are coming and going so much that that's what I'd watch for."

"I could wait across the street," I offered. "In a coffee shop or some other place."

"Better off in the lobby here. It's big enough. Besides, they say another cold snap's coming, bringing more snow off the lake." Finley glanced at my only jacket. "I'll find you something better, along with a warm hat. If I was a betting man, I'd wager you'll be out in the air keeping up with this lot."

Finley was right. It began to snow that evening, and I first caught sight of Beall soon after the flakes began to fall. It was about eight o'clock when he entered through the hotel's front doors and made his way to the bar. From behind my paper, I watched him briefly talk with two other men. They soon departed. Only Beall lingered, nursing a cocktail. When he headed for the stairs, I stepped up to the bar, at the same place where he had been. The bartender was tidying up, and I saw a matchbox for a local business, Carlton's Transport, which I pocketed.

"What can I get you, ma'am?"

I ordered a Bourbon Old Fashioned. While I'm no teetotaler, I rarely take the opportunity to imbibe. Still, as I took the first sip, feeling the warmth seep down my throat, I decided I had made a good choice. I was once again in over my head, and any fortitude that I could find was something to hold on to.

The next morning, I awoke early, thankful for the heavier coat that had appeared outside my door from Finley, folded and wrapped in paper. For a time, I waited downstairs, but there was no sign of the rebels. So, I decided to find Carlton's Transport. The shop was located several blocks away, and inside they had all kinds of rigs—carriages and even bicycles.

"Can I help you, ma'am?"

"I'm sorry, kind sir. I just stepped in for a bit of warmth," I said, glancing about. "It is such a chilly morning."

"And we button up and forge ahead, don't we?" the man behind the counter said. He was taller than me, which most men cannot claim to be, with a starched white shirt that was protected by an apron.

"Things must slow down for you this time of year," I said, making chit-chat, stalling as I tried to determine Beall's interest in such an establishment.

"Not necessarily," the storekeeper said. "Certainly, the snows make it difficult for rigs with wheels and alike, but we also rent sleighs and teams. No better way to get around when the winds howl in off the big lake. Horses seem to enjoy pulling those outfits. A change of pace for them, too."

"Has business been good?"

"Couldn't be better, ma'am. Only have a few of the sleighs left. Been a good run on them. Mostly out-of-towners. They seem more interested in the pending weather than the locals. A dapper gent with a cane rented several of my biggest rigs through the end of the week.

A real industrious chap with all these questions about the best ways in and out of town. He paid in advance, too."

54

"They'll be on the train arriving at five tomorrow afternoon," Martin said.

He and Headley, the ones that Beall trusted the most, were in his suite that evening, putting the finishing touches on the attack plan.

"We'll take the sleighs from the depot," Beall told them. "They've already been reserved. In addition, there's a hint of snow in the air, so that will help cover our tracks. Pass the word that we'll meet at the depot at noon sharp."

"I'll chisel the rail," Martin said.

"Three sleighs then?" Headley asked. "Each with a pair of horses?"

The rebel leader nodded. "Make sure that kid Anderson is in my rig. He's as shaky as a peach tree heavy with fruit."

"And what if he runs?" Martin said.

"I'll shoot him," Captain Beall replied.

The others exchanged surprised looks.

Late the next morning, they entered the depot in Buffalo individually and soon gathered at the rear of the cavernous building, where the rentals were doing a brisk business. Martin and Holt got away first, followed by Headley and Hemming, then Captain Beall and Anderson. While traffic was thick on Main Street, leading south out of town, soon they reached the countryside, where they located the rendezvous spot Beall had previously decided on. Here they hid the sleighs and horses in a nearby stand of trees. Then Martin, with Hemming's assistance, began dislodging the rail. An experienced cavalry raider, adept at breaking things apart, Martin used a sledge hammer and chisel to pry away the beam. His plan was to lay it across the track; then the eastbound train would be flagged down by Headley swinging a lantern.

Dusk was fast approaching by the time Martin freed the rail from the cold hard ground. With the help of several others, he was about to lay it across the track when in the distance they heard the whistle of an oncoming train.

"It's early," Headley shouted.

"Get it across, get it across," Beall shouted as Headley stepped forward, swinging the lantern.

But it was too late. Already the beam of the train swept around the turn, bearing down upon them. The men dropped the rail across the tracks and jumped to either side. Barely slowing down at the sight of the lantern, the locomotive struck the loose rail, sending it pinwheeling into the air. Somehow the train stayed on the rails. As the engineer sounded the whistle, the locomotive screeched to a stop. That shrill sound echoed throughout the woods. The train, ten cars long, safely came to a rest several hundred yards up the track. Already, men with lanterns of their own, as well as firearms, were stepping down to investigate.

"To the sleighs," Beall ordered, but his men were well ahead of him. The mission's commander was the last one to reach them, and they fled as soon as he was pulled aboard.

"They'll soon be onto us," Headley said.

"Break into smaller groups once we reach the depot," Captain Beall ordered. "Every man for himself. Get across the border as best you can."

55

It was well after closing time when the heavy knocks on Wreet's door rustled the bell atop the frame.

"Keep your shirt on," Wreet shouted. "I'm coming."

When she unlocked the door, she found Constable Peabody, hat in hand.

"Begging your pardon, ma'am," he said. "There's been another raid."

I hung in the shadows, listening to every word. Captain Beall's rebels had tried to derail the Lake Shore train south of Buffalo, and they were now on the run, perhaps heading in our direction. Word of the failed raid had spread to Buffalo, and I was ready to assist in the efforts there. But I was told there were plenty of sentries already on the border at Buffalo and the authorities there had no role for me. In fact, they couldn't be bothered with my questions or eagerness to help. So, I'd returned to the Falls on the late train. All the while, I kept an eye out for Beall and the others. Yet there had been nothing. No sighting or word—until now.

"If they reach Canada, they'll get away scot-free," said Wreet and Constable Peabody agreed.

"But at this late hour," Wreet added, "there's only one path left to them—if they've come this way."

"The Suspension Bridge," the constable said, finishing her thought.

Wreet turned to me, and that's something I'll always treasure about her. Even though I sometimes confounded her, she wanted me to accompany her once again.

"Fetch your new coat, Rory."

The winds that evening blew a gale from the north, funneling down the canyon of the Niagara River. The two of us wrapped ourselves in scarves, hats, and mittens, and nudged our chins beneath the coat collars as we made our way by foot to the station. Entering the New York Central Railroad depot, which, unlike the larger downtown terminal, stood in the shadow of the Suspension Bridge, Wreet studied the time schedule on the wall. Overhead, the large clock read ten o'clock.

"The next train to the other side isn't for another hour," Wreet said, surveying the nearly deserted terminal. "It's the last one until morning."

"What should we do?" I asked.

"If they walk across, we have no way of stopping them," Wreet said. "Not without more help." She nodded at a pair of Niagara City police officers near the newsstand at the far side of the terminal. "And they'll be off duty once the last train departs."

"So, we wait?" I asked, and Wreet nodded in agreement.

The two of us huddled in the far corner on what appeared to be a fool's errand. Even the pair of policemen soon ambled outside, about finished for the night. Yet a half-hour later, two men entered through the main doors. The taller of the two, barely in his twenties, was dressed in a workman's jacket and cap. The older man wore a tailored suit and bowler hat. Both were haggard and exhausted.

"Is that who I think it is?" Wreet said.

"John Yates Beall," I whispered.

"They must be the stragglers," Wreet said, keeping her eyes on them. "Look at them. They're dead on their feet."

And that's what was keeping them from simply walking across the Suspension Bridge's lower level to safety. They were too exhausted to make a run for it.

"What should we do?" I asked.

"Find those policemen," the older woman said. "Even in their weakened state, we're no match for a pair of rebels."

Outside, in the howling winds, I walked nearly completely around the stone building until I found the two policemen sheltered out of the wind, smoking cigars.

"Kind officers."

"Ma'am," said one as the other snubbed out what was left of his smoke. "What seems to be the trouble?"

"There's some men inside," I began.

"Passengers for the eleven o'clock train," one interrupted.

"And I don't like the looks of them."

"You don't like the looks of them, ma'am?"

"That's right. My auntie believes they could be persons acting under the direction of the authorities in Richmond. Rebel commandos."

"Rebels?" the one officer smiled, giving his partner a bemused look. "What makes you think that?"

"You saw the papers this morning, didn't you?"

"And were given a directive by our captain about it before our shift began, too," the other policeman said.

"Well, perhaps you should take a look at these two."

"Were they disturbing you, ma'am?"

"No."

"Besides, you look like you could take care of yourself," the first policeman said.

"It's my auntie I'm worried about. She's getting all in a tizzy about this. Please help us. Just come back inside and give them a look-see. My auntie and I will be forever grateful."

The first one shrugged, and together they made their way toward the front doors, with me trailing behind them. Inside the terminal, the two officers eyed Captain Beall and his younger accomplice. Both of them were sitting on the bench nearest the door to track. Their heads were down. Eyes closed.

"Excuse me," one officer sang out, taking longer strides toward the two rebels.

Beall's eyes fluttered open, while the younger one scrambled to his feet, eager to make a run for it. The other policeman was ready for him and caught him on the shoulder with his billy club, knocking him to the floor.

"Now, let's stop right there," the first policeman said. "I'm Niagara City Officer Charlie Jenks, and this is my partner, Solly Sanderson."

As Jenks spoke, he patted down Captain Beall and pulled a Colt revolver from his inside coat pocket.

"Now, this is an impressive piece," Jenks said. As he spoke, the younger one tried to slip away again, only to have Officer Sanderson force him down to his hands and knees. "And who might you be?"

"W. W. Baker," Captain Beall said.

"You look like a troublemaker, perhaps a spy of some sort to me," Jenks said. "Just the kind we've been warned about here along the border."

"No, sir." Beall blinked his eyes and gazed about the terminal, focusing for a moment in my direction. "I'm just accompanying my young friend here. We're going to visit his family across the river."

"And where in Canada might that be?"

"Near Hamilton," Captain Beall hesitated. "I've forgotten where exactly."

"I see," Jenks said. "I think the two of you best come down to the station."

"But our train?"

"There's another one bright and early in the morning, and another one right after that. If your story pans out, you can catch any of them."

The police officers, with their pistols drawn, began to lead the two rebels away when Officer Jenks turned and came back to me.

"You know them?"

"Not the young one, but the other one is John Yates Beall."

"And who might that be?"

"The most dangerous rebel in the borderlands."

As soon as the words were out of my mouth, there was a commotion near the terminal entrance. The younger rebel was wrestling with Officer Sanderson, and Beall had somehow disappeared.

Despite the frigid evening, the Bystanders were moving about at the entrance to the lower level of the Suspension Bridge. None of them was Beall, however. A glance down the wooden gateway, the pathway stretching out like a tunnel leading toward British Canada, revealed no one of his stature or gait, either. Where had he gone? He couldn't have simply disappeared into thin air.

I looked to Officer Jenks, who was as befuddled as me. Around us the Bystanders moved about like ghosts from the underworld. The policeman quizzed them, asking if they had seen someone matching Captain Beall's description, but they weren't about to tell a man in uniform anything. Mum as church mice, they were. That's when I drew the attention of one Bystander, and he simply stared at me, as if he was greatly annoyed that I was there, as if he somehow recognized me from another time long ago. That's when his eyes briefly looked upward, nodding to the upper deck overhead, where the trains ran. Then he turned away, leaving me to realize that's where the rebel leader had gone.

"Up top," I told Officer Jenks, pulling on his arm.

"Are you daft, woman?"

Yet I was already heading up the stairs leading to the upper level. The wooden banister and roughshod risers weathered by the winds and mists of the Falls reminded me of the staircase at Ferry Landing, the one leading to the raging river.

"The train," Officer Jenks shouted as he began to follow me. "Ma'am, it'll be here any minute."

As we reached the top level of the Suspension Bridge, the train was slowing, preparing to pull into the station. Its beam of light flashed past us, and as I followed the line of illumination, further down the track I saw a lone figure, hobbling toward the border in the darkness. It was John Yates Beall.

"Hold it at the station," I told Officer Jenks. "I'll get him."

With a relieved look, the policeman retreated in that direction.

Stepping from rail tie to rail tie, I began to move across the upper level of the Suspension Bridge, and, at first, I thought my eyes had been playing tricks on me. I didn't see Beall anywhere. Yet as the train arrived at the station its beacon light, like an orb of God, once more streamed down the rails, and there he was. Beall had to be halfway across the upper level by now.

Moving fast, I began to gain ground on him. Around me, the wind gusted. Several times I feared that its very force would topple me over the edge and down into the chasm far below. To this day, I don't know which crossing most unnerved me—going across the first time by boat, through Niagara's rapids and whirlpools, or stepping as lively as I could that night in the wind and the snow in pursuit of the rebel captain.

The lights of the other side were breaking through the mist and snow when I finally reached him. Without thinking twice, I brought Beall down by driving my shoulder hard into his back. While my time in the 138th may have been short, my service had taught me how to fight.

"But I'm past halfway," Beall protested as I pinned him to the tracks. "I must be in Canada proper."

I looked around us, and we were well past the midspan. Technically, he was correct. Yet that had never helped the Black people who previously tried to escape across this span. The ones my mother and those at the Cataract House had assisted in their flight. Why should such particulars and specifications now benefit a rebel who fought to keep them enslaved? That's what flashed through my mind at that moment and, as a result, I refused to let John Yates Beall escape.

Arguably, life would have been easier for us, all of our fates more bearable, if I had simply let him go. Watched him stagger the remaining distance across the top of the Suspension Bridge to British Canada. Of course, I didn't know any of that at the time.

Together, with both hands firmly grasping his arm, I led Beall back to the American side. Out in front of us, the train started to move slowly in our direction, its bright beam bearing down on the scene, and for an instant I feared the locomotive might run us down. As it neared us, though, the train seized to a stop, with the hiss and screech of brakes, a bank of steam rising upward.

All around us, the air grew alive with noise and distraction, so loud that it momentarily drowned out the roar of the rushing waters far below. In fact, our immediate world was so frantic with activity that I didn't hear the low chuckle of laughter boil up from deep inside John Yates Beall until I realized that his arm, his very torso, was beginning to shake. I stared at him, still hanging on tight, wondering if the man had snapped, gone completely off his rocker. That's when the rebel captain turned toward me, wild-eyed, with a maniacal grin breaking across his face.

"Just another soldier in this fight," he said. His voice had become a low growl that only I could hear as the authorities drew closer. "For that's what I am, Miss Chase. You and I both know it. If they strike me down, a legion will rise in my place. Mark my words. There's nothing more powerful than another who dares to suffer. Another who believes in the cause."

Thankfully, the two policemen and a swarm of others in uniform soon reached us, taking John Yates Beall away. They handcuffed him and led the rebel leader to the train, with me trailing behind. When we were all aboard, the train slowly began to edge backward, returning to the American side of the Falls.

56

I returned from the Prospect Point overlook to Wreet's store. In recent weeks, I had fallen into the habit of viewing the cataract nearly every morning, regardless of the weather. For some reason, I found that the raging waters soothed my soul.

As I opened the door, Wreet was waiting for me.

"There you are." The older woman held out a small sheet of paper. "Ronnie from the telegram office dropped this off while you were out and about."

The notice read that I had been summoned to New York City, to the police headquarters on Mulberry Street. "What's this about?" I asked, handing it to Wreet.

She studied it and replied, "Reading between the lines, I'd say that Beall now realizes what dire straits he's in, so he's lying about his true self. As a result, they're summoning those who can positively identify him. Unfortunately, you're one of them."

"What if I don't go?"

A pained expression came over Wreet's face. "My guess is they won't take no for an answer, Rory. They're asking politely now. Next time will be more of an order."

I glanced again at the notice and then folded it in half and folded it again, as if I was some kind of mad magician who could make this part of my life simply disappear.

"Major-General John Dix is heading the investigation. We've all heard of him."

I nodded.

"Determined fella," Wreet said. "I'd imagine he knows who he's landed with John Yates Beall. What the Rebs have been up to with him as a ringleader. I'd imagine he's assembling an air-tight case against Beall, and he's leaving nothing to chance. Such steps begin with a positive identification."

"This cannot all be on me."

"Exactly," Wreet answered. "From what I know of him, Dix will bring in anyone and everyone who can help prove his case. That would include witnesses from Buffalo, certainly Ohio. I wouldn't be surprised if he's turned some of Beall's own recruits against him, got them to talk. That's Dix's way."

"If he has so many others, why does he need me?"

"I only met Major Dix once. He came through Buffalo and the Falls early last year to inspect our operation. Truth be told, Dix wasn't pleased with what he saw here. He thought we were too skittish, too unsure of ourselves to do an effective job, and he was probably right. We are amateurs compared to him, a real military man, and we've tried to improve our methods since then. About the only one who impressed him was our Mr. Douglas. You think I'm a tough old goat? Dix is that in spades. What I'm trying to say is whether he needs you or not, he'll stay after you, Rory, until you do his bidding."

"I'll just disappear for a while."

"No, please think this through, Rory. Dix is not the kind you want to upset. Take the morning train tomorrow, and you'll be in New York by nightfall. Help them identify Beall, then leave as fast as you can. You'll have done your part, and you can be left alone."

As soon as I came off the platform from the Hudson River Line, a pair of policemen fell in beside me.

"Ma'am, we're to take you downtown," one of them said. Soon enough, our carriage pulled up in front of the Mulberry Street station.

Inside, I was led to the booking desk, where Sergeant Kane was waiting for me.

"Best to go over matters thoroughly before heading downstairs," he said as he led me toward his office. I saw that a policeman had stationed himself outside Kane's door.

Kane followed my eyes and said, "That's for your protection."

"Or to make sure I don't flee," I answered.

"Major-General Dix knows you're a valuable piece of this investigation, so he's leaving nothing to chance."

"And where is Mr. Dix?"

"You'll meet the major-general soon enough. We have some work to do first. The suspect is being held one floor below us. The cell isn't large. Five by eight feet, so don't let the conditions throw you. This is a police station, after all. I hope you'll remember that he has been issued a mattress and blanket. He isn't uncomfortable."

"Who else have you brought in to look him over?"

Kane paused before answering. "Well, I guess it won't do any harm to tell you. Earlier today we had in Walter Ashley, part-owner of the *Philo Parsons*, the vessel the rebels commandeered to cross Lake Erie. Yesterday, it was the boat's fireman. You've read the reports. Undoubtedly, you know the names. Much of the setup."

I wouldn't tell him that I knew more than perhaps anyone about how the attempt on the *USS Michigan* had been launched.

"Your other visitors?" I asked. "They said it was Captain Beall?"

"That they did," Kane replied. "But none of them were around him as much as you, Miss Chase. After all, you met him in Niagara Falls, traveled with him to Ohio."

I couldn't disagree with that.

"You're an important set of eyes for us," Kane said. "We need to be certain before going ahead. He keeps insisting that his name is actually Baker, not Beall. He's gone as far as to try and bribe one of the watchmen to let him walk in the middle of the night."

"And if I identify him as John Yates Beall?"

"Then he'll be formally charged as a foreign combatant."

"And if sentenced?"

"He could hang."

I shook my head. "So, you're asking me to put a man to death."

"No, ma'am. Simply verify that he is who he is. And then let the evidence decide what happens to him. He'll have his day in court, or at least in front of a military tribunal."

Was there no end to this nightmare?

"The two men from the *Philo Parsons* have already picked him out of a lineup," added Kane. "Did it right quick, too, so there's no need for that. We'll keep him in his cell. As I said, it's not very big, so we'll walk you by once or twice, as many times as you need. We'll douse the lights in the hallway, which will keep you back in the shadows. We can even dress you in a hood and cloak to better disguise your presence, if you'd like."

"I walk by and do what?"

"You take a good hard look at him. You can take as many passes, linger as long as you need to. We need to know, without a doubt, if this is John Yates Beall or not."

"And what if I refuse?"

"I wouldn't advise it, ma'am. The major-general is eager to move this case forward. Let's just say that the man can make things difficult for those who cross him."

Soon afterward, I followed one of the guards down the backstairs to the first level of cells. Kane trailed close behind me. I wore the long cloak and pulled the dark hood as closely as I could around my face.

"He's in the second cell on the left," Kane whispered, and together the three of us filed past.

The person accompanying the space wasn't a big man and at first glance he sported a strong resemblance to Captain Beall. He was huddled on his bunk, face turned away from the door of bars, and I lingered as long as I dared before moving past.

When we reached the end of the dark hallway, Kane drew alongside.

"Well?"

I found that I was holding my breath against the stench of the place.

"I'm not sure. I couldn't see enough of his face."

"All right," Kane said. "We'll try again."

The guard turned to go back down the hallway, and I reluctantly fell into step behind him, with Kane again on my shoulder. As we neared the cell the second time, Kane stepped forward and ran his baton along the cell's bars.

"Baker, is that you?" he shouted, and the figure in the shadows turned toward us. His face was bruised with welts, and he hadn't shaved in days. While there was none of the madman's bluster that I had witnessed that night on the Suspension Bridge, there was no mistaking those intense eyes. They fell upon me and briefly grew wide in recognition.

"Miss Chase?" Beall exclaimed, and with that Kane led me by the elbow, down the hall and out of sight.

57

Major John Bolles began his closing arguments in the crowded courtroom at Fort Lafayette, the island fortress in the narrows of the New York harbor, by saying, "The witnesses have clearly and unequivocally placed John Yates Beall at the center of several serious crimes against the Union. These include the taking of the *Philo Parsons* and then the *Island Queen*, which were part of the attempted attack on the *USS Michigan*. As we have shown beyond any doubt, this was an integral part of an organized plan to free the Confederate prisoners on Johnson's Island near Sandusky in Ohio.

"The witnesses and further documentation also place the defendant at the raid just south of Buffalo, New York. Fortunately, this brazen attack did not result in any loss of life. And John Yates Beall was then apprehended during his attempt to cross over the border to a safe refuge in Canada on the Suspension Bridge in Niagara Falls."

Here Bolles paused to survey the small courtroom, which was standing room only. I sat near the back, in the second-to-last row. In addition to me, the prosecution had brought forward five other witnesses: Walter Ashley, the co-owner of the *Philo Parsons*; William Weston, the vessel's fireman; Charles Jenks, the officer who had officially arrested Beall at the Suspension Bridge; Edward Hays, the doorkeeper at the Mulberry Street police headquarters, the one Captain Beall had tried to bribe; and George Anderson, the seventeen-year-old who had been arrested with the rebel commander at the border at Niagara Falls.

Anderson had left no doubt about the scope of the Buffalo raid, confirming that it was done to free the Confederate generals and bankrolled by Jacob Thompson and the Northwest Conspiracy.

"And it's this particular point that I must underscore in my final words to you," Bolles told the courtroom. "You have heard a great deal of talk during these proceedings about what constitutes a spy. John Yates Beall's defense has offered up letters and documentation from those in Richmond and Jefferson Davis himself that the planned attack on the *USS Michigan* and the later raid south of Buffalo were a part of the war effort. That it was, in essence, business as usual during such horrific times. I could not disagree more."

Bolles paused and faced the table where Beall and his attorneys sat. He stared at the rebel commander, who glared back.

"These so-called commandos wore civilian dress and assumed aliases. Their actions were hundreds of miles beyond any battlefield, and innocent people were caught up in their web of deceit, several of whom you have heard from in this very room. The defendants want to cloak themselves in the honor and respect awarded to regular soldiers, but to do so becomes a corrupt action in this particular case. For John Yates Beall and his men do not deserve any respect. The only words that apply to what they have done are pirate, guerrilla, and, most of all, spy.

"That's why I beseech the court that the only sentence for such action is death."

A gasp ran through the courtroom. Major-General John Dix had entered the courtroom by this point. He stood along the far wall, not far from me. I saw Dix give a slight nod of appreciation in Bolles's direction.

Within the day, a verdict was handed down by the military tribunal and endorsed by Major-General Dix himself. It stated that John Yates Beall was deemed a spy and ordered to be "hanged by the neck until dead on Governor's Island" in four days' time.

I couldn't believe that my testimony had led to this. Helped send a man to the gallows.

In the hubbub after the verdict was read, Bennet Burley's warning flashed through my mind. How the worst outcome would be to turn Captain John Yates Beall into a martyr. Someone the rebel cause could rally around for years to come.

58

"Rory, it is not within my power to pardon him," Secretary Seward said. "Only the president can do that."

Once again, I found myself sitting on the opposite side of a desk from one of the most powerful men in the Union. The study in his Washington residence bore a striking resemblance to the one in Auburn. Once again, my friend Fanny stood near the door, hanging on every word.

"Then when can I speak with him?"

"The president?"

"Yes, sir."

Secretary Seward turned toward the window. His Washington residence overlooked Lafayette Park, and beyond that stood the White House itself. By the grave look on the secretary's face, however, I knew that my request wouldn't be fulfilled as easily as I wished.

"The president is a busy man," Secretary Seward began. Then he paused, as if unsure how to continue. "He's pleased with your fine work regarding the warship, the *Michigan*. He appreciates it whole-heartedly. But right now, so much is riding upon day-to-day, even hourly decisions."

"The war is finally winding down," Fanny interjected.

"It's not over yet," the secretary warned. "So much remains open-ended until Richmond falls."

"But I'll only need a few minutes of the president's time."

"That's nearly impossible right now," Secretary Seward answered. "I'm sorry, Rory."

Minutes later, I was ushered from the secretary's office, walking with my childhood friend to the parlor. It wasn't yet nine in the morning, and Secretary Seward would soon be leaving for his official office, a few blocks away, closer to the Capitol.

"Thank you for getting me in to speak with him," I said. "I didn't realize your father would be so busy this early in the day."

Fanny smiled, "It's like this all the time now. Everyone knows the war is racing to a close. With General Grant in full command, Lee cannot hold on much longer."

The two of us sat by the window overlooking the square and listened to the front door open. Someone else asked for the secretary.

"I've been after Father to hire a doorman," Fanny said. "He won't hear of it, of course. He takes after the president in that way."

"Can you get me in to see President Lincoln?"

"I don't know, Rory. From what we've heard about John Yates Beall, his attempt on the *Michigan*, now this Buffalo raid—"

"Fanny, if he hangs, others will cherish his memory. Take up this evil cause. It's best to do as Mr. Douglas once told me: 'Lock him up and throw away the key.' Let the world forget about him."

My childhood friend took a deep breath. "I'm not one to argue with Mr. Douglas," she finally said. "Few know the ways of the world, the good and the bad, better than he does."

"So, let's stop the killing then. At least this time."

Fanny considered this as the room once again grew silent. I looked out the window at the small park and the people moving past. Everyone in the nation's capital seemed to be in a hurry—eager to recast themselves before their world was transformed into something else, something new and bold and perhaps more reasonable.

"I don't like working behind Father's back," Fanny said. "But I'll see what I can do."

59

At dusk, one could better picture what kind of city Washington might grow up to be. Even though whores, swindlers, and monkey grinders populated the muddy streets near the White House itself, and an open sewer ran along Connecticut Avenue after a heavy rain, the boulevards themselves were constructed wide enough, daring to stretch away in every direction from the blocks-long strip of land of meandering carriage paths and trees called the Mall. I didn't consider myself much of a city person. I would always be more accustomed to the rhythms and the light to be found in the country, or certainly a smaller town. Still, I had to admit that I enjoyed walking many of Washington's streets, especially as night approached. At dusk, amid the gathering shadows, one could better recognize what this world might one day be.

As I entered the Sewards' home, Fanny called for me to keep my wrap on. In fact, Fanny was pulling on her coat and grabbing an umbrella from the canister near the coat tree.

"Let's go before Father is any the wiser," she whispered, grasping my hand. "President Lincoln will see us now—if we hurry."

From the Sewards' home, it was no more than a five-minute walk to the front door of the White House. No doubt the secretary had moved into the three-story town house to be closer to the president and available whenever he was needed.

At the White House door, Fanny was immediately recognized, and the two of us were ushered inside, where the advancing darkness had already cast many of the rooms into shadow and hushed conversation. If I had been on my own, I knew I would have been stopped here. My childhood friend was a familiar face, though, and soon we were heading farther into the gloom, which was becoming speckled with candlelight.

"Miss Fanny?" a boyish-looking man called out. "Is he expecting you?"

He was sitting at a small desk inside the door to one of the next rooms we passed by. Fanny refused to stop or directly answer.

"It's important, Mr. Hay," she said over her shoulder as she continued to nudge me along until the two of us nearly spilled into the adjoining room, with John Hay, the president's private secretary, hurrying after us.

Once inside the room, I wondered if anyone was actually there. Without enough light, the place's dimensions seemed to stretch forever, mimicking how the streets outside were laid out.

"It's all right, John," said a bemused but weary voice. "I'm always at Miss Fanny's beck and call."

In lieu of any formal introduction, the president stepped into the half-light, and Fanny said, "Mr. President."

"What can I do for you, child?"

"I brought a visitor."

"I see you have. A friend?"

"A good friend, sir. We've known each other since we were children, growing up in Auburn."

"Then I'm delighted to make her acquaintance," Lincoln said, nodding for each of us to sit in one of the upholstered chairs across the desk from him. "We have a few moments before the next round of scheduled interruptions. Come, let's see if we can solve something that's amiss with the world."

As we sat down, Hay remained by the door, unsure of what to do.

"You must be Miss Chase," the president began.

"Yes, sir. How did you—"

"You see, I know our Miss Fanny. And she usually teases things out in a cool, measured way. Like a cat with a fair-sized ball of yarn. For her to come in unannounced, to get my Mr. Hay all agitated and bothered, something very special must have happened, or she would not conduct herself in such a contrary way. And one Rebecca 'Rory' Chase is about the only reason I could come up with on such short notice."

"Rory was in New York," Fanny began.

"At the trial of John Yates Beall?" the president said.

"That's correct, sir."

"His actions and arrest are most unfortunate," Lincoln said, stroking his forehead. "The war may soon be over. If he could have steered clear of trouble for a while longer, he would have been forgotten. Allowed to fade into what many of us desire after these long years of war—being unrecognized by fate."

"Couldn't you still offer him that choice, sir?" I asked.

"You mean pardon him?"

"Yes, certainly you could find it in your heart, Mr. President."

Lincoln chuckled faintly at this. "Ah, Miss Chase, if you hang around this town long enough, you'll soon hear that pardoning supposed sinners is all I'm good for. Isn't that right, Mr. Hay?"

His secretary, still standing in the doorway, didn't reply.

"I've pardoned more men than anybody in this place, the people's house, can remember by this point. My military men say I sometimes mock them with another stroke of my pen."

"So why not spare another one?" I said, daring to press the point.

"But my generals say that if John Yates Beall and his men had secured the *Michigan*," the president continued. "Oh, the damage they could have done to the Union. Some, like Fanny's father, have also advised me that it could have damaged my campaign to win the presidency for another term."

"Yet they didn't, sir."

"I know, Miss Chase. I have you to thank for that as much as anyone. Your work in Sandusky to keep the prison at Johnson's Island secure, the *Michigan* in safe hands, was exemplary."

"Thank you, Mr. President."

Lincoln tapped one of the many stacks of paper on his desk with an open palm. "I must admit that I don't fully understand why you are coming to his defense now, at the eleventh hour. Especially considering that you helped derail his plans."

How could I explain that I didn't wholly understand my desire to save Captain Beall either? President Lincoln was right: it didn't make much sense at all. None of it did anymore. Except something deep inside me kept saying it was the right thing to do. Especially now that the war was nearly over. Too tongue-tied, I simply sat there, staring the floor.

"If it's any comfort, you're in good company," President Lincoln said and again lightly patted a stack of papers on his desk. "All of these are letters urging me to pardon one John Yates Beall. And their ranks include several Congressmen, members of the military on both sides of the conflict—in fact, even members of my own cabinet. Isn't that so, Mr. Hay?"

"Afraid so, sir."

"It seems Mr. Beall has a great many friends, ones willing to vouch for his character."

"So why not let him be?"

Lincoln brought his long bony fingers into a steeple and rested his chin upon them.

"Because one man is adamant that I don't pardon him."

"Dix?" Fanny asked.

Lincoln smiled. "You are correct, my dear. How long have you been coming down from the north woods with your father? I bet it amounts to a significant tenure by now. Still, you know more about how Washington works, who is who, than almost anyone. I should have made you a general, Miss Fanny."

"Please don't tease me, sir."

"I'm not. Not at all. Your father has a great asset in you, and once again you've hit the nail on the head. Yes, Major-General Dix feels that we need to make a statement here. One that not only our side and the Confederates will recognize, but one that the British and even the rest of the world will understand as well. That such skullduggery will not be tolerated. That if we let the ways of war soar so far beyond what we accept as the proper limits, how can we push them all back behind the curtain again?"

"Do you agree with General Dix, sir?" I asked.

"I see you're as fast on your feet as your childhood friend, Miss Chase. For you're right, the final decision is mine. The curse of being president, I suspect. It makes you wonder why men will move heaven and earth to win this very office, doesn't it?"

"But if Beall is executed," I began. "I worry about what the future may hold. That some who share his beliefs may uphold his memory. Make him a person who's not so easily forgotten."

"Make him a martyr?"

"Yes, sir."

"What a frightening concept," Lincoln said. "John Yates Beall was certainly once a threat to the Union. Again, if he'd seized the *Michigan*, who knows what harm he might have caused? But in the end, I doubt that the history books will remember him as they will Robert E. Lee or Stonewall Jackson or other Confederate generals."

Fanny and I fell silent, waiting to hear more, as the president himself paused for the longest time, lost in his thoughts. His last sentence reminded me of the echoing note for some impressive yet unfinished piece of music.

Finally, Hay broke the spell. "Sir, the military attaché is waiting," he said.

"I'm sorry, Miss Fanny, Miss Chase," said the president. "Someday this war will finally be over, and we will have time for an honest conversation without so many constraints upon our time."

"Ladies, I'll accompany you to the door," Hay said, and reluctantly we stood to leave.

"I know you deserve a more definite answer," President Lincoln said. "In some ways, I do, too. Many a night I've stayed awake, waiting for a glimmer to fall from above. Sometimes it happens, too. Unfortunately, it's not enough to make me truly happy."

The way he spoke reminded me of when I walked above the Niagara River, waiting to hear more from those who haunted my days.

"Rest assured that I understand your concerns, Miss Chase," the president said. "Pray for him, pray for our nation."

60

At one o'clock in the afternoon, on February 24, 1865, John Yates Beall walked up the steps to the gallows that had been erected in the small courtyard outside the jail on Governor's Island. Despite appeals for mercy from the Reverend John Bullock, a well-known Presbyterian minister in Baltimore, as well as several members of Congress, its chief librarian, the governor of Massachusetts, and members of his own cabinet, President Lincoln let the matter be decided by Major-General Dix. The Union commander had declared that Beall "was not only acting the part of a spy, in procuring information to be used for hostile purposes, but he was also committing acts condemned by the common judgment and the common conscience of all civilized States." Such charges were read out loud one last time as the prisoner stood on the platform awaiting his fate. At one point, Beall shook his head and half-heartedly laughed at the reasons for his execution.

Although Dix had turned aside the claims for clemency, he had allowed more than fifty of Beall's supporters to be in attendance that afternoon. Word had it he wanted as many witnesses as possible to convey the event back to Richmond and even throughout the land. One of them was me. Along with the others, I watched as Beall turned to face south after the noose was brought down over his head.

"I protest against the execution of this sentence," he said in an unwavering voice. "It is a murder. I die in the service and defense of my country. I have nothing more to say."

Moments later, a flash of the sword was seen behind Beall, a signal to the executioner. The doors below the rebel leader opened, and he swung in the air until he died by hanging.

61

It had been raining for several days in Washington, and as the Seward carriage drove along Pennsylvania Avenue, toward the eastern front of the Capitol, the side streets were thick with mud and pocketed with large puddles. Despite the weather, a vast crowd had gathered. The Seward family, with several guests, including myself, made our way to our seats. We were there to hear President Abraham Lincoln's second inaugural address. He had become the first sitting president since Andrew Jackson to win re-election.

Just before noon, the president arrived to loud cheers from the overflow crowd at the Capitol. Within weeks, the Confederate capital of Richmond was destined to fall, with the president himself walking the streets there and even sitting in Jefferson Davis's chair. Yes, the war was coming to an end, and many in the crowd were eager to hear Lincoln declare victory and put an end to the national nightmare.

As we were finding our places, we saw a handsome man with a mustache, dressed in a black coat, holding his ground as the crowd flowed by on either side of him.

"That's John Wilkes Booth," Fanny whispered. "The famous actor."

I almost told her friend about being introduced to Booth that night along the border. Yet it could wait, I decided, and my eyes followed Booth as he eventually joined Lucy Hale, the senator's daughter and rumored to be Booth's fiancée.

Those in attendance, braving the drizzle and overcast skies, had already endured a long, rambling speech by Vice President Andrew Johnson inside the Capitol, in the Senate Chamber. To many of us, he appeared to be drunk, and his address veered from one subject to another, sometimes delivered in a whisper and at other times almost shouting.

But out here, on the East Portico, it was finally the president's turn. As he stood to take the oath of office for the second time, the sun broke through, bathing the moment in a reassuring, dare I say a heavenly, light.

While the vice president's speech had been far too long and filled with hateful language, Lincoln's was short—only 701 words, I was later told. While some in the crowd found it too brief for such an occasion, it reminded me of what the president had said at Gettysburg two years before. It emphasized how Lincoln was determined to bring a ravaged nation together.

"With malice toward none, with charity for all, with firmness in the right, as God gives us to see right," he told the crowd, "let us strive on to finish the work we are in, to bind up the nation's wounds, to care for him who shall have borne the battle, and for his widow and his orphan . . ."

Almost as soon as the speech had begun, it was over, the words still echoing off the nation's newly refurbished Capitol building in the background.

I fell in with the Seward family, a hand on Fanny's shoulder, as the crowd of dignitaries surged forward. While they congratulated the president, I stepped back and tried to remember as much of the day as I could. Already the sun was disappearing behind the gray clouds, and more rain was predicted. However, just for a moment, everything seemed to be right with our world again. As the crowd dispersed, some were repeating the words the president had said. Certainly, Lincoln could have spoken for longer, yet everyone had to agree that there were some memorable passages, lines that wouldn't be forgotten, in his address.

I took a last look around, searching for John Wilkes Booth. But the actor had already disappeared into the crowd.

By mid-afternoon, the Sewards had returned to their town house facing Lafayette Square. Soon they would be heading out for the first of many inaugural parties that evening. Perhaps it was due to all the years I had known them, growing up as Fanny's best friend, but I had no difficulty being at home in their company. Even on a night like this, with her brothers Frederick and Augustus going up and down the stairs, calling out to their little sister that the carriage would soon arrive, how they wouldn't be kept waiting, it felt comfortable and familiar to me. Like I was a member of the family.

I changed into the gown that Charles Cole had insisted that I wear in Sandusky, the night of the grand ball, and found a quiet place in the parlor to wait. That's where I was when William Bell, the downstairs servant, found me and held out a letter.

"This came for you, ma'am," he said.

I took the thick envelope from him, seeing it was from Wreet in Niagara Falls. Opening it, half-expecting to hear an update about life along the border, I found another envelope, a smaller one, instead. Attached to it was a short note from Wreet, telling me this had arrived the week before. As I studied the handwriting, the postmark from Montreal in French Canada, I realized its author was Bennet Burley.

Dearest Miss Rory:

I post this before boarding a ship bound for Plymouth and then traveling by train to London. I feel like a dog going home with his tail between his legs. But at least I am no longer in that shambles of a jail in Ohio. Thank you for setting me free.

I suppose I should go directly home to Glasgow, but that would require too much of me right now. Trying to explain what I did during the War between the American States. Indeed, how to explain such a thing when I don't rightly know myself.

I hear talk that it will be nothing but blue skies now that "Honest Abe" has been reelected. But I caution you never to dismiss the hatred that some in the South hold toward the Union, especially those in Washington. I partnered with such individuals for longer than I like to admit. And while some—certainly John Yates Beall comes to mind—remained gentlemen until the end, I cannot say the same for others I met during my time in America.

Your humble servant,

Bennet Burley

I reread the letter, hoping to find more in it. Perhaps a degree more fondness. But I knew that wasn't his way, and I was happy that Ben Burley had gotten away, able to start anew.

As I folded away his letter, I realized that if I'd learned anything during my time in the Falls, overlooking those raging waters, trying my best to play spy, it's that the past is difficult to escape. In helping capture John Yates Beall, I had done my part, my supposed duty. I knew I should be proud. But I couldn't help believing that God, or the Fates of Greek mythology or whomever guides our affairs from the shadows, already mocked such efforts.

Our great conflict would soon end, and the strength and initiative that had been so necessary to carry the day would do us little good once Lee's army surrendered. There had been the "war before the war"—the heroic efforts involving Mother and others at the Cataract House and elsewhere along the Underground Railroad. But unless we shifted our approach, our very temperament, there could well be a "war after the war." For President Lincoln had been correct in his inaugural address, emphasizing "malice toward none, with charity for all." And the longer I lingered here in Washington, caught up in Fanny's world of posh dinners and eloquent posturing, the more I wondered if we had enough mercy and understanding to take on a new role. Or had the war exhausted and hardened us forever, and Beall would become a martyr after all?

62

A few days later, my bags were packed. Despite Fanny's protestations, I had decided to return north. To stop by Auburn and try to determine what was left for me there and then to continue onward.

"Home to Auburn?" Fanny asked as the servants loaded my bags into the carriage trunk. "I cannot think of anything drearier."

"I'll start there for a time and then perhaps go farther west."

"You're going back to your friends in Niagara Falls?"

I tried to shrug off her keen observation.

"Rory Chase," Fanny said. "That place has gotten under your skin. You need to be careful about that. Life along the border can be beguiling—too much so, I fear."

Outside, Fanny's brother Frederick had the carriage door open, and the secretary himself came out to join us.

"How good of you to say good-bye," Fanny told her father.

"I thought I'd join you," said Secretary Seward as he gazed up at the brightening April skies. "Spring is in the air, and I thought a trip to drop Miss Rory off would do me good."

Fanny, Frederick, and I climbed into the carriage, while the secretary took a seat alongside the driver. Rides about the city gave him an excuse to light up one of the Cuban cigars he favored, which his daughter secretly detested.

We had gone only a few blocks when the coachman dismounted to secure one of the doors, which kept sliding open. He was fixing the trouble when the carriage suddenly lurched ahead. Fanny and I were flung back in our seats, and out the window I saw the reins dancing wildly in the air. With the horses soon at a full gallop, we edged on to the sidewalk, brushing against several trees and heading alarmingly close to the brick corner of a house.

"Father, are you all right?" Frederick shouted. Then we heard a loud crack, which echoed down a nearby alleyway.

Frederick kicked open the door and climbed out. "Brother, be careful," Fanny said, but he was already making his way forward, shouting for his father.

Moments later, the carriage came to a hard stop, and we heard screams. As we hurried outside, I saw a figure well behind us, motionless, on the street. It was Secretary Seward.

Frederick was soon at his father's side, and we rushed to follow. As we drew closer, I feared the worst had happened. In trying to rein in the horses, Seward had fallen hard upon the street. I kneeled down next to Frederick, feeling the secretary's left wrist for any sign of a pulse. Holding my breath, I felt it. *Faint. So faint.*

"He's alive," I said. "But he needs help."

Frederick flagged down a pair of policemen farther up the block. They ran toward the accident, and Fanny waved for them to hurry. As the crowd gathered around them, I stayed at the secretary's side, one hand still on his wrist, the other smoothing the hair back from his forehead, praying that he would live.

Due to his severe injuries, the secretary was confined to bed and required around-the-clock care. While the doctor had ordered no visitors, one exception was made. When President Lincoln returned from Richmond, with his blow-by-blow account of the Confederacy's collapse, his first stop was the Sewards' home. As Fanny and I watched from the hallway, the president detailed how General Grant's Union forces had trapped General Lee and what was left of the rebel army at a small crossroads somewhere in the Virginia Piedmont. A place called Appomattox.

"There old Ulysses got ahead of the rebels," Lincoln told his friend. "Did what we've been urging every general we've had during these long years to do. Stop Mr. Lee in his tracks and make him fight on our terms."

Though the secretary could barely speak, his eyes were bright with enthusiasm.

We exchanged surprised looks as the president then stretched out on the bed, right next to his good friend, to better detail his incredible trip into Richmond itself, the seat of the Confederacy.

"Of course, the general populace in Richmond didn't know what to make of me," President Lincoln said. "But I didn't feel threatened. Not one minute while I was there. In fact, I felt at ease walking through that ravaged city. The authorities, the rebels themselves, ordered much of it burned. Such a waste. But as I took it all in, it didn't matter if it was whites or Blacks in my wake. We were all one now. We've made sure of that, my friend."

That evening, when I told Fanny that I wanted to stay a while longer, my friend's eyes glistened like her father's had while lying next to the president.

"Thank you, Rory," Fanny said. "The family needs you here."

63

As Fanny expertly guided the Sewards' "piano box" buggy up the Seventh Street Turnpike, I thought of another carriage ride, not that long ago, when she retrieved me after my dismissal from the 138th.

With her father doing better, I reminded myself that there were far happier times ahead for us and the nation. Despite the early hour, barely past seven in the morning, people were out and about, going about their business in a vigorous manner. We had already passed the corner of Vermont and L Street, where Fanny said the poet Walt Whitman regularly waited for the president to pass by, bowing to acknowledge his presence.

"As far as I know, the two of them have never met," Fanny said, flicking the reins. "Still, it's like they share this bond, this love for country."

Soon the city center fell away and farmland, rich and ready for planting, spread out before us. Fanny was telling me about Confederate Jubal Early's attempt on the capital only a few months before, when the only ones manning Fort Stevens, another mile or so up Seventh Street, were boys and old men. The Union Army had gone south to lay siege to Richmond. Despite the danger, President Lincoln couldn't resist riding over to Fort Stevens to witness the action himself. He'd stood on the rampart, in plain view of the Confederate snipers, until a federal officer ordered him to "Get down, you fool," and take shelter. The event soon became the buzz around town.

A half-hour from Lafayette Square, we came up the drive to the Soldiers' Home, which Fanny said had become the Lincolns' summer residence. She told me that the family began coming here after its middle son, Willie, died of typhoid fever. How the youngest son, Tad, had been befriended by the soldiers of Company K, the so-called Bucktails, from the 150th Pennsylvania Volunteers. And how the president had written much of the Emancipation Proclamation here.

"I believe he thinks best in this place," Fanny said as we pulled into the semicircular drive of crushed stone. "As we know, the White House can be such a viper's nest. All glad-handing and interruptions. Father says Lincoln has become so enamored with this particular locale that he sometimes rides here alone. Does so even though Father and Mary Lincoln warn him to take the proper precautions. That it's too dangerous."

As we stepped down from the carriage, the arched doors opened and William Slade—Lincoln's valet, a freed man—stepped into the morning sun.

"Right on time, as always, Miss Fanny," he said. "And good—you've brought your friend."

"Is the president up?" Fanny asked.

"As you know, sometimes sleep is elusive for the poor man. So, he went riding early this morning. Here he comes now."

We turned to see President Lincoln, with a two-man military detail far behind him, in full gallop as he swept past a castle-like building nearby.

"That's the old soldiers' home," Fanny said to me. "The president often visits when he's here. And beyond that is the cemetery that became so filled that they had to take over Bobbie Lee's house across the Potomac in Arlington."

"At the height of the war," Slade added, "we had up to forty burials a week here."

We grew quiet as the president slowed his mount to a trot and came alongside us.

"You are angels for agreeing to meet me at this early hour," Lincoln said. He was slightly out of breath, yet in good cheer. "I feared that I sent you word too late."

"We wouldn't have missed it," Fanny replied. "Besides, Rory and I have been up for hours."

The president chuckled as he dismounted. "Perhaps our Miss Rory is up with the dawn," he said. "But I know that you can be the life of any party, dear Fanny. You love to observe all the goings on. Write them down in that diary of yours. My guess is you're more of a night owl. Like me."

President Lincoln gestured for us to follow Slade through the front doors and into the dining room, with its towering octagon-style windows. There a fine table had been laid out with eggs, bacon, grits, wheat toast, sliced fruit, dark coffee, and decanters of juice. We took our seats—Lincoln at one head of the table and Fanny at the other, with me once again in the middle of it all.

Our breakfast appeared to be an impromptu gathering. Still, if I'd learned anything during my short time in Washington, it was that such spur-of-the-moment events were rarely as they seemed.

The president began by asking Fanny about her father, how he was recovering, and then he thanked me again for my efforts in Ohio. He wanted to know "from an eyewitness whom I can genuinely trust" how close the rebel steamer had come to the *USS Michigan*. What would I have done, what could I have done, if they had actually seized it?

"Absolutely nothing," I told them. "That's where Mr. Douglas and his men from the Cataract House saved the day. Confusing the rebels to the point of bewilderment when the fireworks lit up the sky."

" 'Oh, for a muse of fire that would ascend,' " Lincoln began, " 'The brightest heaven of invention.' "

" 'A kingdom for a stage,' " I dared to answer, " 'princes to act.' "

Lincoln grinned, "You know it? You both do?"

"*Henry the Fifth*," Fanny said. "Shakespeare's opening."

In response, Lincoln briefly raised both arms into the air, still holding his knife and fork.

"I'll take that as a grand sign," he declared. "A harbinger of better times to come. What could surpass breakfast with two lovely ladies who know the Bard? It gladdens the heart, and now I'm wondering what I shall endeavor to write today. Thankfully, I have fellow muses in you two and, perhaps most importantly, I have dear Mr. Slade to take care of me."

"How's that?" asked Fanny.

"Throughout the day, when ideas come to me, I jot them down upon slivers of paper and place them under my hat," he said. "Still, it's a slipshod system at best. Pieces of paper fall out, and dear Mr. Slade must gather them up. He places them in the left-hand drawer of my desk upstairs here or under a paperweight upon my desk at the White House, the one in the shape of a shepherd. For that's what I've felt I've had to be during these long years. A shepherd trying to keep the lamb and the wolf apart."

"And you have been," Fanny said. "You did so to save the Union."

The president nodded in gratitude. "It's usually only at night that my mind slows enough for me to think. That's when I find the slips of paper that Mr. Slade has tucked away for me. That's where I found one that I had scribbled about John Yates Beall."

"Captain Beall?" I replied.

"Yes, you were there for his execution, weren't you, Miss Chase?"

The president undoubtedly knew this, for I hadn't kept my attendance a secret.

"I was," I said in a low voice.

"And when they brought the noose down over his head," Lincoln continued. "He insisted upon turning toward the south. To somehow pledge his allegiance."

"Yes, they allowed him to do so."

For a moment, we all grew silent. It was if the war had somehow returned to us, creeping out of some far corner where we prayed it had been placed forever.

"Miss Rory, I owe you an apology," the president finally said. "I fear I was too much the brute when you both visited me at the White House. How dismissive I was as you advocated for me to spare John Yates Beall's life."

"You're being too hard on yourself," said Fanny, ready to smooth things over.

"No, no, dear Fanny," Lincoln said. "I am being quite candid. Miss Rory was right in trying to keep Beall from the gallows."

"But he was as evil as they come," Fanny insisted.

"That's for the history books to decide," the president replied. "Still, at that moment, Rory, you spoke the unvarnished truth. I've done my research, asked around about you, especially among your comrades in arms in Niagara Falls."

I didn't like the way this conversation had turned.

"Your friends Wreet and Mr. Douglas believe that you may have helped the other rebel, Bennet Burley, escape."

"Sir, I didn't—"

"Now, now, this isn't any kind of interrogation," Lincoln said. "It's more of a revelation on my part. That you could be that compassionate, especially after losing your Uncle Frank—arguably your mother, too—to this conflict. And then to rise to the occasion, doing what you had to do to arrest John Yates Beall on the upper trestle of the Suspension Bridge in that raging storm. You are indeed a person of contradictions and greater honesty and courage than most."

I didn't know what to say to this.

"You were right to argue for Beall's life," the president added. "I was only seeing the man's dire plans and the near consequences of his actions, and I forgot to search for the human face behind the attempted crimes. Be more curious about where his personal philosophy went awry. But also not to allow the man to perhaps become a legend for all the wrong reasons. My God, turning south as a testament to his beloved cause? I realized last night that I need to strive to be more like you, Rory Chase. If not, our peace may be as contentious as the war."

Soon afterward, Mr. Slade entered the dining room and servants began to clear away the dishes. Another day for the president was fast upon him. He walked us back outside, into the bright sunshine, where Fanny's buggy was waiting to carry us back to the federal city.

"If I'd planned things better, I would have returned with you," Lincoln said. "For I need to be back at the White House later on. Plenty of festivities in the works, aren't there? That said, I'll linger here for the morning and then allow the military guard to squire me back. Today I'll follow the rules. Be under their guard and watchful stewardship. But who's to say what happens tomorrow and the next day?"

Then he smiled and briefly nodded to us, perhaps like he did to the poet Whitman when they passed each other on Washington's streets. As we pulled away, the president stood by the front door, a long arm held aloft, and watched us go until we fell from view.

64

A more prudent man would have been home by now or at least heading back to the British Isles for Easter and the rolling away of the stone. But Bennet Burley found that he couldn't leave this part of the world. Not yet. Montreal had been thick with rumors, so much strong talk that John Wilkes Booth was incensed by Captain Beall's hanging. So much so that he was returning to the US capital as an avenging angel. Sources told him that Miss Rory was in Washington, staying with her childhood friend, Fanny Seward. As a result, Burley felt he had no other choice but to steal back across the border for a final trip south.

It was April 14, 1865, Good Friday, and from across Lafayette Square in the District of Columbia, it was easy to spy upon the Seward residence. Burley settled into the background and stood watch as this day, a supposed time of reckoning, faded to evening. Why didn't he simply walk up to the front door and announce himself? Despite the war being over and the world seemingly eager to move on, Burley knew he remained a wanted man, a rebel with a bounty on his head. While transferring trains in New York, he had kept his hat pulled low, not wanting to draw attention to himself. Besides, he didn't want to put Rory in a dodgy spot by forcing her to explain who this gentleman with the Scots accent was at the front door of her best friend's home.

Instead, Burley kept watch from the park itself, following the comings and goings at the Sewards' residence. Between family and well-wishers, it was a steady trickle. A few evenings before, it had been the Night of the Illumination, an attempt to turn night into day by deploying every available source. House lights and streetlamps were left aglow, with bonfires in the grassy areas near the Capitol and in the middle of Lafayette Park itself—all to celebrate the South's recent surrender. After so many years of war, a buoyant mood had swept through the city and the northern lands.

Even though he'd searched the streets between here and Union Station earlier in the day, he'd seen nothing of Booth, nor the members of the Surratt family, who the actor was supposedly in league with now. He'd even passed by the Surratt boarding house on H Street, and it was locked up tight. Still, Burley couldn't dismiss those who had warned him about Booth being here. Somewhere the devil was afoot. He could feel it in his bones.

Late that afternoon, Miss Rory and her friend Fanny Seward stepped out for a walk. Uncertain what to do, Burley withdrew into the alleyway as they passed by. When they returned home after dusk, from the lights and shadows upstairs it appeared that they stopped by to check on the secretary in his bedroom on the top floor of the three-story town house. He'd learned that Secretary Seward was in a bad way; his upper torso shattered by the fall from the carriage. He was on painkillers, barely able to talk above a whisper due to a metal brace that held his broken jaw in place. He expected that Rory tried to stay out of everyone's way, content to hide in the small guest bedroom at the far end of the ground floor. But Fanny apparently insisted that she accompany her on visits to the upstairs bedroom, two levels above, where her father was in a large bed, propped up by pillows.

Dinner that evening appeared to be a haphazard affair to Burley. Through the window, he was able to make out Fanny, her brother Augustus, and Rory eating leftover chicken and twice-baked potatoes. Burley moved closer, until he was able to hear much of what was said. He overheard Fanny mentioning that she would take some of the food upstairs on a tray to her father and the army nurse attending to him, one George Robinson. It was well after sunset by the time Fanny's other brother, Frederick, arrived home. He was now the assistant secretary of state, taking over many of his father's duties since the carriage accident.

Frederick foraged for what he could find in the kitchen as the others asked about his day.

"Blessedly uneventful," Frederick told them.

"And the president?" asked Fanny, reentering the kitchen.

"In good spirits," Frederick replied. "So much so that he and Mrs. Lincoln are going to Ford's Theatre tonight. She wanted to see the play there, *Our American Cousin.* From what I understand, the president would rather stay in. The Grants were scheduled to accompany them, but they left on the late afternoon train for New Jersey. Tad, the Lincolns' young son, is on the town as well. He's going to see *Aladdin* at the National."

"Good for them," Fanny said. "They deserve a little fun."

Soon the Seward residence grew quiet for the night. Frederick and his wife, Anna, had already retired. Augustus indicated that he was ready to do the same, and Fanny returned upstairs to check on her father. That was when Burley caught a glimpse of Rory, in her nightgown and robe, in the guest room. She held a slender book, which he recognized as his *Shakespeare's Sonnets*, in her hand. He thought about rapping lightly on her window pane, but he was never afforded the chance. Too soon a sharp knock came at the front door, and Burley stole around for a better look.

When no one answered, a louder round followed, and the house servant, a Black man, finally opened the door.

"I have medicine for the master of the house," a towering figure said, holding out a vial wrapped in butcher paper.

"I'll take it," the servant replied.

The visitor was well over six feet tall yet, despite his size, the skin of his face was smooth, resembling a boy's. He had dark hair and blue eyes, which searched the interior hallway of the Sewards' home in an eager manner. He was a stranger to Burley and certainly not John Wilkes Booth.

"I'm not leaving it with the likes of you," the intruder said, pushing past the servant.

By now, Burley was near the front door, already concerned about what might transpire.

The commotion brought Frederick to the top of the first flight of stairs.

"This is medicine," the stranger repeated as he held out the small vial.

"Wait here," Frederick said, and he walked up the second flight of stairs and poked his head inside the secretary's bedroom.

"He's asleep," Frederick said, returning to the man.

Then the uppermost bedroom door reopened, and Fanny said, "Father is awake now."

"Is he asleep or not?" the intruder called up the stairs. He was well into the foyer, moving toward the stairs.

"He's terribly tired," Fanny shouted down.

Frederick nodded for her to go back inside the bedroom, telling the man, "I'll take the medicine."

The stranger was almost at the top of the first flight of stairs, and Frederick came down a few steps to confront him. With wild eyes, the visitor still held the vial in his hand, seemingly lost in thought. Then, in a blink of an eye, he came at Frederick, pulling a revolver from under his coat. Before anyone could move, the intruder aimed the gun at Frederick's temple and pulled the trigger. Thank God, no shot fired. The gun had jammed.

For a moment, a spell of shock hung over the Seward home. In a perfect world, the intruder would have lost his nerve right then and there, hurried down the stairs, and escaped out the front door. Instead, he deftly pivoted the revolver in his hand and brought the butt end down on Frederick's head. Then he did the same thing again and again until Frederick fell to the floor. The servant shouted, "Murder, murder," and ran out the door.

Pulling her robe about her, Rory raced up the stairs to help. By then, the assailant had reached the top floor, forcing open the door to the secretary's bedroom. There he was confronted by a man whom Burley recognized as Robinson, the secretary's nurse.

By this point, Burley was inside the entranceway, and he saw that the intruder also had a Bowie knife, which he was swinging wildly, catching Robinson across the forehead. Holding his head with both hands, Robinson toppled over, his eyes wide with shock.

"Don't kill him," Fanny cried out. The assailant punched her hard in the face, knocking her backward. Burley dashed up the stairs.

The secretary's bedroom was nearly pitch black. Burley saw Secretary Seward roll away from the man with the knife, trying to hide between the mattress and the wall. As the man stabbed repeatedly at the secretary, Rory jumped onto the man's back, scratching at his face. But the man reached over his shoulder with his free hand, grabbing her by the back of the neck. With a dismissive grunt, he tossed her hard to the floor.

Rory's efforts, though, did allow the secretary's older son, Augustus, to reach the bedroom, where the intruder caught him several times with the knife. That's when Robinson, the male nurse, was able to rejoin the battle. Regaining her senses, Rory somehow staggered to her feet, too. Seeing one figure after another rise from the shadows, ready to take him on, the assailant finally decided to escape. As he headed down the stairs, Burley ran after him, freezing a few strides from the bottom of the first staircase. The madman whirled, then took a wild swing at him with his gleaming blade. Once again, in his fevered mind, Burley was back along the docks in Sandusky, about to be badly cut. Blessedly, this time the man with the knife missed him, even though Burley heard the sing of that sharpened edge as it passed under his chin. The intruder fled, yelling, "I'm mad, I'm mad," as he disappeared into the night.

"Ben?" Rory was beside Burley now. Despite the danger, she had chased the assailant down the stairs. Above them, on the upper floors, the Seward household was in turmoil. "What are you doing here?"

Burley was light-headed from his close call. "I thought I could stop them," he babbled. "Stop Booth."

"But that wasn't John Wilkes Booth," she said.

"I heard rumors in Canada," he tried to explain. "So much talk that I had to come."

At that moment, both of them realized that Burley needed to get away, too. Flee before the roof came off the Union capital and he was caught up in the accusations and his previous associations with the likes of Booth and John Yates Beall and rebels of their ilk. Already, the Seward children were calling to each other on the floors above them as a crowd gathered out front. Off in the distance came the shrill of police whistles.

"They can't find you," Rory said. "Not here, not now."

Realizing that she was right, Burley plunged out the door, pushing past the bystanders before anyone could stop him. Without looking back, he was soon lost in the nightmare of that cruel night, intent upon making his getaway from this cursed land.

Epilogue

Eighteen Months Later

Mr. Douglas later told me that Harriet Tubman had a premonition about Fanny Seward's passing. Moses claimed to have witnessed a flaming chariot streaming south across the sky at dusk, a vision that so unnerved her that she ran to the home of her minister in Auburn, arriving only moments after word of Fanny's death reached the man himself. Tuberculosis was the official cause of death, and Fanny was laid to rest at the Fort Hill Cemetery on October 31, 1866. Generals, cabinet members, ambassadors, and even President Andrew Johnson had gathered in Auburn a few days earlier for her church service. But today's event, her burial, was deemed to be only for friends and family—those who had known her since she was a child.

My dear friend died eighteen months and two weeks after that dire night in Washington. Her beloved mother had died two months after the assassination attempt. What occurred at the Seward home soon became a footnote to history as that same evening, only a few blocks away at the Ford's Theatre, John Wilkes Booth assassinated President Lincoln. Booth himself would be shot dead twelve days later in a barn in the Virginia countryside. The man who tried to kill Secretary Seward was identified as Lewis Powell. He was soon captured and executed with other conspirators—David Herold, George Atzerodt, and Mary Surratt—on July 7, 1865, at the Washington Arsenal in the District of Columbia. The metal brace that Secretary Seward had worn for his broken jaw deflected Powell's knife blows from his jugular vein. Yet the secretary's face was forever disfigured, cut along the jawline for several inches on the left side.

As Fanny's burial drew to a close, Secretary Seward nodded for me to join him. Despite the line of carriages ready to return everyone to the main house, he wanted to walk down the hill and the remaining blocks into town. The secretary extended his arm, I took it, and side by side, with Augustus falling in behind us, we made our way down into Auburn. The first of the leaves were beginning to fall, and anyone in these parts knew that winter would soon be upon us.

"I've decided to take a trip," the secretary told me. "An extended one."

"Is that right, sir?" I replied.

"Yes, plans are being made to travel to Oregon, California, Mexico, perhaps to Cuba and on to Europe," he said. "Despite my best intentions, I realize I'm not getting any younger. That makes one more urgent and forthright about such things."

I glanced at his face and saw that it would never be close to the same. Some would say that the secretary had never been a handsome man. Yet he had a spirit and humor about him. Such characteristics were still there, of course, but one needed to linger on his words in encountering him these days. To let their gracefulness and eloquence move one past the scars left by the war years and the attempt on his life.

"I would like you to join me, Rory," the secretary said, and I paused, with Augustus coming alongside us. I wondered if the son knew what his father had in mind.

"I'm not sure what to say, sir."

"You don't have to say anything now," Secretary Seward said, "or even tomorrow or the next day. We have some time as I make the necessary arrangements."

"I'm honored that you asked me."

"Honor has nothing to do with it, my dear," he said. "It seems to me that both of us find ourselves very much alone in the world at this point. I know that time is running out for me. I was reminded of it again as they were lowering our dear Fanny into the ground. I have so much more that I want to do. But I need help. I need your assistance."

That evening, I slipped out the Sewards' front door and found myself again walking the streets of Auburn. A few blocks away, closer to downtown, I paused in the shadows by my mother's old house. She had died twenty-two months before "the war came," as President Lincoln said in his second inaugural address. The Seward family had been gracious enough to pay for her plot in the far corner of Fort Hill Cemetery, which I would visit again before returning to the Falls. If the war hadn't occurred, if she had lived, I could have stayed in this house and tried to make it more of my own. But with all that had happened, it seemed better to let such memories go.

It was well after eight o'clock when I returned to the Seward house. From the brick walkway, I saw that only a few lights were still on. One of them was in the secretary's study, and I decided I'd best decline his kind offer.

"May I come in?" I said in the doorway.

The secretary looked up. In the kerosene glow, he looked even older, more ravaged by time and events.

"Miss Rory, please have a seat." He nodded at the chairs across from him—the same place I found myself when he first proposed that I join the war by becoming a courier, a spy, along the border with Canada.

"I've been thinking," I began.

"So have I," the secretary interrupted. "After we spoke, Gus pulled me aside and pointed out the poor position I was putting you in. How it could be embarrassing for a single woman such as yourself to join an old codger like myself, no matter how well intended, for a grand tour of distant places. How people could talk."

"That doesn't bother me. I just don't think I'd be very good company for you."

The secretary smiled at this. "You're being too polite to an old friend," he said. "You've practically grown up in this house. If anyone knows what you've been through, it would be those who reside here, under this roof."

"Yes, I know. But—"

"If the war has taught me anything," Secretary Seward added, "it's that life cannot be taken for granted. If one has a good notion of how things can be, then he or she needs to find a way to make it possible, if they can. That's what I was thinking tonight, especially after I was told you'd gone out for a walk—probably to figure out a way to decline my invitation. So, I have an idea. Please hear me out."

"All right, sir."

"A young woman joining an elderly man in his travels?" he said. "Yes, my son is right. People would talk, and that wouldn't be fair to you. But they wouldn't if that couple was father and daughter."

"Father and daughter?"

"Yes, Rory Chase, I'd like to adopt you as my daughter."

Stunned, I sat there, not knowing what to say.

"I realize that this is all very unexpected," he said. "But I've talked it over with my son, and he appreciated how it made sense, even if in an odd kind of way."

"But Fanny?"

"You're not taking her place, Rory. No one can. We both know that. Those times, those struggles are over. And now I would very much enjoy the kind company of someone I can travel with and see more of this world with, a person I trust and respect. That's why I'm eager to make this work. Because right now, at this station in my life, you're the only one I can rely on for such a role."

"I promise I'll think about it," I said, dropping my gaze.

"Please don't," the secretary said. "Thinking too much only muddies the waters, makes it too easy to say no. You know who used to say that?"

"President Lincoln?"

"Absolutely right," the secretary smiled. "And like many of his words, those are ones to remember. So, no more thinking. Yes or no? Tell me your decision right now."

For an instant, I thought back upon everything that had happened in recent years—the war, the heartbreak, the times along the border. I could see no reason to refuse such an invitation from an enduring family friend.

"Yes," I said, without hesitation.

That autumn, after Secretary Seward spoke to the Houses of Parliament and was resting back at our hotel in London, I went for a long walk. Passing one of the bookstalls along the Thames River, a title caught my eye—*Along the Border: My Time during the American Civil War* by Bennet Burleigh. After purchasing a copy, I found a nearby bench.

Flipping through the pages, back to front, I saw that Bennet Burley was now a foreign correspondent for the *London Telegraph*, and I couldn't help but smile at his ability to recast the past. He had even changed the spelling of his surname.

As I studied the cover, a seascape of a steamer heading for the far horizon, I found myself borne back to those times on the Union side of Lake Erie. I recalled gazing down upon the Sandusky harbor from our window in the West House, with the mighty warship resting at anchor. Once more I could see myself, pencil in hand, sketching another scene from that epic time and war-torn world. And so often, against my best intentions, I remembered how my hand would slow when I heard Ben Burley enter the room.

Soon I reached the first few pages, the dedication, and what I found there took my breath away. "For Rory," it read. "The one who set me free."

> *When Lee surrendered*
> *At Appomattox*
> *They said the war*
> *Was over.*
> *I didn't believe it.*

> *When they cornered*
> *Booth in a Virginia barn*
> *And shot him dead*
> *They said they had rid*
> *His kind from this world.*
> *I still didn't believe it.*

When they say
The struggle has
Come to an end,
I know events will
Keep tumbling ahead
Like the waters
Over the Niagara.
I know it's never done.
Never.

JOHN DOUGLAS

Acknowledgments

When I decided to go in search of those lost to time, barely footnotes or passing mentions in current works, I knew I would need a lot of help. Thankfully, I was assisted by several exceptional editors. Dean Smith agreed that this tale could be similar to my earlier novels regarding Fidel Castro and Cuba, in that it would be more effective as fiction than a more scholarly work.

Still, I wanted this novel to be as historically accurate as possible, and that's when Michael McGandy came to my rescue. Not only were his edits thoughtful and precise, but he knew the historical backdrop of upstate New York, extending from Niagara Falls eastward to Auburn, the home of the Seward family.

Despite such insight, the novel wasn't finished until Mahinder Kingra stepped to the forefront. Even though he was new to the project, Mahinder found time for careful line edits and in-depth questions about the time period and the novel's overall structure. From there, Jennifer Savran Kelly and Carolyn Pouncy guided the manuscript through the editing process and made crucial suggestions along the way.

Thanks to Nalini Akolekar at Spencerhill Associates, who fought for this book in the marketplace. And a special nod to my longtime friend Donna Pieszala.

Burt Solomon and Amy Foster offered key suggestions about the characters and this tumultuous period in our nation's history. Richard Peabody of *Gargoyle* magazine published an excerpt about the Suspension Bridge, while John Stoll helped me better understand Sandusky's distant past. Others who are in my corner include Jim and Nin Andrews, Molly Ascrizzi, Erik Brady, Marie Colturi, Jock Crothers, Paul Dickson, Marilee Enge, Bob Fonseca, Len Forkas, Tom Harry, Chae Hawk, Michael Kinomoto, Claire Lilly, Mark Lorenzoni, Howard Mansfield, E. Ethlebert Miller, Diane Naughton, Lelia Nebeker, Gerry Rosenthal, David Rowell, Aran Shetterly, Tom Stanton, Carol Stevens, Todd Wait, Paul White, Gregg Wilhelm, Rick Willis, Richard Woodbridge, Brock Yates Jr., Dan Yates, and Mary Kay Zuravleff.

I wouldn't have made it this far without the support of Johns Hopkins University (JHU). Decades ago, David Everett asked me to teach a fiction workshop there, and since then my compadres have grown to include Cathy Alter, Mark Farrington, Karen Houppert, Melissa Hendricks Joyce, and Ed Perlman. In addition, I've been fortunate to have a great many outstanding students throughout my time at JHU, including Nicole Chung, David Frey, Craig Gralley, Monica Hesse, Alma Katsu, Sascha Klein, Will Potter, Mark Stoneman, John Trumbo, and Erin Williams.

The Hopkins' connection extended to Jim Gillispie, at the Milton S. Eisenhower Library in Baltimore, who located the vintage map of Niagara Falls.

When I began to write fiction, I first found a home at the Community of Writers in northern California, where Alan Cheuse, Carolyn Doty, Richard Ford, and Oakley Hall helped show me the way.

In subsequent years, I attended the Sewanee Writers' Conference in eastern Tennessee, learning from John Casey, Greg Downs, Holly Goddard Jones, Randall Kenan, Margot Livesey, Brendan Mathews, Alice McDermott, and Cheri Peters.

Kiara Santiago and the staff at the Niagara Falls Underground Railroad Heritage Center answered my questions about the Cataract

House hotel and detailed how that landmark, which unfortunately no longer stands, was once the last major stop for enslaved people escaping to Canada.

A final nod goes to a specific locale rather than a particular person or group. For me, Niagara Falls remains one of the wonders of the world. Look beyond the casinos and carneys, the shopworn buildings and crowds of tourists. Glimpse the mist billowing to the heavens from the cataract below and hear the roar of the Falls. At such moments, you can be carried back in time, witnessing it all anew.

Tim Wendel
Charlottesville, Virginia

AUTHOR'S NOTE

Even though they are reminiscent of Shakespeare's Rosencrantz and Guildenstern, almost entirely overshadowed by other characters and events of the day, Captain John Yates Beall and Bennet Burley nearly tipped the balance of power toward the end of the Civil War. They were actual Confederate spies, briefly mentioned in Carl Sandburg's *Abraham Lincoln*, Doris Kearns Goodwin's *Team of Rivals*, and Amanda Foreman's *A World on Fire*. In addition, Beall's memoir and an account of his trial can be found at the Cornell University Library.

Desperate for assistance along the US-British Canadian border, the Union scrambled to set up a spy network, and its members sometimes included the waiters at the Cataract House, a luxury hotel that was a stone's throw from the American side of the Falls. Before the war, many at the Cataract House helped escaped enslaved people cross the Niagara River to Canada and freedom. Their leader, John Morrison, was the head waiter at the Cataract Hotel, and he is now remembered in several exhibits at the Underground Railroad Heritage Center in Niagara Falls, New York. For this story, I've renamed him John Douglas, in honor of a childhood friend who died far too young.

This was also the time of great advances in the world of photography, as tintypes gave way to *cartes de visites* (postcard-sized reproductions) and larger photographs called "Imperials." These were enhanced by artists using crayons, watercolors, or oils. All the while, such photographers as Alexander Gardner, Timothy O'Sullivan, and Mathew Brady headed into the war zone, transforming how the conflict was portrayed to and understood by the general public. Brady was a major force during this era in the nation's history, as highlighted by *Mathew Brady's Portrait of an Era* by Roy Meredith, *Mathew Brady and the Image of History* by Mary Panzer, and *Mathew Brady: Portraits of a Nation* by Robert Wilson.

To learn about the Seward family, I turned to *Seward: Lincoln's Indispensable Man* by Walter Stahr and *Fanny Seward: A Life* by Trudy Krisher. In addition, I toured the Seward House Museum in Auburn, New York, several times.

In this novel, I've added several characters, notably Rory Chase, who is a composite of a childhood friend of Fanny Seward, the secretary's only daughter, and Olive Risley, who became Secretary William Seward's adopted daughter and traveling companion after the war. Today, a statue of Risley stands at the corner of Sixth Street and North Carolina Avenue in Washington, DC.

For insight about espionage along the border during the Civil War, as well as the role of the Underground Railroad, I'm indebted to *A World on Fire: Britain's Crucial Role in the American Civil War* by Amanda Foreman, *The War before the War: Fugitive Slaves and the Struggle for America's Soul from the Revolution to the Civil War* by Andrew Delbanco, *The Civil War Years: Canada and the United States* by Robin W. Winks, *Wild Bennet Burleigh: The Pen and the Pistol* by Graeden Greaves, and *Rebels on the Great Lakes: Confederate Naval Commando Operations Launched from Canada 1863–1864* by John Bell. For an overall history of Niagara Falls, both sides of the border, I recommend *Niagara: A History of the Falls* by Pierre Berton.

More than fifteen thousand books have been written about Abraham Lincoln, as exemplified by the thirty-four-foot-tall tower of titles at the Ford's Theatre Center for Education and Leadership in Washington, DC. Among that sea of information, I found *Lincoln and Whitman: Parallel Lives in Civil War Washington* by Daniel Mark Epstein, *Abraham Lincoln in the National Capital* by Allen C. Clark,

Lincoln's Citadel: The Civil War in Washington, D.C. by Kenneth J. Winkle, *Manhunt: The 12-Day Chase to Catch Lincoln's Killer* by James L. Swanson, *Mr. Lincoln's Washington* by Stanley Kimmel, and *Lincoln's Other White House: The Untold Story of the Man and His Presidency* by Elizabeth Smith Brownstein to be very useful.

Of course, the Civil War has long been a fertile ground for historical fiction. My favorites, and the authors in whose footsteps I aspired to follow, include *The Murder of Willie Lincoln* by Burt Solomon, *Neverhome* by Laird Hunt, *Confederates* by Thomas Keneally, *Lincoln in the Bardo* by George Saunders, *Open Country: A Civil War Novel in Stories* by Jeff Richards, Ralph Peters' Civil War series, *Booth* by Karen Joy Fowler, and *Killer Angels* by Michael Shaara.